OF SHEPHERDS AND MAGES

Of Shepherds and Mages

Book 1: The Wise and the Faithful

ALI JON SMITH

JD Smith Imprint

Contents

1	The Magnolia Court	3
2	The Fool	26
3	Necessary Evils	51
4	An Emperor's Funeral	78
5	Call to Arms	92
6	War Craft	117
7	Elsiren's Tomb	139
8	The Mages	156
9	Invasion	176
10	The Battle for Serra	200
11	Aftermath	221
12	Hidden Mercy	235
13	Flotsam	260
14	The Battle for Adlan	275

15	Negotiations	291
16	Voyage Beyond	322
17	Approaching Storms	341

About The Author 363

Many people helped me in the creation of this book: Chiefly my wife, Zaynab, who provided constant helpful feedback. I must also thank my first English teacher, Jan Galpin, who helped me love words on a page at a time when I struggled to read.

The cover art is by Ahmad Hosseini-Khorrami, a generous and talented man if ever there was one.

The Hublands

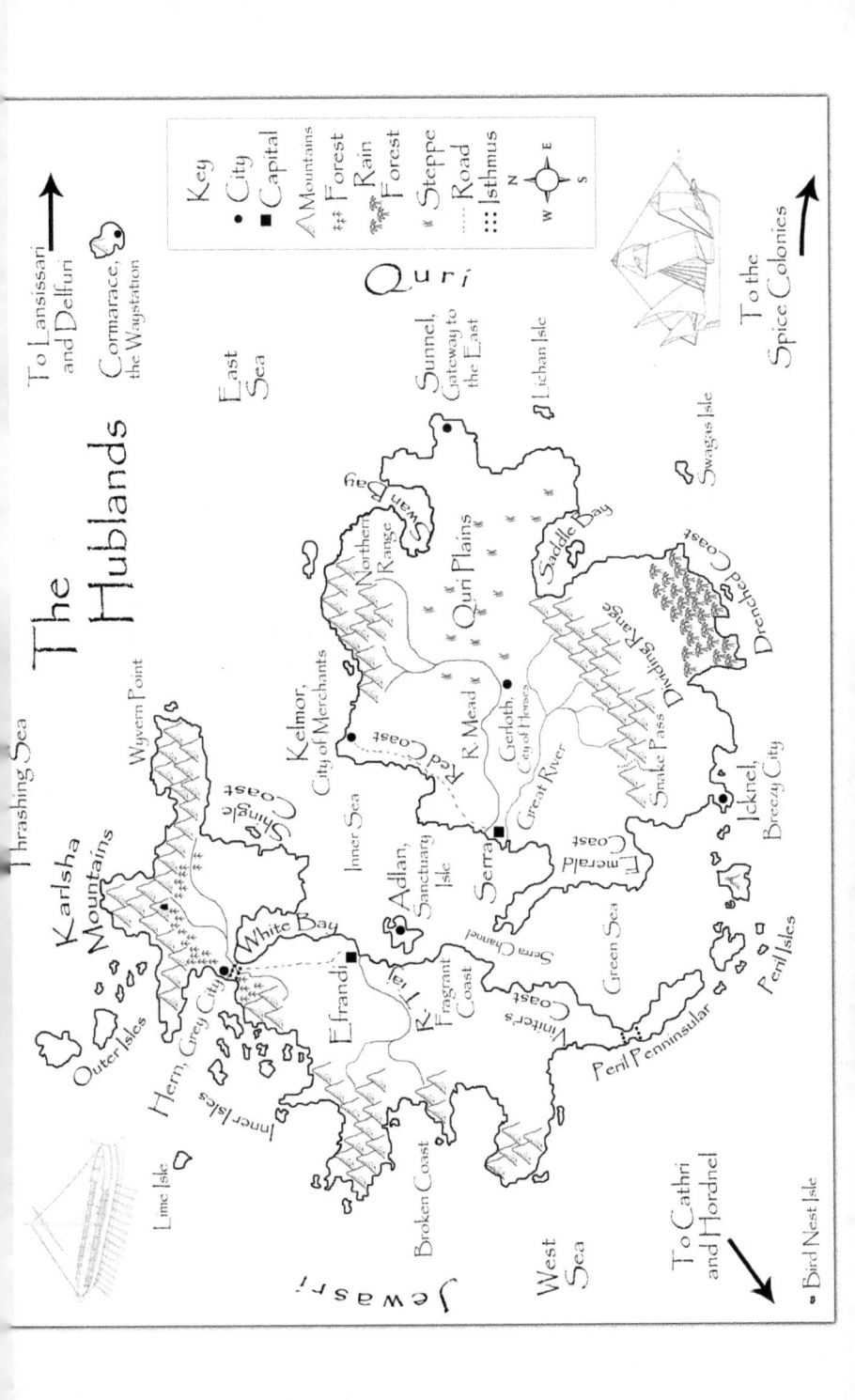

A Quick Note to the Reader on Gendered Language

Dear reader, the world I have sketched is (or at least begins as) a Bronze Age utopia, somewhere between what the ancients would have recognised as such, and what our modern western sensibilities allow. The two ideals do not always sit happily and nowhere do they clash more than when it comes to gender roles. I have chosen to be anachronistic in this respect and craft my world as a place of equality where men and women are expected to do and say almost the same things. To highlight this I have actively chosen to de-gender many nouns by choosing to use the most common variant for both sexes. For example, both Kirrie and her husband Duarma are referred to as 'the Emperor' (as opposed to 'Empress and Emperor') and both men and women are called 'widows' (as opposed to 'widower' and 'widow') when they have lost their spouse. I hope this does not cause confusion or detract from the story.

Chapter 1

The Magnolia Court

Wind whistled through marble fretwork as the unseasonable gale brought a distinct tang of salt to Duarma's tongue. Far below their balcony it was whipping waves to foamy crests and spraying white flecks against the palace tower. Duarma squeezed his wife Kirrie's hand anxiously.

His ship might be out there. Your throne might yet be safe.

Her expression did not crack; she was already wearing the stony mask of a young Emperor, ready for her courtly duties. Then he felt the reassuring pinch as she squeezed back. Kirrie was nervous as well. She was dressed in her best imperial robes; blue and white silk trimmed with silver to contrast with her deep black skin. Although the clothes were simply cut, she looked every bit the Emperor of all cherno. She was three-hundred years old, but in the way of their race, time had not yet wrinkled her smooth skin, or added a grey hair to her long black locks. As Duarma often reflected, she had barely changed since the day they married.

Kirrie turned to her chief meteomancer.

"Mordhai, you are sure this storm is magical?" she asked the ancient mage.

Mordhai shut his eyes and rested his bent frame heavily on his staff as he allowed his farsight to range out into the currents of air on the distant horizon.

"No doubt, my majesty. It has been diverted from the White Sea north of Efrandi," Mordhai answered.

Efrandi, seat of the Archlord Tisenin. Just as Duarma had suspected. *Who else but Tisenin could summon such a wild wind to aid his travel?* Kirrie must have had the same thought, but it did not seem to bring gladness to her face.

Duarma looked out across the windswept ocean, where the sky and the waves blended into misty grey, and saw a single galley moving into the estuary of the Great River. It was cruising on the sweet spot at the fringe of the gale, with a full-bellied sail and the white flash of oars pulling it to shore as fast as it could move. When it emerged from the distant murk it was clear to see the bulging sail was embroidered with a purple chevron; Tisenin's crest. He was cutting his visit fine, but at least the powerful wind he had summoned showed he was doing his best to reach the assembly on time.

When Duarma pointed the little galley out Kirrie gave an uncharacteristic sigh of exhaustion.

"It doesn't please you?" asked Duarma.

"I should be glad I suppose. I know we need him to stop this whole thing turning into a farce." She let go of Duarma's hand and dug her nails into the alabaster of the balcony rail. "But I am weary of his constant mental fencing. Every assembly my cousin asks for what I cannot give. And always more lords side with him. Every time it is the Ban," she said. "It has been almost a hundred years now."

The Ban. Always the Ban.

Duarma wrapped an arm around her shoulders, "I know, my love, but I fear it must be endured. I was frightened he would boycott your court altogether."

Kirrie nodded in resignation. She shifted over to the tower's other balconey, which looked into the palace courtyard and the nobles who gathered in its blossoming orchard. So painfully few. Over the years they had grown used to being marginalized. In the days of the first Emperor, no lord of any merit would have missed the assembly. It would last for weeks with feasts and politicking beginning long before the formal ceremony. Now when they did come it was just for a day or two, and most of the time they sent representatives. The office of Emperor no longer held sway like it once did. Archlords in prosperous and distant parts of the Empire – in the cool forests of Lansissari, the horse plains of Delfuri and mineral rich Cathri – no longer looked to her as the centre of authority. Fewer and fewer came to her Magnolia Court.

But the day Tisenin rejected her would be the day she ceased being Emperor. He was the most important man outside of their own palace. He was the Archlord of the Empire's second city Efrandi, heir of Elsiren, second in line to the throne and Kirrie's only blood cousin.

Kirrie hugged herself to her husband's chest. "Duarma, it was simpler in the days before I was Emperor. I remember when we three were children. Then our arguments had been about who could win a race, or who could throw a stick furthest? Who knew the most disgusting thing humans did? Those things had a simple resolution, not these drawn out ideological battles."

It was merely an attack of pre-performance nerves, and they both knew it. Kirrie had ruled for a hundred years now and the prevailing wisdom was that she would go on doing it successfully for another seven-hundred. But she was never more on display than when she presided over the Magnolia Court. This issue with Tisenin and the Ban was a recurring thorn. That, and this year the added insult of the girl Hilsi from Cathri, but she was another matter entirely.

"You will judge with dignity and wisdom, as you always do my love," assured Duarma.

Kirrie patted his hand.

"Imagine how much simpler this would be if I had given up the role to him. We have equal parts of the blood of Elsiren. The mandate passed to me by a slim margin."

"You are by far the better of the two cousins. The Celibate Fish knew it long before you were elected. Remember when he proposed? What was that if not the most obvious move to align himself with your popularity."

'Celibate Fish' was their pet name for Tisenin. He had famously rejected every romantic advance made towards him, leading to the suspicion that he intended to reproduce by spawning in the water.

"Ha! You can scarcely call it a proposal. He said, '*it would be good for the Empire. Produce a purer line.*' He was always too serious for his own good."

"I'm glad you had better taste than to settle for him," said Duarma.

Kirrie pushed her lips against Duarma's.

"Ahem!" interrupted Mordhai. "The ship has entered the royal canal. It will be at the quay shortly."

"Then I shall make my entrance and begin the formalities," said Kirrie.

As Kirrie and Duarma descended down the tower, Mordhai the meteomancer remained on the balcony. He could feel the tingle of magic being worked on the gale. A molecule here, a molecule there, slowly accreting the kind of changes needed to make the winds shift back round to the northwest. It was delicate and exhausting work, but there was a lot of mana being put into it. That kind of weather manipulation usually took days to effect, but the cluster of mages on the ship seemed to be attempting to do it in a matter of hours. Whoever was on that ship really wanted to get back to Efrandi quickly.

* * * * * * *

The Magnolia Court was a large shady garden within the palace walls, open to the sky and peppered with beautiful magnolia trees in the flush of bloom.

They were always in bloom.

In her youth Kirrie had visited the cold northern colony of Lansissari during the spring and had been awestruck by its wonderful magnolia trees. They bloomed with large, elegant pink flowers sprouting in architectural forms. Morning dew twinkled on their petals and made the sky look like it was filled with jewels. Serenus, the Archlord of Lansissari, had noted her wonder and made the Emperor a gift of a box full of magnolia seeds and one of her best treesingers to attend to the saplings. The treesinger made them grow in the arid soil of Serra and kept them in a permanent state of bloom. Kirrie let cherry trees grow here as well so that once a year the magnolias could be seen amidst the snowflakes of falling white blossom. The Magnolia Court was Kirrie's favourite place in Serra.

Duarma noted with gladness that Serenus's youngest son was here representing her today. Handsome Jandor was fast becoming a court favourite. He did his best to fit in, dressing like a native of Serra, in white cotton robes with a coloured silk sash rather than the heavy woollen clothes of his native Lansissari. His only concession to his origins was a small, brightly woven scarf depicting the pride of his nation – its ever blooming trees. He always spoke with reason and due reverence, like a consummate ambassador, and it was well known that he had his mother's ear in every matter.

If only the representative from Cathri was so fitting, thought Duarma.

Kirrie took her seat on the wooden throne in the centre of the courtyard and gathered loose material into her lap. The back of the chair was carved into the form of an eagle, symbolising Elsiren's journey on Earth before the great exodus. Duarma took a less elaborate seat beside her and a symbolic guard representing her imperial authority stood behind her. The lone guard had a huge axe, so impractical that he had to rest the haft of it on the floor in order to keep its butterfly-shaped head aloft in a stately manner.

The worthy lords were all arrayed in front of Kirrie. The relatively minor aristocrats with country estates were towards the back of the assembly. Those few who were paramounts of the fifteen noble dynasties were allowed a little closer to the Emperor, with the three great colonial representatives, the archlords, right at her feet. The turnout was very poor; in particular few of Tisenin's supporters from Jewasri had bothered to come. Duarma knew Kirrie would have to make some formal complaints; though the sea may have created a mental barrier, the passage from Jewasri was short and they had no excuse for their absence. She could not let herself be snubbed so easily.

Snubbed so easily. The words echoed ironically in Duarma's head. *The first complaint has to be with the Archlord of Cathri.*

Kamil ap Hexin, who held great tracts of land on the continent southwest of Jewasri, had never come to Kirrie's assemblies and had always been slow to react to her dictates. But this year he had gone too far. He had sent his adolescent niece to be his representative.

Kirrie called the girl forwards.

"Hilsi ap Hexin, you are a newcomer to this court. Before we start formal petitions would you like to introduce yourself?"

Hilsi stepped forwards and bowed. She was seventy years old, barely into her first blood. For the cherno, a species who regularly lived for a thousand years, entrusting power to an adolescent under a century was just insulting. At Hilsi's age, she should have been tying lovers' feathers in her hair and learning her first craft; not representing the most prosperous colony in the Empire. Her smooth black face and wide eyes had not even set into their final adult features. But the eyes met Kirrie's with an arrogance that said *'I've already seen enough, I already know it all.'* In that respect at least, she was like her uncle Kamil.

"My dear Emperor, I am here at the behest of Kamil ap Hexin to represent the interests of Cathri. I look forwards to addressing the assembly on Cathri's behalf. I have also brought your majesty a fine and unique set of gifts which I am confident you will delight in," Hilsi squeaked.

Ignorant girl...

Duarma had to exert a measure of self-control not to flinch on the girl's behalf. It was very bad etiquette to speak of gifts before the start of the assembly. It stank of bribery and favouritism. Politeness dictated that the gifts were to be given after politicking was done.

She obviously had no idea of court protocol, but no one openly corrected her; it would have caused further embarrassment. Even so, Duarma saw Kirrie's lips crease down a fraction. She wanted her displeasure with the candidate publicly known.

"Archlord Kamil must have *remarkable confidence* in you to send one so...young and new...to the court," said Kirrie.

The fire in the girl's expression flared up. "I can *assure* your majesty that my uncle is *fully* confident of my abilities to talk for my people at this assembly." The muscles in her jaw stood proud as she clenched her teeth.

Petulance of a child, thought Duarma. *She has the raging temper of a human; no concept of how to handle a reproach with dignity.*

Jandor put his hand on Hilsi's shoulder to calm her down. "My dear Hilsi, do not think that people question your good self. One is scarcely to blame for receiving high office at a young age, or following the bidding of one's lord. Rather, we are surprised with Archlord Kamil."

The subtle distinction Jandor made seemed to take the fire out of her face. She crinkled her nose.

"Then let my actions be testament to my Archlord's judgement," Hilsi proclaimed.

"No one asks more or less," said Kirrie.

Before Kirrie could interrogate the newcomer any further, they were interrupted by the sound of many sandals slapping flag stones. The crowd of nobles parted around the courtyard gate to allow Tisenin and a large train of Jewasri lords into the orchard.

Ah, so the Jewasri lords have chosen to travel as a single delegation; that explains their absence, thought Duarma with a sense of relief. A token of their solidarity no doubt.

Some whispered words flew around the court about being 'disrespectfully late,' but Kirrie chose to ignore them. When Tisenin reached the middle of the court he stopped and knelt.

"My dear Emperor, I apologize for my late arrival. I had to make some vital last-moment arrangements in Efrandi. For this I and my fellow lords were detained overnight."

Kirrie was magnanimous, "Tisenin, think nothing of it. I can tell you have pushed your ship to get here in due haste." She motioned for him to rise.

It was often noted that you could tell a lot about a cherno noble by the way they dressed. Tisenin was wearing at least four layers of silk robe tied in the complex manner of those from the cold Jewasri mountains. The hem was folded precisely one finger above the top of his foot and the long loose sleeves rested neatly on the crease of his wrist. It required discipline to maintain the delicate formal dress code. All four layers were dyed with shades of an expensive purple from the Peril Isles, which complimented his warm, dark skin. His long black hair had been tied into tight ringlets and intricately interwoven so that (even after sailing in the gallant breeze) no hair was out of place. He was showing he was a man of Jewasri with patience, discipline and significant wealth.

"Can I trust you will be making the usual appeal at this assembly?" asked Kirrie.

There was a flutter of laughter from the nobles, but conspicuously not the ones who had just arrived with Tisenin.

Tisenin forced a smile. "You can. I will address this council on the familiar issue, but I hope this year it might elicit a different response." He bowed deeply and slowly at the end.

"Very well." Kirrie let her diaphragm relax and projected her voice for the entire courtyard to hear. "And so, to begin. I first invite Tisenin ap Elsiren, Archlord of Efrandi, to speak his petition."

Tisenin stepped forwards, placed his hands in the sleeves of his robes and began to pace up and down as if remembering the lines of a well-rehearsed speech. He spoke calmly and with every word carefully measured out, so that it filled more space than it normally ought to.

"I thank your Majesty. I have asked the same thing of this court for almost a hundred years now and my mages tell me that if we do not act soon, it will be too late. So I will make this promise, this will be the last time I make the plea. And I will keep it short, I know everyone here has heard me speak before," assured Tisenin.

People mumbled agreement. *The last time?* Duarma saw Kirrie's eyes brighten with those words.

"Not me," interjected Hilsi.

Tisenin turned and smiled at her, noticing the newcomer in the position of honour at the foot of the Emperor for the first time.

"You must be Cathri's new representative," Tisenin surmised. The novelty of her adolescence fazed him for less than a heartbeat before he seemed to understand the significance of her presence.

He always was sharp, thought Duarma.

Hilsi nodded, "It is so."

"Then what I am about to say is especially for you," said Tisenin with a small bow of courtesy.

"I know all about the Ban. About the simurgh and the death of magic," snapped Hilsi, clearly worried people thought her youth equated with ignorance.

"Yes the simurgh! That is the place to start. Back on Earth, in the great desert, the simurgh split our seed from the humans and bred magic into us for one purpose – to use our power to weave the Ban and sever that very magic from our world for eternity. They feared magic as the greatest evil, but it did not flow in their veins like it did for us. When the great spell of the Ban was finished, our ancestors were mana-blind and found their existence utterly intolerable. They rebelled and broke out of the simurgh's desert prison. Only Elsiren was able to save us from the Ban. He united the disparate tribes of cherno and forced the simurgh to make us a new home where magic could flourish — here, this Haven."

As Tisenin paced around the court, he seemed to be spending more of his time talking to the assembly than to Kirrie. It was a little disrespectful. However, protocol aside, they all knew the only way Kirrie would agree to his request was if there was overwhelming pressure from the assembled lords. At the front, Jandor seemed unimpressed with Tisenin's words, but Hilsi was following them carefully. Duarma hoped it was only because she was a little taken with his style of oratory. For all Tisenin's coolness in private, he was very charismatic when given a chance to preach.

Tisenin continued, "Elsiren negotiated at every opportunity he got. He took pains, wooing factions for decades. But when negotiations failed, he used force...No! Let me be more honest with my words! He *killed* over the Ban. Can you imagine how desperate our ancestors must have been to shed kin's blood to save their magic? That is the situation we are moving towards now. Like a slow cataract, the Ban has expanded from Earth and now reaches us here."

Tisenin turned away from the assembly and gazed up at the falling cherry blossoms. He sucked in a long lung full of the perfume. "This orchard, to our Emperor's credit, one of the loveliest places in these isles, would not exist if it were not for magic. I would not have made it here today if it were not for magic speeding my ship. Who among us would even dare cross the great ocean if it were not for the meteomancers guiding our ships in safety?" He stared intently at Hilsi, who had obviously just made the months long voyage from Cathri.

"Not me," she finally admitted under Tisenin's gaze.

Rather than grin at this small victory, he looked grave and concerned, like a worried father.

"I don't believe it," interrupted Jandor. He took both of Hilsi's hands and squeezed them reassuringly. He always managed to seem like a pillar of warmth and clarity no matter what was going on around him. "No one who can speak so easily in front of the Emperor can be called faint hearted. Surely it is only the novelty of the suggestion which makes you hesitate?"

"Maybe. Perhaps I would cross without magic if it were *really* important." The unintentional implication being that she did not consider the Magnolia Court to be important. Duarma made special note of that for later consideration.

Nothing in Tisenin's demeanour changed to suggest anger, but now he turned his attention to Jandor, which rather implied he disliked being undermined by this young noble from the forests.

"Jandor, you are an ap Suvix, a line of great mages. Tell me then, the villages of Lansissari are built with enchanted wood, like this orchard, and your borders are defended from the humans as much with magic as those of Cathri are with stone. Could Lansissari survive if the magic failed tomorrow?"

Jandor was cool and honest, "No Tisenin, my country would be ruined. But you know very well that is not the situation we face. The Ban is not merely a slow cataract, it is an achingly slow one. It will not strip us of our powers for at least a thousand years. Long enough for us to change. My mother has already begun the work."

"You mother Serenus? Who managed to push our understanding of magic and living flesh further than anyone predicted it could go? Woe to us that such an innovator is resigned to her doom. What could she do if she turned her mind to the Ban?" Tisenin wisely did not give Jandor a chance to reply. Instead he whirled around and directed his final plea towards Kirrie herself. "It fills me with fear to think that when I am old enough to be called venerable, my magic will be no stronger than a mere human's. This is why we must act now, when we are still strong, or not at all. Think of the bleak future we condemn our children and grandchildren to! Life in darkness!"

Tisenin knelt before Kirrie on her throne. Duarma had never seen him so vocally animated before, not even in speeches; he was usually so controlled and precise about everything. His face was pleading and pathetic. *If it was anyone else he would be expecting to see tears on his cheeks soon. That would be a first.*

"I ask you my Emperor, my cousin, one last time. Allow those with the skill and knowledge of the Ban to find a way of bending it, so it might bypass this world and it might stay our Haven. Please, act now, before we are unable to."

Kirrie took a deep breath before replying. It was important to have her words right and her reply clear.

"Does anyone have anything to add before I pass judgement?"

There was silence from the court. It was a well worn topic that had been discussed everywhere and without resolution for as long as it was apparent that Elsiren's Haven was just a temporary reprieve from the Ban.

"...Very well, I will pass judgement. My honoured cousin Tisenin, we have all been impressed by your arguments and touched by your dedication. But the issue has not changed since you first brought this plea to my court, forty seven gatherings ago. We are bound by oath to honour the agreement our ancestors made with the simurgh. We were only ever granted a temporary reprieve from the Ban. The simurgh and students of the Ban both insist that any attempt at alteration risks unravelling it all – and the consequences of removing the Ban are infinitely more dangerous than losing one of our seven senses. One without balance may learn to walk by sight. One without sight may learn to navigate by sound and touch. One without magic may learn to cope. So, on grounds of honour, I must deny your request. And on grounds of the safety of my people, I must deny your request."

Tisenin bowed his head in resignation.

"It is as I expected, my Emperor." Then he did something unexpected. He reached up and hugged her around her waist, so his head lay in her lap. Kirrie was completely taken aback. Duarma and the rest of the court stared incredulously at Tisenin hugging her. Even for a close relative this was informal courtly behaviour; for the Celibate Fish it was unthinkable. "Kirrie, we have fought for so long on this subject. It brings me such grief. I must beg your forgiveness."

Kirrie was initially stiff and awkward in Tisenin's embrace, but when she looked down and saw how humble he was, she eased a little. She laid a hand against Tisenin's soft black cheek and beckoned him to rise.

"My dear cousin, you have it. You have only argued in our people's best interest as you see it."

"Thank you, your majesty, it means a great deal."

Tisenin did not stand, but instead slowly drew from his sleeve an ornate metallic object. Kirrie opened her hands out to receive the gift. Duarma strained his neck to see what it was.

But Tisenin's own body blocked the view of him plunging the knife into Kirrie's chest.

It was so quick, not even Kirrie realised what had been done to her until a scream ripped from her own lips. There was a split second everyone there that day would remember forever when Tisenin and Kirrie just stared at each other and no one else knew why the Emperor had screamed.

Before anyone could act, Tisenin withdrew the knife and dashed through the magnolia trees to where his fellow Jewasri lords were clustered near the courtyard gate. His body seemed to melt into them and they smartly closed the gap behind him. In a calm, practised manner they filtered through the gate and out of the palace.

Duarma and the other lords had not even grasped what had happened until they saw the fierce plume of blood spewing from Kirrie's chest and puddling in her lap. There was an outcry and the lone palace guard ran after Tisenin.

Duarma was filled with panic. He pushed his hand against Kirrie's wound, but there was no chance to staunch the blood; the blade had passed very precisely through her heart.

Kirrie knew she was very nearly dead. In her last few seconds she looked at Duarma and smiled as if experiencing a moment of profound prescience. It would take Duarma a very long time to decode that smile, but eventually he thought he understood.

It said, *'I am the luckiest person in the courtyard. It is better to die here and now than live through the times that are about to unfold.'*

* * * * * * *

Akai saw his lord Tisenin running for the galley and got ready to pull him aboard. The deed was done, and now they needed to make an escape. Tisenin planted one foot on the side of the galley and leapt over the rail, only needing Akai's hand to stabilize himself. People made the mistake of thinking that someone as cool and wise as Tisenin must have the icy joints of a scholar, but Akai had often seen him hunting with a javelin in the grounds of his manor, where he displayed the agility of an athlete.

Tisenin collapsed onto the wooden deck, his back against the rail. His eyes were glazed and his breath came hard.

"Are you alright, Archlord?" asked Akai.

"Yes, see to the others," he ordered.

The other Jewasri nobles were following out of the palace and down to the quay in a tight gaggle. They huddled to the side of the galley and Akai and the rest of the sailors hauled them aboard one person at a time.

There was some kind of commotion at the back of them as Kirrie's bodyguard tried to force his way through to Tisenin. His giant axe was in hand, but he seemed reluctant to use it as anything more than a staff to clear his path. In a few seconds he was mobbed by Tisenin's followers and the axe was ripped from his hands. He was kicked and punched to the floor whilst everyone boarded the galley.

The very second the last person was aboard, the oarsmen pushed the vessel away from the quayside and started rowing for the open ocean to the sound of a beating drum.

Specks of glittery sweat appeared on Tisenin's face and he called out for some water. Before the last syllable had left his lips, Akai had placed a cup sweetened with rose petals and saffron into his hands.

"Thank you, dear sailor," said Tisenin in surprise. "I have seen your face before. What is your name?"

"I am Akai, from Efrandi."

Tisenin sipped from the cup and shut his eyes, but it seemed to bring him no relief.

"Archlord, would you like me to clean that?" asked Akai.

Tisenin looked at Akai quizzically for a second then realized he was talking about the bloody dagger he still clutched in his hand, as if he had forgotten it was there.

"No Akai, I will do it later." Tisenin sheathed the blood-slick dagger in a small pouch within his robes. It was as if to say, *'This is my blood-debt, it will stay with me forever.'*

Akai placed a basin of water in front of Tisenin so he could at least wash his stained hands. Tisenin dipped them in and watched the swirls of red float away. The vortices seemed to mesmerise him. Akai could tell that something deep down in Tisenin had changed the moment the knife went in and Tisenin was contemplating what it was. He felt compelled to say something comforting.

"Archlord, they say that when the simurgh made us from the humans, they did more than just give us control of magic and extend our lives," said Akai.

"They slowed down our reproduction, made us submissive and docile. They did everything they could to make us easy to manage."

"What is your point Akai?"

"My point is that they made us slaves. We cherno are not naturally inclined to acts of violence or rebellion. Archlord, I just wanted to say *thank you*. It was a brave, selfless thing you did. I could not have done it," said Akai.

"I hope the rest of the Empire sees it the same way," said Tisenin. "You have wisdom in excess of your occupation. Tell me, how old are you Akai?"

"I am three-hundred, Archlord."

"Ah, the same as me. And how long have you been a sailor?" asked Tisenin.

"Three-hundred years, Archlord."

"What, you have only served in one trade?" said Tisenin, baffled by the concept of such a restricted life.

"Fishing, sailing the trade routes, chartered voyages. All the ports from Cathri to Sunnel. I've been hauling the produce from your estates for the last few years. Everything I own I can carry on my back and every week I am in a new place meeting new people or visiting old friends. Never wanted anything else, except maybe to someday see the whole world."

Tisenin scanned Akai looking for symbols of his eligibility, and finding none, concluded he must be married. "What about raising children? That must be difficult on a ship?"

Akai forgave the assumption. Most childless cherno wore their hair long and loose, or long and braided, like Tisenin. But Akai had given up trying to tame his salt-encrusted hair at sea and just let it grown out as a mossy afro.

"Aye, that too, but I would have to find a wife first. Not many women have the strength to haul hemp on a ship and still fewer are willing to put up with a perpetually absent husband. Like most sailors who do the long Cathri run, I've probably had more men, but not found a soul-mate among them," lamented Akai. "That is my excuse, what is yours, fellow bachelor?"

"Ah, I have just never found a woman worthy of my ego," joked Tisenin. Akai detected just a hint of something darker beneath his reply, but Tisenin quickly switched the subject back to Akai. "The trick for you would be to find a sailmaker, a bronze smith or cartographer and have her serve aboard the same ship. Some trade every ship would benefit from."

"Alas, I would have to be the captain to hire my choice of crew. And that will not come to me for a few centuries yet."

Tisenin held his hand out so Akai could help him up. "Then it sounds like you could use a friend with many ships." Tisenin cracked a wan smile, acknowledging his gratitude for Akai's help, then he regarded the six mages sat on the prow of the ship. They were shivering and sweating with the exertion of changing the winds. "How much progress have they made?"

"They say it will be a few hours yet until we have the wind behind us," said Akai.

"Good, then the sails will be useless until then. Get the white one down and change it for the black. We shall let our allies know that the deed is done."

"Aye, Archlord!"

Akai went about his business, proud to be at the centre of the turning wheel and proud to have shared a few words with his cynosure.

Chapter 2

The Fool

Zanthred was on one knee, holding a goose feather up to the woman who was widely credited to be the most beautiful woman in the world. Everyone in the inn was staring at him in outright astonishment, not least the woman he was propositioning.

"My lady Janistor, I would be the most honoured man in the world if you would consent to take me as a troth."

"I'm sorry... do I know you?"

Zanthred choked a little. Of all the possible responses that had gone through his mind, this was not one he expected. The little grey feather wobbled in his hand.

"Er, yes. I am Zanthred. We danced here not two nights ago."

Janistor's features settled into a smile.

"Ah, I am sorry. I dance a lot."

There was a titter of laughter from the group around her. One young man raised a scented handkerchief to his face to conceal the broad grin that had formed. It did not do a very good job.

"So tell me Zanthred, I have heard nothing of your deeds. Are you perhaps famous in the lands across the sea? In Delfuri or Lansissari where the world is yet wild?"

"No my lady, I am from a village north of Icknel, I have never journeyed out of Quri." There was a peel of laughter from the room at the response.

"Are you perhaps a great artist, who has taken me to be your muse?" asked Janistor.

"No, though you are muse enough, I am but a humble amateur in all the arts." Another round of laughter. The man with the handkerchief was virtually having to stuff it in his mouth to keep quiet.

"Dear Zanthred, are you here in Serra to compete in the athletics games and win fame across the land?"

"No my lady, I am here to do my civic service. Twenty years tilling the fields for the Emperor." The hilarity multiplied with each utterance. The crowd were no longer disguising their amusement. Zanthred could feel his face flush with heat and he began to sweat.

"Do you have a rare gift for me to show your fortune, maybe a fine mare? Or perhaps something won with courage and skill? A scale from a blue dragon or the pelt of a shadow panther?"

"No my lady, I only have this simple goose feather and my devotion to offer you."

The room erupted in fits of glee. Zanthred had never heard such a spontaneous outburst from an entire room of people before. Even Janistor was joining in with a slight chuckle. But with an eye to propriety she forced herself back to a serious demeanour and signalled for the rest of the room to calm down.

Once there was quiet enough to speak she delivered her verdict. She took the little grey feather and held it in her hands. Not for the first time, Zanthred was awestruck by the number she already wore in her hair. No less than twelve – twelve troths, twelve men who were content to share her and perhaps call her a 'lover.' Twelve rivals from who she would eventually pick a single husband. Zanthred had known his chances of joining them were slim, but after the dance...he had just got a feeling that something special had passed between them. He was starting to doubt that intuition.

"Dear Zanthred, I am sorry, I cannot accept you as a troth, but I consider it an honour to have one so...*bold*...devoted to me." She took the feather and tied it to a band at her wrist. That was meant to dull the blow; the wrist meant *'I can't see myself loving you, but I'm happy to have you as a friend.'* It was small consolation. There were already about thirty other feathers tied to that band.

Zanthred got up from his knee and planned on saying something expressing gratitude, like he had practised in his head. However, his embarrassment was so deep that he just wanted to get away from her and her friends as fast as possible, so he automatically beat a hasty retreat to the other side of the inn, chased by howls of laughter.

"Zanthred! Did you just do what I think you did, or am I hallucinating?" asked his friend Mille. Pure shock radiated from her face.

Zanthred sighed as he sat down at his familiar table, "No Mille, you're not hallucinating. Get me some more mead will you, I need to drink."

"I can't believe you just tried proposing to Janistor! Look at her!"

"I don't want to look at her. That's the very last thing I want to do. In fact, I think I want to see if I can slowly melt through this wall and leave without anyone noticing me."

"Stop being such a child, it was your choice. You can't sit here sighing all night going 'aye me'. Look at her!"

Zanthred slowly pulled his head round. She was in high spirits, giggling at what just happened. And every time she came to the punch line one of the crowd around her would shoot a mirthful glance in Zanthred's direction, leaving him in no doubt as to what they were finding funny.

A hundred years of life had resulted in little more than Zanthred learning the name of every star in the heavens, absolutely everything there was to know about sheep tending, and almost everything about fresco painting. It was this last facet of knowledge he could use to analyse Janistor's face. There was a rare symmetry in her features; a careful positioning of her wide eyes, delicate nose and full lips that suggested some artist had already been responsible for what he saw. He knew which pigments he would use for her skin. Raw umber mixed with burnt sienna, to get that dark brown and just a hint of ultramarine to add depth. A trace of golden ochre would fetch the sheen of her iris, although the pupil and her hair needed the blackest bone char. When he looked at her, he could see himself dabbing the delicate brush onto damp plaster, already knowing and cursing the fact that he could never do her face justice with his commonplace skill.

But that was not really what went through his head when he looked at her. It was more like: *Phwaar, she's gorgeous!*

"Zanthred, you see that long red feather in her hair?"

"Yes," he droned.

"That was given to her by Malichar ap Sunnar, son of the Lord of Sunnel. He climbed to the top of a mountain and plucked it from the tail of nesting eagle. And you see that green and purple one?"

"Yes."

"That came from Callin ap Elsiren, a distant relative of the Emperor. He personally went to the spice colonies and had to fight off an attack by the tribals to get that feather from a rare parrot. Rumour has it he would have challenged her last would-be suitor to a duel to the death if she had not intervened. And you see that black one?"

"I get your point Mille."

She thumped the table. "The point I'm making is that some of the best men in the Empire have done some of the most romantic things imaginable to get her attention. And you offered her a grey goose feather."

"I thought it said something like 'forget the hype, I like you, you like me, that's all that matters'."

"A hundred years old, and you don't know the first thing about wooing," tutted Mille in her big-sisterly way.

"I've not had much practise. Fifty of those years I spent on a hillside with sheep, doing nothing but stargazing and shooting hares."

"Yes, and I spent the same amount of time doing the same thing in the valley next door, but I know damn well not to go making a fool of myself in public. I wish you'd run this past me before you tried that. I'd have stopped you."

"I know you would have. But I wanted to take the risk," insisted Zanthred.

"Risk? You really don't get it do you! You can spend a hundred years building a good reputation, but you can lose it all in one misjudged action. By the morning everyone in Chepsid will know who you are and what you did."

Zanthred groaned, put his head flat against the table and pointed to his empty beaker.

"Mead! Or wine if they've got it."

Mille consented and got up to ladle some more drink into their beakers.

At least this happened in Chepsid, thought Zanthred.

Chepsid lay across the great river from Serra. It was a town on the outskirts of a city where all the young cherno went for entertainment. It was full of cheap hostels and wine parlours where labourers performing their civic service could unwind or look for a mate. Actors, comedians, acrobats, singers and poets all flocked here to practise their acts before taking them to the market square in the centre of Serra. The township had a reputation for raucous behaviour and much of what would never be tolerated in the proud and duty-laden world outside passed by here unnoticed. Zanthred just might get through this episode if he could convince people it was a moment of Chepsid madness.

Mille returned empty handed.

"Baytee, our host wants to talk to you," she said.

Zanthred looked up to see the woman who ran the establishments looming over the table. Baytee was in her six-hundreds and had grown broad from all the cooking she did and all the wines she tasted. She had her arms crossed about her bosom with a jug held temptingly in one hand.

"My good host, how can I serve you?" said Zanthred.

"You've done me more good than I could have asked already, young one. That was quite a laugh you gave us! I thought I would bring this wine for you and your friend. It is one of our best. From the Emerald Coast." She placed the wine down. It was a large quantity; more than two could drink in the night and retain their senses.

"Thank you! I am only sorry that I currently lack the means to repay your kindness. Perchance you have work you need doing around your household?" offered Zanthred.

"Work and workers aplenty I'm afraid. But if you could bear to separate from your blue cowry, I would be greatly pleased. Such a token would carry no little weight in Chepsid, now you have made a name for yourself."

Zanthred's hands shot to the little blue cowry shell at his neck. It was the first time someone had asked for one of his cowry; he just wished it was for a different reason. Although everyone in the inn wore one or two of the shiny cowry shells about them – as earrings, beads or toggles on clothing – the blue cowry they wore around their necks was special. It signalled "I'm available and looking for a partner." Janistor still wore one, despite the twelve feathers in her hair. It had been all Zanthred had been able to focus on when he had been swirling around the room with her in his arms. That little shiny jewel on her long brown neck, telling him he had a chance.

Collecting cowry from notable people was something everybody did and giving them was a good way to discharge your debts. There was nothing one would call a currency in the cherno world, but the bright little shells came close to small change. Only, Zanthred felt awkward about giving his blue cowry away before having found a wife. He had had visions of it being some kind of solemn occasion. But what choice did he have?

"Of course, I consider myself blessed to know it is in your good care." He untied the pendant and handed it over.

"Thank you. I don't know where you are lodging, but I have a few spare spaces in my hostel. You are welcome to stay until you begin your civic service."

"Really?" squeaked Mille. "It's an honour. We shall come over tomorrow."

The Perched Sparrow was not so much an exclusive establishment as a notorious one. It had a reputation for attracting the best poets and musicians among Serra's youth and was always busy. There was no distinction drawn between young nobles like Janistor and her troths with their bright, finely woven silks and long, intricately styled hair, or the plebeian likes of Zanthred and Millie with plain, well-travelled clothes and rustic dreadlocks. If you were serious about musical appreciation, as Mille was, then you did not turn down the opportunity to stay there. The room went deathly quiet for a moment and the three of them at the table glanced to the door. There was a man in respectable garb holding a chest at the threshold. He looked very sour faced.

"I wish to speak to Baytee, the host of this inn," said the man.

"It is I," said Baytee.

"I am come from the palace. After today's terrible events the great banquet has been cancelled-"

"...Terrible events?" interrupted Baytee.

"You have not heard yet? No one came to tell you?"

"There have been high winds all day, perhaps no one dared cross the river. The waves come up to the breast of the bridge. But what is this event?"

The palace porter drew a heavy-hearted sigh, "The Emperor Kirrie is dead, slain by the hand of her cousin Tisenin. The palace is in uproar." There was a general gasp of disbelief, then a clamour of questions were thrown at him. "I will tell all I know! But first I must speak with Baytee."

"Then speak," said Baytee.

"The feast was cancelled and so, as protocol dictates, the perishables are to be given to the guilds of the city. Given the Emperor's love for this tavern, I thought it best you were included." The palace servant opened the box and revealed what looked like a series of white cocoons, each as large as a man's fist. "These are a rare ingredient from Cathri, bird nests I believe."

"Bird nests?" Baytee repeated, confused.

"A gift to the Emperor from Archlord Kamil ap Hexin. Apparently they are produced high in the caves of a single island in the western ocean, and harvested at great risk. Apparently the soup they make with them is in vogue in Cathri. Kamil's niece, Hilsi, was kind enough to provide instruction on how they are to be prepared."

"Odd people, out in the colonies. But I am honoured to receive such a rare gift and doubly honoured to be remembered as the Emperor's friend." Baytee motioned for one of her residents to take the box over to her stove. "It will be a privilege to serve what was meant for the Emperor's table at our own. I know my guests have unbounded creativity. Please, let the Emperor's widow know we will compose an elegy for dear Kirrie. It will be delivered by morning."

"I will convey your offer to Duarma," said the porter.

"Why us? Why not the palace laureate?" whispered Zanthred.

Baytee overheard, but addressed her reply to the whole room, "This generation is too young to remember, but a paltry two hundred years ago, Kirrie, yet to be Emperor, sang in this hall and danced with her only troth."

An audible flutter of excitement went round the room; to compose for the dead Emperor was one thing, but to know that you and she shared a common bond made it even more compelling. Almost straight away the patrons gathered together in small groups and started making notes on scraps of paper or strumming experimental bars on their instruments. Baytee began following the recipe provided with the box of white cocoons and people crowded round to ask the place servant questions about the terrible murder.

"I can't believe it," muttered Zanthred. "I can understand being scared of the Ban, but murder?"

"I know," said Mille.

It was not long before Baytee was dishing up, ladling a bowl full of soup in front of each person. They spooned it into their mouths in silence. Any other time and Zanthred might have enjoyed the salty taste and sticky texture, but that was impossible with what they had in their minds.

When everyone was done, Janistor picked up her lyre and stood in the centre of the room. She began singing the *Lay of Finasa*. It was a song about lost love and wasted life, and popularly held to be the saddest song ever written. Her fingers barely touched the lyre and she let her voice carry the full weight of the words in long sonorous notes.

Her soft voice cut right to Zanthred's heart and he was not surprised when tears started streaming down his face. Mille was also crying next to him; in fact, everyone in the Perched Sparrow had water on their cheeks.

When the last lonely notes of Janistor's lyre had been plucked and her voice came to rest, one of her follows joined her in the centre of the room. It was the man with the handkerchief, now using it to dab his eyes.

He addressed the whole room, "My friends, I propose that whoever should write the elegy for Emperor Kirrie, Janistor should be the one to perform it."

There was a clamorous assent of pots ringing on tables and shouts of 'aye.' Janistor looked well pleased and smiled eagerly at her advocate.

A thought struck Zanthred; a plan to make Janistor his, perhaps the only shot he had.

"I know what you're thinking Zanthred," said Mille. "I can see it on your face. You *can't* write a song by the morning and you *can't* make Janistor love you for it."

The plan shattered before his eyes.

"No, I suppose you're right."

"We'll find you a new blue cowry in the morning, and hopefully a new girl to go with it. Until then, let's drink and talk sheep."

They drank as much of the wine as they dared to retain their senses and occasionally danced when a lively troop took to the floor. Their fun was only spoilt when some raised voices on Janistor's side of the inn seemed to indicate a fight was about to break out.

"WHAT DO YOU MEAN YOU AGREE WITH TIS-ENIN!?" The man with the handkerchief seemed to have cornered a young man against a wall and was shouting right into his face. His words were slurred as if heavily weighted with alcohol.

"I didn't say I agreed with him killing the Emperor, I said I agreed with him that something radical needs to be done to stop the Ban. If we are going to act, it has to be now, before our powers are reduced too far."

"You are an insult to our race. We should stone you to death where you stand!"

Shouts of thuggish agreement sent a chill down

Zanthred's spine. Luckily, Baytee pushed her way through the crowd and raised her voice over the antagonists.

"We'll have no more kin-slaying today. If you can't argue civilly, get yourselves a table at either end of the inn." There was a good deal of force in her voice and she was held in high esteem by the patrons. So, sluggishly, they pulled themselves away from the confrontation and the cornered man slunk out of the door. Baytee interposed herself at the entrance just in case anyone decided to follow him and continue the argument.

The man with the handkerchief begged leave of his friends and wandered around to cool his temper. He was the most richly dressed man in the room with an airy satin robe and a firmament of little yellow gems in the braids of his black hair. Unfortunately, he wandered straight over to where Zanthred and Mille were stood. When he recognised Zanthred from his earlier exhibition, he paused.

"Ah, you are the latest love rival, yes?"

"For Janistor?" asked Zanthred.

"Of course, who else?"

"And you are?" interrupted Mille.

The man pointed to Janistor, "You see that purple and green feather in her hair? That is mine. I am Callin ap Elsiren."

"Oh," said Mille flatly. "I've heard of you, by reputation."

"Yes, I forget that newcomers might not know me

in person. You may have gathered I have quite the hot temper." He dabbed the handkerchief to his mouth and took a breath of whatever scent was infused on it, presumably in order to calm his nerves.

"Yes..." said Mille, recalling the story about the threatened duel.

"I just wanted to let you know Zanthred, that although Janistor may consider it an 'honour' to have one so 'bold' as a suitor, I find it rather insulting that a pleb like you would hold yourself to be my equal."

The insult bit deep in Zanthred. In cherno society such comments were rarely used without the malice implied. He did not know what to say back, so he just held his tongue.

"I think in future Zanthred, it would be better if you found a different place of recreation so we didn't cross paths again."

Zanthred was about to make for the door when Mille placed a hand on his shoulder to hold him back. "Oh dear Callin, you see what you've just done?" she said. "You've just made it impossible for Zanthred to spend his evenings anywhere else! He's already made a fool of himself this evening, so he couldn't possibly be made a coward as well. One flaw is quite enough to mar a man's life."

Callin starred down at Mille for a pregnant couple of seconds. Zanthred gritted his teeth.

"Humph, well quite. At least you, my dear one, have sense enough for the both of you. Goodnight."

He turned to leave, but Mille called him back.

"Callin, how does it work? The twelve of you with Janistor?"

Callin turned again with a scowl on his face. "Adequately. We nobles are often called away on hunts or to do deeds worthy of our stations, so we time matters so that there are rarely more than three of us in Serra. Still, as to the matter of who goes home with her at night...that is up to Janistor." He looked over at where she was laughing and frolicking with her friends; there was one handsome man she was staring deeply in to the eyes of, giggling coquettishly at his every comment. Callin did not look pleased. He no doubt suspected it would not be his turn this particular night. "Still, it is not like I am without obligations of my own." Callin stroked a hand through his hair, drawing attention to the three feathers perched there.

Zanthred and Mille distinctly felt the lack feathers in their own hair and got the feeling that Callin had won this round. He left and Zanthred breathed a sigh of relief.

"Thanks Mille, you saved my reputation there."

"I know, you can thank me properly some other time. For now, I'm taking this wine of yours. There's a timid looking girl by herself over there and I'm going to see if she is open minded about which gender she beds."

Zanthred looked over and saw a short mousy girl sat by herself with a quill and some parchment. She was splitting her time between furiously scribbling and nervously looking up towards Janistor and her clique.

"Need some help wooing her?"

Mille shot him a look of pure scepticism.

* * * * * * *

Duarma clutched Kirrie's broken body and wept profusely. She was limp in his arms and her limbs sprawled uselessly on the floor. He was not sure how much time had passed. He was only vaguely aware of the other lords arguing around him.

"That damn fool Tisenin. What did he think he was doing?"

"He knew exactly what he was doing. He is next in line to the throne. He will declare himself Emperor."

"But surely he cannot think that anyone would accept him after he has done this? Kin-slaying is for the humans, we have never tolerated it."

"Except from the line of Elsiren."

"Elsiren had no choice!"

"And Tisenin will argue that neither did he."

"Would anyone follow him?"

"No one in their right mind!"

"You saw how many of the Jewasri lords he had with him. And how many still here secretly sympathise with his position, if not his method?"

"We must already have a new Emperor by the time he makes his position clear and we must back that person unanimously."

"There is none with a stronger link to Elsiren than Tisenin."

"They do not have to be of the line of Elsiren,

providing they already have some strong stake in governance."

There was a distinct lull in conversation. Duarma had no idea how long it lasted for before he became aware of it and looked up.

The lords had formed a ring around him and were staring intently.

Haddra ap Woodrin seemed to have blustered his way to the front of them. Haddra was the last of the great colonial archlords represented in the assembly, and the only one to have done the honour of coming himself. During Tisenin's speech he had stayed silent with a look of disdain. His lands were in Delfuri, the great eastern plains where they raised horses, sheep and little else. He was eight hundred years old, with heavy, creased eyes and greying hair to match, yet he was still famous as a war leader and master horseman. Like most of his generation, he had an undue reverence for title and ceremony; it could take months to get here from the eastern plains of Delfuri, but he made the trip every time Kirrie held the Magnolia Court. *You could tell a lot about a cherno lord by the way they dressed*, and nowhere was this more obvious than with Haddra. He had gone past the point of dressing to show standing. He could rely on his reputation alone to do that now. Today he wore plain blue linen riding trousers, fresh with mud from a morning gallop.

He held out his hand to help Duarma up. Duarma did not take it.

"Duarma, I know you want the time to grieve for your wife, we all want time to take stock. But we don't have it. Duarma, you must be our new Emperor. Have some courage and take this gnarled oak hand of mine," insisted Haddra. His voice was grim and practical.

Duarma's tears were making everyone's faces blurry and it took a while for him to discover that each lord was assenting. It took him even longer to realise the magnitude of what was being asked of him.

"That's ridiculous," Duarma sobbed. He clutched Kirrie's body tighter and wished everyone else away. "How can I lead the Empire? Why would anyone follow me? Pick some archlord or paramount of the clans."

Haddra knelt down and gently pulled Duarma's arms from Kirrie's body. "I'm the only archlord here and no one wants this crude-talking colonial as a leader. A paramount? Sure, but which? There are fourteen noble dynasties. *Ap Lunis or Sunnar? Ap Hexin or Ranra?* It would take time to argue which clan chieftain takes the throne. None of us have time for luxuries while your wife's murder escapes. Kirrie chose you as a husband, not because you were handsome or of particularly noble birth, but because of all people, you shared her thoughts most closely. That much is common knowledge. And that fact makes you as valid a successor as Tisenin's blood makes him. Now we have some hard decisions to make and we need you to make them. We will offer our guidance, all you have to do is legitimate our orders. Will you do it?"

Duarma slumped to the floor and looked up at all the expectant faces gathered round him.

"No," he said.

Jandor touched a hand to Duarma's shoulder. "Think of Kirrie's reign. She rarely stinted from her duties. Of that I'm sure you know more than anyone. Her every waking thought was of how to use her position to help the people of the Empire. To refuse this burden now is to make a mockery of her hard work."

A sore lump came to Duarma's throat; he knew what Jandor said was true.

"...If you think me worthy, I will do the task until someone more suitable can be found," he finally consented.

"That is all I ask," said Haddra. He raised his voice so that everyone could clearly hear it. "First issue of the Magnolia Court. I propose that Duarma ap Brazini, widow of the former Emperor Kirrie, become the new Emperor of all cherno lands."

"Agreed!" came the shouts from the nobles.

"Does anyone dissent?" asked Haddra. There was silence. "Good, then it is unanimous. Secondly, what do we do with the traitor Tisenin ap Elsiren?"

Duarma rose to his feet and clenched his fist. He found his grief could be converted to anger easily when he imagined the look of supplication on Tisenin's face just before he plunged in the dagger. "We send to Efrandi immediately and demand that the people of the city and good subjects of the Emperor turn him over to face a trial in Serra."

"Then we must act with all haste," said Haddra. "What is the state of the wind between here and Efrandi?"

"My Lords, I believe I can answer that." It was Mordhai the meteomancer, who had come down from the tower when he had heard the commotion. "At the moment the winds blow southeast, directly against us. But I could sense mages aboard Tisenin's galley trying to swing the winds in the opposite direction. Within four hours they will turn northwest and blow directly to Efrandi. We could speed that up if I gathered the mages at the Guild."

"Good, do that Mordhai," said Jandor.

"The coward must be desperate to run back to his home," said Haddra. "With the wind behind it an imperial catamaran can beat his galley to Efrandi easily. He will be arrested as soon as he steps ashore."

Jandor raised a note of caution. "We should not assume he will be so easily captured. This act has clearly been pre-planned, there will be some contingency. He may not even be heading for Efrandi. What would you have us do, Emperor Duarma?"

Jandor was spelling out a problem and an obvious response, but he was trying to have Duarma make the decision and look like an Emperor. In his current state, Duarma was grateful for Jandor guiding his hand.

"That seems sound reasoning, Lord Jandor," said Duarma. "Then we must send fast ships to all quarters of the Empire and let them know what has happened. Tisenin will only have the human lands to flee to."

"I will also gather some proven soldiers in case he and his fellows resist arrest. I know many veterans of Delfuri who have fought in our border wars with cutthroat humans and have retired to Serra. There will be no soldiers in the Empire with greater experience. I'll have a hundred ready before the end of the day," announced Haddra. He could not help a measure of pride, boarding on boastfulness, leak into his words as he talked of his country's warriors.

"It is as well," said Duarma.

"If there is a shortfall, people who have lived on the borders of Lansissari and Cathri can serve in their stead. All the colonies have problems with humans," said Jandor. He looked around to get a confirmation from Hilsi, but he could not find her. "Where is Hilsi?"

Haddra scoffed, "Bah! The timid creature fled at the first sight of blood. She's probably already back on her ship, running off to her uncle in Cathri as we speak."

"Then make sure someone else sends word to Cathri," said Duarma.

One of the minor Serra lords volunteered to arrange all the messages.

"There is not much more to be done now, we should let the people of the city know so that the mourning can begin," said Haddra.

"I am sorry, my friends, there will be no feast tonight. I fear I cannot play the host," said Duarma.

The other lords nodded in understanding and began

to disperse; each small group talking of what might be in the days ahead.

A servant took Duarma's arm and began leading him away to his chamber where he would be allowed to wail himself into exhaustion alone. However, just as they were leaving the courtyard, he caught sight of the bodyguard who had stood behind Kirrie during the conference. Duarma had forgotten all about him. The guard's face was now swollen and bruised and he walked with a limp as if someone had stamped on his leg.

Duarma heard himself speak without any conscious input. "Why didn't you save her? Why didn't you stop Tisenin?"

The man swallowed hard and looked ashen. "My Lord, I did not see. I could not catch him."

"Why!? It was what you were supposed to do! It was your job!" Duarma began to blab uncontrollably and punched the bodyguard in the chest. "Why didn't you save her!"

Duarma's fists rained down on the bodyguard as he poured out his frustration. The bodyguard stoically stood his ground and allowed Duarma's hands to pound his already battered body.

"I'm sorry, my Lord," was all he said. He did not flinch from a single blow.

Jandor pulled Duarma away and tried to talk him back to sense.

"My Lord, I'm sure he did all he could. He is of the Shadow Guard, he should need no more recommendation than that."

Duarma's raging spirit broke and exhaustion weighed his arms and legs like lead. He allowed himself to be led away. He dimly knew there was no sense in his rage; he had been as close as the bodyguard when the attack happened, and he had the better view. It should have been himself who saved Kirrie.

That knowledge burned at him.

On the way back to his chamber they passed the great hall. There were piles of boxes outside which had not been there a few hours before.

"What are these?" he asked his servant weakly.

"Emperor, they are the gifts from the nobles. They were supposed to be presented during the banquet. I have made a list so you can return the compliments...at a better time."

"Thank you. Are there any perishables?"

"Already dealt with Emperor. Lord Jandor prompted me to disperse them while you were...indisposed."

"It is as well."

"All the guilds sent their condolences. The residents of the Perched Sparrow offered to compose Kirrie's elegy."

Duarma remembered long nights of laughter and mirth before any sovereign responsibility had been placed on his troth's shoulders.

"Tell Baytee I would like that dearly."

"I will make sure it is done, Emperor."

Emperor. The title felt like a joke hung around Duarma's neck.

The servant finally managed to get Duarma into his room and let him collapse onto the floor mattress, then quietly shut the door on his way out.

Duarma's eyes welled up and tears streaked down his face. He knew he would be crying for some time.

* * * * * * *

Hesiad the bodyguard was so full of guilt that he could barely maintain his legs. He had been an arm's length from Tisenin. But the truth was, he just was not paying attention. Nothing like this had ever happened before. The butterfly axe was supposed to be symbolic. It had never even crossed his mind that a favoured noble, let alone the Emperor's cousin, would try to assassinate her in broad daylight. But perhaps if he had paid closer attention, he might have seen the dagger, he might have reached Tisenin in time. He could not face looking into Duarma's eyes again. He had failed. He would have to go back into exile. For the second time in his life, he walked down to the docks and away from his home. He would have to work his path out of shame as a penitent.

Only, he was not sure how long that would take a second time, or if there were any deed that could make up for his failure.

Chapter 3

Necessary Evils

Akai saw the imperial catamaran behind them when it was just a speck, but it closed the distance alarmingly quickly. The tiny catamarans were the royal messengers and with a good wind could make the journey from Serra to Efrandi in half the time their own galley could. Its prow blades sliced though the water sending up a frothy white surf and its silk sail kept full without billowing or tearing in the strong wind. High waves rolled straight over the top of it without the least danger of damaging the vessel. It was made for pushing straight through storms, even hurricanes.

Akai wished they had similar advantages. The wind was so strong that they were having to travel at half sail to stop the mast from splintering in two and the waves were splashing over the sides, drenching the oarsmen. There was no doubt they were about to be overtaken by the nimble catamaran.

The spray from the waves had drenched Tisenin, pasting his expensive silk robes to his body and making his legs run with purple dye, although the comedy of the scene was robbed by his serious expression. Akai knew something similar was happening to his hair; he could feel the weight of water in his woolly fro dragging it down to his scalp.

"Akai, you have plied these waters for decades. Will you give me your opinion?" asked Tisenin.

"That is the Captain's place, Archlord."

Tisenin looked to the Captain, but he was more than busy shouting orders to the sailors trying to tame the wind in their sail.

"I have no doubt you are an able sailor Akai. How long until that catamaran reaches Efrandi?" asked Tisenin.

"An hour, Archlord."

"And how long until we could be seen from the harbour?"

"At this rate? About two hours."

"And with the oarsmen going at their fastest pace and a full sail?"

"Perhaps an hour and a half, maybe less. But I wouldn't advise it. The men are already tired and the mast is not designed for this kind of weather. If the mages could calm the wind a bit, our oars would give us the edge."

They looked over at the six mages. They had kept a vigil up for days and were now so exhausted that they had collapsed on deck where they were being treated by a worried cook hand.

"I doubt we can expect any help from their quarter," said Tisenin. "Never the less, we need to get back to Efrandi as quickly as possible."

"I will speak to the Captain," promised Akai.

Within minutes the drum was beating double time, forcing the oarsmen to heave their chests and thrash the water with their blades. The sail was drawn high and the mast began to creak in protestations. Dark waves crashed on the prow and the hull raised up, skimming through the white froth.

Despite their measures the imperial catamaran caught up to them fast and it was easy to make out just three crewmen on its deck. They had tied themselves to the mast so that they might control the sail without danger of being swept overboard. The vessel was cutting a course very close to their own and as they passed by the imperial messengers looked across to their galley and eyed Tisenin with pure contempt.

"We need to move faster," he said.

Akai had a moment of inspiration, "Archlord, is there anything on this vessel we need except ourselves?"

"No."

Akai did not wait to check if his idea was acceptable to Tisenin or the Captain, he just shouted it out. "All spare hands, grab whatever we don't absolutely need and throw it overboard!" The crew would not normally take orders from someone as young as Akai, but with Tisenin beside him people seemed to obey straight away.

The stone anchors went first, cut from their lines. Then all the barrels of fresh water and food. Spare ropes, nails, pitch, cloth and wood next. And lastly, they grabbed all the boxes of gifts that had been intended for the Emperor, had she changed her mind. A king's ransom of riches was cast overboard; brocaded silks, plum wines, rare indigo dyes from the Peril Isles, spices, jewellery of gold and ivory, cut translucent stones and arts and crafts of every description. They floated away in their transport crates or slowly sank, never to be appreciated again. The galley's speed picked up a little and the burden of the oarsmen was reduced considerably.

A cold crosswind suddenly tugged at Akai's neck and made the main sail luff. A rope snapped and one of the lower booms whipped round. There was a second of recollection in him and he saw the danger in where he was standing. He grabbed Tisenin and threw them both to the floor just as a loose cable from the boom lashed out over their heads.

"Are you okay?" asked Akai.

"Yes," replied Tisenin. "You saved me."

Akai pointed to a thin scar that ran under his eye.

"I was caught by a loose cable and a crosswind once before. Knocked me clean unconscious and almost took an eye. Experience is the finest tutor."

"Well Akai, I shall not forget this debt I owe you."

Then he looked out over to the catamaran which was pulling clear away from them towards the rocky shore of Jewasri. "Assuming of course, we make it in time."

* * * * * * *

The catamaran Captain Talyur was glad they were finally coming into Efrandi. The storm had been a rougher one than he would have liked to sail through and the rope tied to his waist had left him with deep friction burns where it had rubbed. The quayside was full of moored ships; no one wanted to be out in this kind of weather. There was only one space near the Harbour Master's house and Talyur and his two crew mates carefully manoeuvred the tiny vessel towards it. There was already a small group of people gathered on the quay, silhouetted by the dark blue sky. They were wrapped tight in hoods and cloaks against the wild wind. One of them had a lantern in hand and was signalling for the ship to come in. *That must be the Harbour Master*, thought Talyur. Imperial catamarans were very distinctive vessels and carried orders directly from the Emperor; it was not uncommon for them to be spotted from afar and greeted in this way.

The harbour stopped the worst of the waves, so they took in the sail and let the wind push the ship gently up to the wooden quay. Talyur threw a rope up and one of the harbour hands caught it and tied it off. Talyur cut the cord around his waist and vaulted up. The Harbour Master greeted him with clasped hands. This master was new; Talyur did not recognise him.

"You have a look of urgency about you, dear

messenger. Can your news wait until after you and your crew have dined with me? It must have been a hard crossing in these winds," said the Harbour Master.

"No, this is of the highest urgency. Archlord Tisenin ap Elsiren has murdered the Emperor and fled the scene. He has been declared a traitor by the Magnolia Court. We believe he is heading here, to Efrandi. All citizens of the Empire are called upon to arrest Tisenin with any accomplices and bring them back to Serra for judgment. This message is to be taken to anyone who can claim authority in Efrandi and is to be repeated to anyone brave and skilled with weapons."

The group of harbour hands shuffled uneasily and the Harbour Master went wide-eyed. Talyur would have expected nothing less.

"Aye, this is urgent news," said the Harbour Master. "But there is one thing you might do for me before we take this news to the people of Efrandi. I think I see another ship on the horizon, but my eyes are poor in this light. Could you tell me what your sailor's eyes see?"

Talyur turned around and stared into the gloom of the distance, drained of colour and blurred by mist from the crests of the waves. There was, he thought, a ship on the horizon.

"Yes Harbour Master, I see a ship. It must be the galley of Tisenin. We passed close by it not an hour ago. We have little time to organize ourselves."

"But its sail looks odd? What colour does it fly?"

Talyur squinted again. There was just a black square against a dark blue sky.

"Black, I think. Yes I'm sure it was black when we passed it," said Talyur.

"Good, that is all I need to know."

Talyur did not see the Harbour Master draw the dagger or see the blade as he plunged it into his back, but he felt the pain as it went in and he saw it dripping with his blood as he staggered away from the injury. The Harbour Master advanced on him to finish the kill, but Talyur reacted fast and flung his wounded body off the quay onto the deck of the catamaran. The other two crew stared aghast.

"Cut the line! Push us out to sea! This is treachery!" Talyur screeched.

The line was cut almost immediately, but the vessel stayed still.

"Push us off, push us off! Take us away before they come for us!" urged Talyur.

"But how Captain? The wind is blowing directly into port."

It suddenly, horribly dawned on Talyur that the wind Tisenin's mages had been summoning had nothing to do with helping him to escape. They were for making sure everyone in Efrandi was trapped.

****

Quinias held his hand over the mouth of the last of the Serra sailors, stifling his screams as he bled out into the water. His body finally went limp on the deck of the catamaran.

"Someone cover these three bodies up and move them on board my galley."

Two of his hooded followers obliged. Quinias clambered back up on to the jetty and snuffed out the lantern to avoid any further attention. There were twenty hand-picked followers here. Friends and servants close to Tisenin and absolutely dedicated to averting the Ban. These were people who knew that words and a single symbolic act of bloodshed would never win victory.

He took two of them aside. Adrin and Dago. They were both the lesser offspring of Jewasri nobles, used to a fine lifestyle but unlikely to inherit a worthy title, much like Tisenin. Adrin wore his trademark coat of lizard skin, which he had taken hunting in Cathri. Dago had freshly tattooed tears on her right cheek; she had fully expected events to come to this and was prepared for a lifetime of remorse.

"My friends, the black sail is flying. We three know our targets. We get them to follow us willingly. If not, we know what we have to do."

Adrin and Dago nodded grimly. The glints of bronze swords briefly shone below their cloaks. They each gathered a handful of followers and marched off into different quarters of the dark city.

* * * * * * *

Akai was glad to awake on a soft, motionless mattress. Tisenin had been gracious enough to let all the sailors from the voyage quarter in his palace for the night. Although, a part of Akai suspected that the main reason was that Tisenin did not want word of events to spread before he had a chance to make arrangements.

Akai got up from the fleeces laid on the floor and briefly stood naked surrounded by the rest of the sleeping crew. It looked like he was the first to rise; everyone else was clutching dearly to the deep, soft sheepskins and light linen sheets. Akai wound a robe round his waist and loosely flung what remained of the fabric over one shoulder.

He wandered out of the hall and into the palace's courtyard where a small fruit orchard had been planted for shade. It was near dawn and the air was still cool and dewy. Birds sang, but the busy insects were yet to warm their wings and begin their infuriating flights. Akai wondered where would be a polite place to relieve his bladder and decided he had best find somewhere outside the inner walls of the palace. He strolled over to the gate and found a man standing there openly wearing a short sword on his belt.

"Good morning," said Akai, warily eyeing the blade.

The guard followed Akai's eyes and tried to smile reassuringly.

"Good morning, friend. Hold no notice of the blade, Archlord Tisenin insisted that we take precautions tonight in case some short-sighted sort should take exception to our acts. Although I should ask you not to stray far from the palace. Tisenin would speak with his esteemed crew early this morning."

"Very well, I seek only to ease my waters."

The guard chuckled at the turn of phrase and allowed Akai to pass.

Akai walked a little way along the wall, raised his robe and relieved himself. He returned to the guard and was about to pass back into the palace when he heard some shouts behind him.

"Kind stranger, please wait!"

Akai turned to see a distraught looking young woman running up the hill towards him. She wore an expensive silk gown, but her hair had loosed itself from an elaborate raised evening style and now partially hung down in slack black coils. There were tears slipping down her face. When she reached Akai, she grasped his shoulder and leaned on him for support, panting.

"Dear stranger, please help me! I am Ashlaya ap Woodrin, daughter of Kesith ap Woodrin. Last night men with swords came to our house and took my father away. When my mother tried to stop them, they took her as well. I have been up all night trying to find someone to help me, but every friend of my father seems to have gone as well and I find nothing but households with weeping servants. Then one of them told me that the men claimed to have acted on the authority of Tisenin."

Thoughts rumbled round in Akai's head. *Blades in the night*. Was it really possible? Akai knew of Kesith ap Woodrin; he was the Paramount of the Woodrin dynasty, ostensibly the most senior lord in the noble clan. He was also one of the great landholders in Jewasri and vocal proponent of the Ban. Before Akai could think any more, the girl dropped to the floor and threw her arms around his knees. It was the ultimate sign of submission.

"And so I find you, about to enter Tisenin's palace and I beg you, please ask him to see me so that I may know the truth. Does he have them? Why? And if not, will he provide me with the good veterans that we need to track down these outlaws?"

Akai looked uneasily at the gate guard, who shrugged. Akai touched the girl's head, beckoning her to look up at him.

"I will of course take this to Tisenin, although I can promise nothing."

"That is all I ask."

Akai re-entered the shade of the courtyard. To his surprise, Tisenin was already up and strolling between the broad leafed trees with a companion in a deep maroon cloak.

"Archlord Tisenin, sorry to interrupt you. There is a distraught girl outside who claims there have been acts of kidnapping carried out in your name. She is most desperate to see you."

Tisenin nodded to his companion and they separated wordlessly. Tisenin came towards Akai. "Thank you Akai for bringing this to my attention. Would you lead the way?"

Akai brought Tisenin to the girl Ashlaya and she immediately fell into a fit of hysterical sobbing.

"Is it true? Did you have my family taken away?" she managed to squeeze out between the sobs.

"Ashlaya ap Woodrin, I know you and I know your father. Although we never shared many ideals, I want you to know I have the utmost respect for him. Which is why it pains me to say, yes I did have him taken away."

"But *why!?*"

"There have been certain political changes in the Empire in the last few days. Changes that your father *would* have opposed. I can only beg your forgiveness for my underhandedness, but I saw it as averting a greater evil by ensuring the transition takes a smooth course. Your family will be returned to you just as soon as everything is set in place and their opposition would be meaningless."

The girl almost screamed in horror at the confirmation, and she recoiled from Tisenin as if he were a poisonous snake. But the moment of dismay soon passed into love for her family and she calmed herself down.

"Archlord Tisenin, I cannot pretend to understand what events have moved you to forcibly imprison my family, but I ask that you take me to them now so that I can see they are alright with my own eyes."

"Dear Ashlaya, I am afraid you must take my solemn oath that they are being treated well and kept in moderate comfort. I cannot divulge their location or permit you to see them through fear that some brave fool will attempt a 'rescue' to everyone's detriment."

Ashlaya's cheeks were marred by a flood of tears. She threw herself to the ground again and hugged herself to Tisenin's knees.

"Archlord Tisenin, please I beg you, let me see my father! You have my oath that I will divulge the location of their imprisonment to none!"

"Dear Ashlaya, I'm sure you have every intention of keeping your oath, but if my three hundred years have taught me anything, it is never to respect a sentiment given in the heat of passion. Besides I could scarcely single you out for special treatment or ask every cherno in Efrandi to clutch my knees and swear a binding oath, when many would rather beat me and break my bones."

Tisenin motioned for her to let go, but she clutched all the harder. His purple robes became streaked black with tears.

"Please Tisenin, *please*!"

She repeated that refrain over and over. Tisenin motioned to the gate guard, who began to peel her arms away. As soon as he was free, Tisenin made for the freedom of his palace.

The girl screamed after him, "Where's my father, where's my father!"

Tisenin shook his head in resignation. He looked across to Akai and saw the shocked look on his face.

"You disapprove Akai?"

Akai looked deep inside himself to see what he was willing to give up for the greater good. The death of an Emperor. *Yes*. Some temporary 'sub-honourable' methods. *Yes*.

"No, Archlord. I did not expect it, that's all. But brief incarceration until matters are finalized is a necessary evil."

"Good."

"Where's my father, where's my father!" rang Ashlaya's shouts from outside the palace's walls. People began stirring and coming out into the courtyard to see what all the fuss was.

Tisenin tutted. "I had hoped to have a few more hours until it was necessary to go public, but it looks like I will have to begin now." Tisenin gathered his household servants and told them to go from street to street and get one person from each house to meet on the polo field to the west of his palace in two hours time; there was important news to impart.

* * * * * * *

Within those two hours, well over ten-thousand people gathered on the polo field outside Tisenin's palace. The field was nestled nicely in some hills which blocked the strong, magic-laden wind that still whipped in from the coast. It had some fantastic acoustics for the occasional open air performance Tisenin laid on for popular entertainment. It was more people than he had expected, but Ashlaya's shrill cries had drawn an audience before his proclamation had even gone out, and people were curious as to the rumours about disappearances at the hands of masked assailants. Ashlaya did not stop her hoarse shouting the whole time the crowd gathered, but eventually, their sheer weight of numbers squeezed out her voice.

When Tisenin climbed the stairs up to the stage, he was flanked by two of his staunchest followers, Adrin with his lizard skin cloak and Dago, who seemed to have tattooed something on her face since Akai had last seen her. Akai had never spoken to either of them personally, but he knew them by reputation. Adrin styled himself the romantic adventure, but his deeds in Cathri had never quite made him the hero of a song and his poetry was never quite good enough be requested by the tavern hearthside. Dago was more of an enigma. She led her life with intense privacy, which was a rare for a cherno. Some fifty years ago there had been rumours about Adrin and Dago being in some kind of delinquent relationship that ended badly. But that seemed to be behind them now; Adrin had shaved his hair, suggesting he was recently made a father, and Dago still wore her blue cowry and long tresses. But she had no feathers. That surprised Akai, because Dago was tall and striking, with a reputation as an accomplished mage and a stake in the inner circles of Efrandi politics. It would take a bold man to turn her down.

Behind them came all the lords who had been in the embassy to the Magnolia Court. In front of the stage a thin line of Tisenin's servants made a solid barrier between him and the crowd. Most of them were openly wearing short swords in their belts and each wore a purple armband; Tisenin's colour.

The crowd hushed as Tisenin stepped to the front. "Dear friends of Efrandi."

A chorus of voices echoed his words in unison. The format was well known to all cherno present. Whatever Tisenin said, the front ranks would repeat so that even those at the back would hear. Additionally, some of the mnemonic masters would remember the entire speech word for word, so it could be repeated to those not present, or transcribed for wider circulation. But Akai needed neither, given he was so close to the front.

"Many of you will know I recently travelled to the Magnolia Court in Serra to petition my cousin the Emperor to save us from the Ban. She refused, and it was nearly the hundredth year of refusal. Things are at a critical juncture. Within my lifetime, the Ban may become too strong to subvert. Therefore I deemed the Emperor incompetent and took the only action I could in the circumstance. I killed the Emperor with my own hand."

The chorus of voices repeating Tisenin's words cracked up on the last line as people were stunned into silence, or disbelieved what they had just heard.

"Speak! Speak!" came the call from the rear as spectators grasped they had missed something important.

Tisenin withdrew the knife he had used to kill Kirrie from its sheath and held it aloft. It was still stained brown with her blood.

"With this dagger, I slew the Emperor Kirrie." This time the line was repeated faithfully and there were gasps and shouts and tears from the crowd. "I know most of you, when you judge yourselves deep within, you will find that the life of one person is a small price for safety from the Ban. I also know, that there are some few among you who will never accept kin slaying or who will never dare alter the Ban. Some I know, would have opposed me with force were they given the chance. And so I have had certain individuals removed from public life until this situation is resolved. I want to assure the family and friends of those who were taken last night, they will be returned to you as soon as is practical."

The crowd became restless. There was some jostling to get to the front by some angry relatives of the 'taken'. Akai thought they might mean to climb the stage and lynch Tisenin, but they stopped dead once they reached the purple line of bodyguards and saw their swords. Just for a split second Tisenin looked nervous, as if he might have misjudged the mentality of the crowd. He began speaking again to regain their attention.

"Killing my cousin does not mean I take her place. I see no reason why the line of Elsiren should continue to rule. I see no reason why a handful of nobles in Serra should dictate policy throughout the entire Empire. We cherno have clung to the ways of our simple desert ancestors for too long. We place too much virtue in lineage and give too much respect to titles, when it is the wise we should revere. Therefore I propose to found a new league of like minded people, a Sagacious League who can look at matters with wisdom; where merit and not birth is rewarded. A Sagacious League where we listen to the fears of the common cherno rather than slavishly follow the dictates of our old simurgh captors."

There were some cheers and Akai felt his chest swell with pride. Everything Tisenin said rang true to him.

"I cannot force the noble cabal in Serra to conform to my will. But together, everyone here, everyone in Efrandi can make them surrender their power and acknowledge the right of the people to have their say. And then, we can decide what to do about the Ban. So here is my plan for the Sagacious League..."

Akai listened with rapt attention as Tisenin detailed his plans. They were bold, humane and justified. And at the end of the speech, Akai was relieved to hear a round of applause; they had the mass of the people on their side.

* * * * * * *

It was not until late in the afternoon that Akai got to see Tisenin again. He had been busy convening small meetings to discuss plans: The Jewasri lords who had accompanied him on his embassy to the Magnolia Court were being dispatched back to their home cities on swift horses with proclamations; Dissenters had to have their fears allayed and be persuaded to stay inactive rather than openly oppose the League's plan; Property owners who were having their ships and lands requisitioned for 'the greater good' needed mollifying; Nobles being stripped of their titles and commoners being raised up needed to know their new duties.

Tisenin looked tired and drained by the time Akai was invited back to the palace to see him. Another man was invited into Tisenin's study at the same time. He wore a large maroon hood and from that, rather than his face, Akai recognised him as the man he had seen with Tisenin in the courtyard at dawn.

"Ah, Akai, please meet Quinias, a man with a mind sharper than any other I have met. He is somewhat my emissary, bringing important people over to my side. And Quinias, Akai is a first rate sailor to be trusted in every way. He may even have saved my life on the voyage back."

Quinias was an older man, perhaps in his four or five hundreds, with just a few wrinkles breaking up his black skin. Akai could not say if he had seen him around the estate before or not. His cloak was common enough – either a noble's rain wear or a labourer's finest – and he had a method of looking out from its hood which obscured most of his face. Akai could see no trinkets or shells to tell of his social bonds. It was as if he were determined to be unremarkable. The only unusual trait Akai noticed was the way he carried his left hand balled into a fist at his side. He did not know if it was merely an affectation or some kind of palsy, but he suspected the latter.

Quinias dipped his head in respect, "Then I thank you Akai, because you may have saved us all from the Ban."

Akai's head swooned with praise but he affected an air of modesty, "Just doing my duty. You could as easily praise the caulker or sail maker."

Quinias turned to Tisenin, "Archlord, I have that *list*, you asked me for. Is this a good time?"

Tisenin waved away Quinias's concerns, "Of course, I would not have invited you both in together if I intended to keep secrets from one of you."

Quinias took a roll of parchment out of a satchel and placed it on Tisenin's desk. He opened it up and pointed out some key details.

"This is a list of my observations at the rally today. The names in black are those who stayed silent or left when you announced our plans. The names in red are those who openly voiced their opposition."

"Good, good." Tisenin looked to Akai. "Just precautions you understand Akai? A list of those who may need watching if the plan is to develop smoothly."

"That seems prudent," agreed Akai.

Tisenin smiled. "Akai, the reason I wanted you to meet Quinias is that he has a galley, but no crew. He could do with a sound-minded captain who knows the waterways of Jewasri and the Inner Sea. You would run the vessel day-to-day and impart advice when Quinias's own sea lore runs short. What do you say?"

"That sounds like a great deal of responsibility. I am still a junior crew member."

"Rank and privilege should come to those who deserve it, not those with mere titles and *age*. At three-hundred I am offering you second command of a small galley; the humans give command of armies to fourteen year olds."

"And surely they suffer for it?"

"Is that a no? Come Akai, do a job that fits your skills," implored Tisenin.

That made it sound like a gift; and how could Akai turn down a gift from Tisenin?

"Very well. Since it is you who asks, I am honoured to accept," said Akai.

"Good!" exclaimed Quinias. "Because I need to go out tonight."

"Tonight!? In this weather, in the dark?" exclaimed Akai.

"Indeed."

Akai tutted, "Then I see why you wanted me, because no grey-haired captain would deliberately go out in this weather so close to shore."

"It will not take long," assured Quinias. "We only need go just outside the harbour."

"Why?"

For a split second Quinias looked at Tisenin nervously, then right back at Akai. It was so fast that Akai was not sure he had seen it. "Private business."

"Alright, sure," said Akai.

"A fine conclusion." said Tisenin. "Akai, you can select whomever you choose to be your crew. You should only need about twenty rowers." He rolled up the parchment Quinias had given him. "Well, sorry for keeping this brief dear friends, but I have other matters to attend to. I will send for you both soon."

Akai and Quinias gave thanks and departed. The two of them agreed to meet at the docks just a few hours before dawn and went their separate ways.

* * * * * * *

Akai arrived at the docks with twenty five of his favourite sailing comrades. They were all young men who owed Tisenin a debt. As they got there, several of the purple armband wearers from the rally were struggling to get some long and obviously obscenely heavy leather bags below deck. When they were done, Quinias whispered to them and they melted back into the darkness of the city.

Quinias greeted the crew and gave them a lightless tour of his galley. Many of them muttered about the madness of night time excursions.

"My crew, on this trip there are to be no lights above deck, nothing to alert anyone that a ship is at sea. No one is to talk about this excursion. If someone sees us and asks you about it, simply say, 'I am sworn to silence,' nothing more."

The mast was stowed to reduce their chances of being seen and the crew set about pushing the vessel out of harbour, gently slicing the water with their oars without raising a froth and trying to hoist in unison without the aid of a drummer beating out a rhythm. It was easy enough within the harbour, where the waves and wind were deadened, but as soon as they were out of the mouth, the ship was gripped by the stormy waters and rocked violently from side to side. The oarsmen's strokes seemed trifling and ineffectual against the power of the water and the ship began to drift to the side.

"This is much worse than it was when we brought Tisenin back. Then we were only at the edge of the storm," said Akai.

"We are perfectly safe, we only need go a few hundred metres beyond the wall, then we can weigh anchor for a while."

Akai looked sceptically at the ship's anchors. "Those pair of stone anchors are too light to hold us in place, they'll drag along the bottom. We need an iron anchor for seas like this. It sticks in the rock below, holds us fast."

"An iron anchor? Is there such a thing? I've never seen a smith able to work anything larger than my forearm."

"I've seen them on ships coming from Cathri. They have good ore there and big furnaces. Mind you they need it. You could fit five of these galleys into one of their junks." Akai spoke with admiration.

"Have you been to Cathri?" asked Quinias. As he asked, he unconsciously rubbed his palsied left fist, as if the two were associated.

"Yes, many times, but it was over a hundred years ago. Such large ships were less common then."

When they were far enough away from harbour, Akai gave the signal to drop anchor and the rowers eased their pace, only moving so as to keep the vessel as static as possible.

"Please join me below deck, Akai," said Quinias.

They climbed down into the pitch black of the vessel's small cargo hold. When the door was securely shut behind them, Quinias used a touch of magic to light a torch. In the dancing light of the torch Akai could make out over thirty of the long leather bags he had seen being brought aboard.

"Let me show you something, a modification to my ship you won't see aboard any Cathri junk."

They had to bend their heads to move around the low beams of the cargo hold and each and every plank gave a groaning creak as the waves rolled by it, tempting it to bend and buckle. Quinias brought Akai to a trapdoor with a lever. Akai assumed there must be a second deck below, perhaps filled with stones for ballast, but when the lever was thrown and the doors fell open there was just a drop into water.

"What is this?" asked Akai.

"Just a fishing hole. They like to swim in the shade and nibble at the seaweed on our hull."

"Aye..." Akai thought it was a little eccentric to put a hole in the bottom of a ship just to fish; what was wrong with dangling a line over the side?

Quinias grabbed one of the leather bags, his frozen fist of a left hand thrust underneath and not slowing him down at all. "Come and help me with this."

Akai obeyed and together they half lifted and half dragged the bag over to the fishing hole. Then Quinias just let the bag drop into the sea. Akai was about to ask what on earth they were doing and what was in the bags, but one look at Quinias's serious face told him that those were questions he was not meant to ask. Akai may have earned Tisenin's favour, but he was not yet part of the inner circle.

They dragged the leather bags over one after the other and sent them plunging into the depths with a splash each time. Akai could feel hard angular things below the surface, like stones. The water that splashed their hands was cold and made the leather slippery. When they were about two-thirds done and just hoisting another bag over the lip of the trapdoor, Akai's hands slipped and the bag crashed down on to the wooden deck, bursting open one of its stitched seams. A few fist sized rocks tumbled out.

Then Akai saw something which chilled him to the core.

Poking out from the bag was a lock of long black hair. At least he thought it was hair; in the flickering torch light it was hard to tell. Deep moral shock gripped him and he found himself unable to move.

Quinias smoothly rolled the bag and its contents the last little bit into the hole. The evidence was gone as fast as Akai had seen it.

What am I doing? Are these...?

Akai found the notion of his idolized master blatantly lying to him almost impossible to believe.

Horse hair? It could have been horse hair!

Quinias was already taking hold of the next bag. He

looked suspiciously at Akai. Clearly he knew Akai had seen something, but he chose not to openly question him.

"Akai, I need your help with this."

Numbly and like a drone, Akai found himself taking hold of the other end.

But whatever one part of him shouted about moral duty, the other just could not countenance that his trust had been betrayed. There were other explanations and to accuse his benefactor of the worst was sheer disrespect.

The last few bags plopped into the water without much mental effort on Akai's behalf. Quinias led Akai back up onto deck and as soon as their eyes had re-adjusted to the star light, he gave orders to raise anchor and return to port.

Akai took up position on the prow, looking for breaks in the frothy waves that might indicate they had moved off-course and were headed for rocks. He could not make eye contact with the crew; he no longer knew his own mind. The broiling depths and empty sky were better places to find himself.

Quinias stood behind him.

"Do you want to talk about what you just saw, Akai?" Between the howling wind, crash of waves and creaking of planks, no one would hear them.

There was a kernel of Akai looking for a way out of the situation. Either he had just partaken in the most immoral act committed by a cherno since the time of Elsiren, or he was mistaken about the hair. The kernel of self preservation pointed his mind towards the latter.

"No, not really," said Akai "I'm guessing we just disposed of tannery waste, or the like. You didn't want the horse carcasses stinking up the city?"

Quinias smiled broadly; Akai did not like that smile.

"You are correct Akai. When we seized the dissident's property, a number of horses were mistakenly killed by an over enthusiastic adherent. We thought it would be better to cover up the little gaffe rather than cause embarrassment to the perpetrator and the greater cause. The horses will of course be replaced before the dissident is released from custody."

"Seems reasonable," said Akai.

Quinias left Akai alone on the prow, but Akai could not get the image of Quinias's smile out of his head. The reason was the smile did not say 'I am amused' or 'I am relieved.'

It said: *Welcome to being one of us.*

Chapter 4

An Emperor's Funeral

Duarma knelt over Kirrie's body and placed the first stone of what was to be her cairn upon her chest. It was a week since her death and her skin was just beginning to turn grey, despite the physician's best efforts. There was a huge crowd gathered, three-hundred thousand perhaps, and they had attentively listened to his eulogy for his dead wife. Now each person who cared for her would place a stone on her grave and gradually cover her over.

This was not a normal funeral. Cherno did not place much importance on burial rites, not like the humans. Cherno knew that the soul resided in the ether, the realm of magic, not in the body or slowly mouldering bones. Usually corpses were buried quickly and forgotten. But her death had been so unexpected and so *dramatic* that the people felt they needed some public event to express their sorrow.

Duarma stepped aside and let the trail of mourners make their way to her grave. Family first, then friends, then loyal subjects. Many stopped to say a few words to the rest about some kind deed Kirrie had done for them in their lifetime: Shelter when their home was taken by a hurricane; generous gifts given to their children during their civic service; sound arbitration in disputes over bad debt and broken troths. Everything he was supposed to do from now on.

When she was alive he had even been a little bitter about having to share his lover with so many other people. Now the thought of spreading himself so thin brought only *fear*.

After they had deposited their stone, many people came over to Duarma and offered their condolences. He was brief in his responses, but people seemed to understand. It was a long day and there were lots of people to see him. Jandor was the only mourner who brought more than words of mere emotion.

"A fine turnout for an honourable woman, Duarma. This must be every able person in Serra and a day's march away."

"Too many. I opened the city's store to provide for the feast and the food has not stretched to half the mourners. Luckily my subjects have opened their own stores as well so no traveller will go hungry. It's so shameful. I remember when the last Emperor died the palace was able to put on a feast of wine and mutton for everyone. I have failed to provide bread and a mouthful of fish."

"No one thinks the less of you or your staff for it. The last Emperor died of a long illness and the palace was able to prepare. And he did not die at the end of the Storm Season when stores were at their lowest."

Duarma cupped his head in his hands. "You know, she had promised me a child when next she reached oestrus? That probably would have been within a year or two."

Jandor nodded solemnly. "I had heard rumours, my Emperor. Kirrie made no secret of the fact she desired to be a mother."

"Seeing all these people praise her and confess how she helped them in their moment of need...It does not make me proud for her. It makes me despise my subjects for monopolising so much of her time, when it should have been spent with me."

Jandor was silent.

"Do you think that makes me unfit to rule?" asked Duarma.

"No. But it will certainly make it more challenging. My mother once told me she had similar feelings when my father died and Lansissari did not suffer for it."

"This past week I have been wondering if the wise and compassionate Serenus would make a better Emperor. Kirrie held your mother as the very paragon of a good lord. Her time in Lansissari was very dear to her. I...well...I half penned a letter...then threw it on the fire. It feels like cowardice to abandon the throne before the current crisis is dealt with."

"Kirrie was also very dear to my mother. Serenus would not happily leave Lansissari, but if you are earnest, she would do her duty by the people of the Empire, I am sure."

"I am. As soon as the situation with Tisenin is resolved, I shall call Serenus to court and name her my preferred candidate for succession."

"You do my mother a great honour." Jandor paused for a second and surveyed the crowd. "My Emperor Duarma, I hate to ask at this time, with so many other people to see you, but has there been any word from Efrandi yet? It should not have taken a good captain more than a week to make the crossing."

"None. The best we can hope for is that their catamaran was pushed off course by the storm. Or perhaps that they deem it unwise to try and return through the strong winds. Mordhai tells me that the Mage's Guild is sure there is still a storm between Efrandi and Serra, maintained only through the most strenuous magics. But I have faith in Archlord Haddra, because even if my messengers have gone astray, he and his company of reavers should have arrived in the city by now."

"Indeed my Emperor, I would not like to find myself on the wrong end of Haddra's barbs in either word or javelin. I once saw him reduce a stable hand to tears for putting the wrong blanket on his horse."

"He is an abruptly practical man," mused Duarma.

"That is rather like calling a thunder cloud 'adequately loud'."

"Indeed." Duarma brooded silently for a moment, before finally deciding to speak his mind. Jandor had a way of making him feel at ease. "Added to all the woes Tisenin brought, I cannot find Hesiad, the guard I so cruelly treated the day of Kirrie's death. He left the palace without telling anyone. I cannot start my reign with such an act of choler left un-righted."

"He will be found eventually and you will have a chance to make amends. No one gives either of you any of the blame for the events of that day," said Jandor.

"I hope it is so."

The day progressed and the mound of stones grew and grew until it was beginning to resemble a hill. Tomorrow they would hold athletic games in her honour; running, javelin throwing, horse racing and the most popular, archery. But for now people were becoming restless, although out of respect they did not like to show it. Palace servants carried water to them, and what little food was available, but Duarma decided it was time they had some distraction. He beckoned a servant.

"Bring me Baytee of the Perched Sparrow."

The servant searched the queue of mourners and quickly returned with a middle-aged woman and gaggle of young followers.

Baytee stepped forwards and bowed, "My Emperor, it is an honour to be called by you."

"Baytee! I have neglected your hospitality for too long. You were very kind to myself and Kirrie when we were young and at liberty. I long for the times when we could indulge our days in carefree song. Tell me, have your patrons succeeded in writing an elegy?"

"They have, my Emperor."

"And who will perform?"

Baytee turned and held out her arm to the gaggle of young followers. "May I present Janistor."

A young woman came forward; she was in a dress which revealed her shoulders and had almond shaped panels cut into the side which exposed the large curve of her hips. It balanced on the line between that which was modest enough for a funeral, and that which was intended for seduction. In Duarma's mind, it fell too far towards the latter. But he could not condemn her for it; his misery should not stop another's joys. Although it seemed she had already had success with seduction enough. He counted twelve feathers in her hair and her wrist was festooned in rejected troths. Then he remembered who she was. Kirrie had avidly followed the gossip about the girl with the greatest ever number of pledged troths. She had even contemplated sending palace invites to her noble suitors on the chance that they might bring her along. However, propriety had always stopped her; there were many established and virtuous subjects in Serra who deserved recognition before an accomplished seducer.

"Ah, Janistor. I know of you by reputation. The reports of your superb beauty are true."

She bowed gracefully, "Thank you my Emperor. Your words are most kind."

"Please, sing for us."

Janistor planted her feet, shut her eyes and opened up her smooth warm vocal cords. The sound that came out was a sheer delight. A mournful, pure sound that instantly gripped Duarma's mind and forced him to look at the long years of loneliness ahead of him. Cold tears trickled down his cheek. The tune borrowed heavily from the *Lay of Finasa*, but the poetic words were unique and surprisingly resonant.

A lullaby on withered wings of grey,
Every moth exists to reminisce,
Faltering into the most beautiful decay.

When Janistor finished the elegy, the whole crowd was silent. Moistness speckled many eyes; the elderly remembered their lost loved ones and the young were plunged into a melancholy of purpose. There was no applause – that would have defied the meaning of the song – but everyone present was aware that they had just witnessed a great musical triumph.

Duarma had to pause whilst his heart left his mouth before he could speak again. Janistor stayed demurely silent awaiting his appraisal.

"That…was a song fit for my wife. You have done me a great service. I can quite see why so many of my young nobles have taken you to their heart."

Janistor bowed with an ecstatic smile on her face. "My Emperor gives great praise."

"Tell me. Who wrote the lyrics of the song?"

"It was a collaboration between myself and the rest of the patrons of the Perched Sparrow."

"Therefore, I am in the Sparrow's debt." Then he looked at Baytee. "In the Sparrow's debt, *even more*."

* * * * * * *

Zanthred was one of those in tears. Millie was not.

"You're just crying because it's *her*," chided Millie.

"That was a damn sad song," said Zanthred. "And I have no reluctance to show it."

"Yes, my eyes watered a little when I read Hanuru's lyrics. They watered less when we'd heard Janistor practise it for the tenth time, but they stayed positively dry just now when Janistor told the Emperor *she'd* written the song."

"She didn't claim it as her own! She said it was a collaboration, which is true."

"Barely!" Millie snorted. "Everyone else together only changed Hanuru's song by a couple of words."

"Well she doesn't seem too upset," scoffed Zanthred.

Millie looked across at Hanuru; she was the small mousey girl she had approached her first night in the Perched Sparrow. Although they had seemed quite compatible, Hanuru held back from any amorous entanglement. And it was no mystery why; then as now she stared at Janistor with dreamy eyes.

"Damn, why am I surrounded by fools who fall for that girl!" lamented Millie. "She's too smitten to see her moment's been stolen. Good singers are common as grass, but good poets? As rare as black pearls."

As they watched, Janistor returned to their little gaggle of Sparrow residents and was hugged and adored by her clique of troths. Callin particularly fawned over her with eyes a-gush, dabbing at them with his scented handkerchief. Hanuru waited anxiously for her to work her way through the crowd of adulators. Hanuru was almost shaking with excitement; it was the ultimate thrill to have her song sung so wonderfully in front of the cream of Serra nobility. It was her way into the world of her crush.

But when Janistor came close, she simply smiled at Hanuru and returned to the embrace of Callin. A visible pall of melancholy came over Hanuru.

"Harsh, no word of thanks, nothing," said Millie.

"Don't be so down on Janistor. She may attract 'fools' like me, but the fault is with the fool," said Zanthred.

"She cultivates it. Do you see that dress she's wearing? Totally inappropriate for a funeral."

"Since when have you judged someone by their clothes? We ran naked as sailors until...well...until—"

"...I know when," for a fraction of a second Millie looked quite pained, as if receiving a pang from a long forgotten wound. "Indifference to clothes is one thing, but clothes designed to attract attention during a funeral is contempt."

"I don't see what's so salacious about it."

Millie sighed and rolled her eyes. "The rule of modest clothing is you can only show off one provocative zone."

"Please! She only has her thighs out, there isn't even a hint of breast or bum."

"Ha! Shows what you know. Men may go on about liking a heavy cleavage or a curvy back, but every wise woman knows the best way to earn that feather is to show off her shoulders and neck."

Zanthred was about to chuckle at the ridiculousness of the statement, but a quick introspective assay revealed that his mental picture of every girl he had ever fallen for, was of a woman in an off-the-shoulder dress.

"Damn. I never realised that's what I was responding to." Zanthred shook his head in disbelief. "So what do wise men wear when they're trying to get a woman's troth?"

Mille grinned evilly. "Prestige Zanthred. Wise men wear other people's respect."

* * * * * * *

Haddra loved the bone crunching jolts shooting through his hips as the horse's feet contacted with the ground. It was just such a shame that it hurt so damn much now he was in his eight-hundreds.

"Not far now men!" he shouted to the hundred Delfuri veterans galloping behind him. "We'll be in Efrandi well before nightfall!"

Their caravel had been forced to divert around the

worst of the storm front and make landfall a day's ride south of Efrandi. There they had cajoled their horses to swim ashore and made all haste for the city, hoping to catch Tisenin and his followers off-guard.

Haddra knew everything there was to know about a fast foray. Horses had been his life. The smell of their sweat, cold air on his neck and the rapid clack of hoofs punishing his ear were what it took to make him feel alive. It did not matter if he was chasing deer, raiding a human camp, or now for the first time, hunting a fellow cherno.

They had struggled to find decent mounts in Serra. Although they had horses aplenty, they were all the big, heavy-boned kind; perfect for short sprints and hauling large loads, but they had no stamina and no sense. Quri horses would run themselves into a lather and then refused to move unless you gave them grain and water. The ponies they bred in Delfuri could run all day and then go and find their own food whilst you set up camp. Luckily some traders had just come down the River Mead bringing some stock from Gerloth. These small sturdy plains ponies were a little more like what he was used to; although they had kicked up a major panic when he tried to get them into the sea.

The landscape around Efrandi was very similar to Quri; rolling hills and numerous small streams which seasonally swelled to raging torrents with the frequent deluges of the Storm Season. Closer to the city, managed woodlands and shrubby hillsides were giving way to fields of grain and terraces of vines, olives and walnut trees. There were hamlets in increasing density; each a cluster of court-yarded houses with gardens dense in aromatic herbs. People came out to see the procession of horses thundering by. Youngsters cheered to see so many riders all together, or else hid in terror from the earth-shaking noise. Although each man in the party carried either a bow or javelins, they did not look much different from a hunting party, save the fact they all wore baggy Delfuri trousers rather than the knee-length riding robes popular in the Hublands. Many travellers on foot were forced to move off the dusty track to make way, whilst the party streamed around bemused wagon drovers returning from a day's trade.

Haddra had no illusions about this going peacefully. Tisenin was too canny to have allowed himself to be arrested by his own people, so they would find him ensconced in his palace, already playing 'Emperor' for those that would listen. A quick, bloody foray would see him in hemp fetters. It wounded Haddra's sense of decency that a man with such noble blood as Tisenin could be so treacherous. He felt a visceral obligation to end this crisis.

The obligation came not only from honour, but precedent. As an Archlord, he was the senior peer in the land now, until another *ap Elsiren* was picked for the throne. Duarma was the perfect seat-warmer, which is why Haddra had been the first to suggest he take Kirric's role; the man had the people's sentimentality on his side, but no real ambition. Haddra could get this bloody business with Tisenin dealt with while Duarma held the Empire together long enough for normality to be restored. In all his days he had not imagined such a perversity could happen at the imperial court and he was damned if he were going to rely on younger folk to fix it.

His pony clambered up a steep slope and he paused on the crest.

Yes the city was here, laid out before him. It was like Serra is so many ways, with row after row of small white houses and the odd dome and spire from public buildings. The big difference was the black volcanic cliffs it was built on, which made the town seem an altogether more melancholy place.

But what Haddra did not expect to see was thousands upon thousands of people lined up outside the city.

One by one his soldiers came to a halt at the crest of the hill and quieted their steeds.

"What are they doing?" exclaimed one of the veterans.

"Some kind of parade?" ventured another.

"No...." said Haddra.

The people in the plains outside Efrandi were arranging themselves in lines and columns around large flags. Some groups were trying to wheel about the flag without losing the formation. Others were slowly processing up and down. It was difficult to see at this distance, but it looked like many of the participants carried wooden poles.

"No," reiterated Haddra. He paused for a moment, looking very worried. "Back to the ship!" he barked. The perversity had worsened.

There was confusion. One of the soldiers pushed his horse forwards.

"Archlord Haddra, we can easily push through those crowds into the city. I've never seen a person on foot stand in a horse's way."

"No, we have something more vital to do than arrest Tisenin now. We have important information to bring back that cannot be risked or delayed."

"What is that?"

Haddra was already urging his steed back down the slope.

"They're practising manoeuvres. They're building an army."

Chapter 5

Call to Arms

When the call went out that Haddra's ship had been sighted, Duarma immediately made his way to the royal dock. He was accompanied by as many of the court as could make it at such short notice, including Jandor. There was also a twenty strong contingent of palace guards (their numbers having swelled since Kirrie's death), each armed with the great ceremonial butterfly axe.

The crowd waited in seething anticipation as Haddra's caravel came into dock and went through the long process of being tied off and extending a gangplank. However, Duarma could tell the news would not be good; he could see Haddra's stony face peering over the railing. When at last the soldiers began to disembark, Duarma could maintain his calm demeanour no longer.

"What news! Is the traitor caught?"

Coming down to the quay Haddra shook his head ruefully. "No, my Emperor. Matters have taken a disturbing turn. The arch-traitor is building an army."

There were gasps of astonishment from the assembled lords.

"Are you sure?" questioned Duarma.

"There can be no mistake. We questioned some villagers outlying the city and they said that Tisenin had seized control of Efrandi by imprisoning potential opponents. He had declared the foundation of a 'Sagacious League' bent on breaking the Ban. They intend to march on Serra and install this League to power. We saw them practising infantry manoeuvres on the plain outside the city. Thousands of them."

"Surely not? How could he gather so many followers?" Duarma shook his head in disbelief. "Do they know what he did to my wife? I expected him to be lynched."

"Apparently they do, he freely admitted it."

"Have I misjudged my citizens' loyalty so badly? How can a whole city be turned against us? Is the Ban worth shedding blood over!?" raged Duarma.

Jandor was in the middle of writing something on a scrap of paper with charcoal. He passed it to a palace servant who took one look and ran off towards the city.

"Speaking as an outsider," began Jandor, "away from the capital there is considerable sympathy for the idea of organized resistance to the Ban, particularly among the young. I never would have thought it would come to this though."

Duarma looked around from blank face to blank face. "...what do we do now?" he asked in vain hope someone had a plan.

Of all the nobles, only Haddra had any gumption. "My Emperor, when presented with an enemy, there four options. Surrender, retreat, defend or attack. I could not bring myself to surrender to the traitor Tisenin or any of his followers. We could retreat and move the capital to another city...maybe Gerloth or Sunnel...but that would only buy time and give Tisenin a considerable licence to do what he wanted with the Empire. Defending is always the safest option, but Serra has no walls and it would take a long time to build them. In any case, it would not do anything to damage Tisenin, merely frustrate his plans. Attacking his forces in a pitched battle is risky, but in my opinion, the best way to bring him to justice."

"How many soldiers could he muster?" asked Duarma.

One of the merchant lords from Kelmor stepped forwards. "If Tisenin has the whole Efrandi merchant and fishing fleet at his command, then he can perhaps move twenty-thousand combatants, plus baggage."

"Twenty-thousand!"

"But Jewasri has not the plains to raise many horses, mountainous as it is. They will deploy as infantry. And if we can gather just five-thousand good riders, it will be enough to carry the day," said Haddra. He had the hubris of a well tested cavalry general.

Duarma found his confidence reassuring. Better by far to let experienced folk deal with this situation. The surety lasted but moments.

One of Haddra's own soldiers stepped forwards. "I am not so sure Archlord. I have served in the western *and* eastern colonies, and those were Cathri formations they were practising. They probably have a Cathri general advising them. And there, most of the troops fight on foot, but are trained to resist cavalry attacks. We should not compare our foe to the craven humans of Delfuri."

"A disciplined body of cavalry might be resisted, but it can't be beaten by infantry," said Haddra.

"A *disciplined* body of cavalry maybe, but what about some hastily rounded-up recruits on nags used to pull carts? I mean, how long do we have?" said Jandor.

Haddra grudgingly shuffled his feet in an unspoken sign of contrition. "I don't know. It'll take time for Tisenin to gather supplies and weapons, but who knows what he managed to stockpile before the Magnolia Court. This was planned. Right down to that storm to stop anyone leaving Efrandi."

The merchant lord shook his head, "No, no. He can't have gathered much during the Storm Season, and before that, not enough to overtly affect the sea traffic, otherwise the Merchants' Guild would have noticed the disruption. It will take a few weeks yet for him to get supplies from the provinces by land and river."

"Then we have...maybe...a few weeks to prepare ourselves," said Duarma. He sighed with a feeling of deep despair. Even Kirrie would have struggled with this.

"We will be able to tell when he sets sail from the intensity of the storm," offered Mordhai the meteomancer. "At least two days."

"Forgive me if I am wrong in any of the details," said Jandor. "But it would be easier to raise and maintain twenty-thousand of our own infantry than try for five-thousand cavalry. Each horse eats twice as much grain as a cherno and each soldier needs at least two horses to be effective, so we may as well be feeding twenty-five-thousand soldiers."

"That's true," conceded Haddra, "but what would you do with infantry? Risk it all in one mass melee? There is no surety in that. The thing hinges on the toss of a single die, and defeat, if it comes, is absolute. I don't know if you've ever seen thousands of people try to rout at the same time because one man panicked, but it's not a sight I want to see again, Jandor. At least not with my friends doing the running."

The palace servant Jandor had given the message to came back. He whispered in Jandor's ear and Jandor thanked him.

"My Emperor, my Lords, permit me to introduce a man I think may be useful to us. Gargrace," said Jandor.

A man in a hooded woollen cloak of obvious

Lansissari extraction slowly limped towards the congress of lords on a solid yew staff. He looked about five-hundred, but his face carried deep lines that suggested a lifetime of worry.

Jandor placed a hand on the man's shoulder, "Please Gargrace, give your credentials so we know that you speak right when you speak of war."

"Very well, m'lud," grunted Gargrace. "I was a captain on the Lansissari border for over three-hundred years. Saw off many an attack, infantry and cavalry. Always leading foot, not hoof. Though I retired here when my leg was ruined." His voice was gruff and coarse, and he showed little deference to his noble audience.

Haddra's eyes narrowed. Up until this point he had been the court's expert on war; even those few others present who had served in Delfuri recognised he had the most experience in the saddle. It was obvious if there was one thing his age, nobility and militant nature could not abide, it was competition to be heard.

"And Gargrace, if we were to face a large force of enemy infantry with raw recruits, how would you propose we do it?" asked Jandor.

"Shooting is the most popular sport in Serra. I'd use that."

"Bah!" scoffed Haddra. "Infantry archers aren't worth having. They don't make a scrap of difference in a melee."

Gargrace looked directly at Haddra and wiped his nose with the sleeve of his cloak. "Begging your pardon m'lud, you're right. A few archers don't make the difference of a piss against an enemy intent on closing with you. But I'm talking about making the *whole damn army* archers." He stooped to the ground and began drawing a diagram in the dust, a big concave crescent representing the archers. "The more of the enemy the better..."

Gargrace outlined his plan for the battle with flicks of his finger showing shooting arcs and disciplined manoeuvres. The result he described was so shocking that one of the lords vomited and two more protested about the cruelty of the solution.

"...That's how we dealt with the humans in Lansissari. A few hundred of us could take on a thousand of them that way. Just have to pick your ground carefully."

"And after *that* happened, they just ran away, I suppose?" Haddra discounted.

"No, they still got to you eventually, but demoralized and in chaos. All you had to do was stand your ground for a minute or two and they were bound to retreat. And if they didn't want to fight us, we were happy enough to shoot them from a distance."

"And you saw this happen with your own eyes?" asked Duarma.

"Frequently," assured Gargrace.

Duarma had little to pick from between the two men's plans. But he had spent the last week trying to scrape enough food together for a funeral. He knew how hard that was. The thought of trying to find and feed five-thousand horses for Haddra was mind-boggling.

"Well, that settles it for me. These rebels who take up arms bring their suffering upon themselves. I will call on every citizen with a bow and their own means of support to join the muster. I would be glad if you, Gargrace, would supervise their training," said Duarma.

"I'll do my best, my Emperor." He did not smile, but he seemed...*smug?*...about getting his own way.

"And I'll call on every citizen with two horses and their own means to join the cavalry, which I will entrust to you, Haddra," said Duarma, hoping the concession would keep his strongest ally happy.

"Gladly," said Haddra. "Although there is one thing I am worried about. Humans may flee at the first sign of chaos, but I wonder about cherno. It is still going to come down to an unpredictable melee."

Duarma wrung his hands with nerves. Then he saw the stalwart palace guards and remembered Hesiad, the runaway bodyguard. He had been a member of the monkish order of Shadow Guard, those ancient protectors of the Ban who had plied their war craft since before the days of Elsiren.

"There is one group of people who will make even your colonial veterans look like amateurs, Haddra. I will go to the Shadow Guard."

* * * * * * *

Zanthred, Millie and Hanuru were sat around a table in the Perched Sparrow. Ever since Hanuru had been ignored by Janistor, she had been much more amenable to the romantic overtures Mille was making. In fact, Zanthred was beginning to feel a bit like his company was superfluous.

Hanuru was a painfully shy girl. You more or less had to ask her a question directly to get her to talk about herself. Then she would mutter quietly and look bashfully away. It was several days before they had learnt she was already a member of the Mages' Guild and one of the prestigious philosophy societies; rare accolades for one so young that would normally be open boasts. She dressed primly and without any of the flamboyance common to patrons of the Sparrow.

Janistor and her crowd occupied the tables across the room. Her clique had swollen somewhat since the funeral as admirers came to meet the singer that had enthralled the noble court. Baytee was mightily pleased with all the visitors; they brought gifts that passed from hand to hand around the inn and mostly ended up in her apron. Those gifts were probably responsible for the better quality of wine that seemed to fill every jug today.

The conversation stopped when a palace servant came into the room and rapped a staff against the door frame.

"Pray all silent for a proclamation from the Emperor." He had everyone's attention. "The traitor Tisenin is massing an army. For the protection of all faithful citizens, the Emperor is forced to do likewise. All able-bodied residents of Serra in possession of their own bow and own means of sustenance are required to step forwards and join the infantry levy. All able-bodied citizens with their own pair of horses are required to step forwards and join the cavalry levy. In addition, any youths yet to undertake their civic service are invited to join the infantry levy at the state's expense. Any volunteers will have their remaining years of civic service halved. The Emperor acknowledges the service rendered to him by the patrons of the Perched Sparrow. Patrons will be allowed to fight in their own company under their own banner. I will stay here for the rest of the day for signing people up."

With that, the messenger took the table nearest the door and set down a wax ledger and a stylus. Baytee was over and talking to him in an instant, asking the inevitable questions.

"Well...*gosh*," said Millie.

"Yes, *gosh*," said Zanthred.

Hanuru said nothing, but developed the kind of glazed look people got when plunged into icy water.

"Tisenin really is rebelling. I never thought I'd see it in my day. I remember everyone was really down on the Ban whenever we went to the market in Icknel, but there was never a suggestion of *forcefully* opposing the protectors," said Millie.

Zanthred could not believe what he was hearing. Killing one person was bad enough. Killing the Emperor was unforgivable. Raising an army to overthrow the whole Empire was so outrageously *evil* that Zanthred felt physical anger in every part of his body. It was overwhelming, every bit on par with lust and deep sorrow. It was a new and horrible sensation.

He thumped the table. "That cur!"

"Whoa, hold up Zanthred, you look like you're actually thinking of joining the army," said Millie.

"Why not? We cannot sit here and do nothing. And what would you rather do, fight or gong harvesting?"

"But we might die," said Millie.

"I'd rather live for what is right and die in the process then let someone as morally bankrupt as Tisenin stroll in here and seize power," said Zanthred.

"Grr...Damn you Zanthred. So would I. That means I have to sign up I guess?"

"But you can't!" protested Hanuru. "That means killing people!"

"Sometimes, you have to retaliate with force," said Zanthred. "It's what we do with the humans. It's what Elsiren had to do when we escaped from the Great Desert on Earth."

Hanuru looked ashen and meek, "...but that's just what Tisenin said before he killed the Emperor."

Millie took Hanuru's hand and spoke to her softly. "I'm as much a pacifist as you. I believe in the moral damage any kind of violence does to the perpetrator and the victim. But, when it's something as fundamental as kingship and the Ban at stake, being a pacifist and doing nothing stains you with as much guilt as a rebel. We can't ask another to slay on our behalf and not be willing to do the task ourselves."

"That's right," added Zanthred.

Hanuru wavered; she was not so sure of her gut-ethics now.

"And what about the simurgh?" said Mille. "You think they will sit by as Tisenin tries to overcome the Ban? We, as a *race*, don't want to make enemies of them. We don't know how far they'd be willing to go to protect the Ban."

Hanuru looked worried, and squeezed Millie's hand. "You think they would attack us?"

Millie dropped her voice to a whisper. "They threatened to wipe us out after the Ban was completed. It was only Elsiren's bargaining that saved us. We don't know what they'd do and we don't know just how powerful they are."

Hanuru swallowed. "Okay, I understand. If...if you join, I'll join."

"Oh thank you so much, Hun." Millie kissed Hanuru's hand and Hanuru's breath came out sharply, as if she had been stung by a pin made of petals.

"It's decided then," said Zanthred rising from his seat. "We three are signing up."

He stepped over to the palace messenger. Three other eager patrons were waiting, so Zanthred queued behind them. When it was his turn, the messenger greeted him with a forced smile.

"Thank you for presenting yourself young citizen. Infantry conscript, cavalry conscript or civic service volunteer?"

"I am Zanthred, from Icknel. I will be a civic service volunteer."

"I thank you for your fidelity on behalf of the Emperor. You are to present yourself to the officer in charge at the athletics field north of the city an hour after dawn in two days' time." The messenger carved Zanthred's name into the soft wax of his ledger.

As they were speaking Baytee came up with a tray of mutton stew and a tall jar of sherbet for the messenger.

"Thank you my dear Baytee, I am honoured by your hospitality. Tell me, is the elegist Janistor in here tonight? I have a special message for her from the palace."

"Hmm? You need me to point her out?" said Baytee, raising an eyebrow.

"I would not like to presume..." began the messenger, clearly looking directly at the girl with twelve feathers in her hair.

"Presume," said Baytee laconically.

The messenger got up from the table and sheepishly approached Janistor. The youths around her parted, afraid they would be pressured by the messenger to sign his ledger.

"Janistor?"

"Yes?"

The messenger took out a small bundle of items wrapped in gold threaded silk.

"The Emperor apologises that he cannot give you these presents in person. He thanks you for your outstanding performance and hopes that he may call on you in years to come to sing again."

She smiled. "Of course, it would be my duty and my pleasure."

The messenger unwrapped the silk and took out what looked like a moth. But it was not a moth, it was brooch made of solid gold and so intricately fashioned that it resembled the real creature in every way but colour. The patterns on its wings were made from tiny coloured gems, with the 'eyes' being deep purple-green pearls.

Janistor gave a cry of suprised ecstasy as the messenger handed the brooch over. She had to steady herself with one hand on a table.

"Why, it's exquisite!"

"This brooch originally belonged to the Emperor Kirrie's mother, a gift from the great artisan Hopini. It has been worn by two Emperors."

Her hands shook as she tried to delicately pin it to her breast.

"And there is this, a bottle of the finest agar wood perfume from the spice colonies."

He handed her a shiny black soapstone bottle, which she briefly unstopped and took a deep draught of. The distinctive smell wafted all the way over to Zanthred. She quickly replaced the lid and bowed before the messenger.

"Please convey my most heartfelt thanks to the Emperor."

Millie and Hanuru were by Zanthred's elbows watching the scene unfold.

"Well, she's got what she wanted," sneered Millie,

"gifts and suitors fit for an Emperor. A pity she's not as generous." Millie looked at Hanuru, but Hanuru said nothing. "Oh come on, Hanuru! You know by rights one of those gifts should be yours!"

"I told her she could say the song was a collaboration," said Hanuru meekly.

"You know and she knows that the writer deserves credit. Everyone who was here the night you wrote the elegy knows it as well. The fact she hasn't given it to you means that either she is afraid you will steal her fame, or that she is testing her hold on her followers – seeing what she can get away with and making them complicit in her own myth. Either way, that makes her a deplorable person. You should call her out on it."

"I c-couldn't!" whined Hanuru.

"Then I'll do it for you," said Millie.

"P-please Millie, don't make a scene!" protested Hanuru.

But Millie ignored her.

Zanthred would not have dreamed of stopping Millie – he had seen her angry before – but he doubted anything good could come from seeing the two most important women in his life clash.

"*Janistor*," growled Millie, interrupting something she was saying.

"...Millie? Is it?" said Janistor.

"Yes. I congratulate you on your prizes and acknowledge your triumphal, melancholy, performance. But I think you are at risk of overlooking those who have helped you achieve your success."

There were stares of grey lead coming from Janistor's clique; Millie's tone was unusually blunt and rude for a cherno. But Janistor smiled instead. She had not become the centre of a social nexus through her looks alone.

"Oh my, you think I have overlooked my duties?" Her mocking reply came with an infuriating veneer of earnestness. "Well, there is one person who I still feel indebted to..." Janistor picked up the black perfume bottle and glanced from Millie to Hanuru. She brushed past Millie and went towards Hanuru; Millie thought her words might actually have had an effect. Then she brushed past Hanuru as well to Baytee.

"Dear Baytee, you have been so kind to me these last few weeks and looked after all of us so well. Please, won't you take this gift from the Emperor?" Janistor proffered the perfume.

Baytee had followed the politics of the room and (thought) she saw straight through Janistor's ploy. She looked sternly at her.

"I can't accept this Janistor."

"You are very gracious Baytee." She turned to the rest of the room. "Does anyone feel they are *as worthy* for this gift from the Emperor as fond Baytee?"

There was dead silence. Hanuru looked very small and withdrawn. No one could speak for her.

"No?" Janistor smiled and returned to her seat in front of Millie. "It seems you are wrong dear Millie, no one feels I have been niggardly towards them. Others might have been angered by your accusation, but I like to think it is concern for me that motivates you, and you have my thanks for that."

Millie bristled with anger. Zanthred could sense the million different retorts and insults swimming in her head, but she chose to hold her words, just like a mature cherno should.

"Well, would you mind leaving me to my companions, we have private matters to discuss," said Janistor.

"Of course, but there is just one thing I'd like to ask."

"Yes?"

"What are you planning to do for your civic service? I imagine it must be hard to contemplate giving up this life of romance and society to work the fields for twenty years. All that mud and hard labour. And you might even get sent away from all your troths to one of the colonies. Worse still, you might end up a gong farmer and turn them away with the stench!"

Millie giggled as if it were a joke, but Janistor went from a smirk to despair in a few heartbeats. She had shuddered at the mention of gong harvesting; it meant cleaning out the sewers and carrying away the effluence for use as fertilizer. Gong farming was the worst civic service that might be given. The places were drawn by lot, so there was always a risk of getting picked for it.

Millie had correctly guessed it was a deep fear of hers.

"I-I have not really considered the matter much."

Zanthred guessed Janistor meant *'I've considered it*

from every angle and the only acceptable solution is a miracle.' She was hoping some noble troth or lordly admirer would concoct a form of civic duty that would be more acceptable. The trouble was, only jobs no one else wanted to do were considered to be legitimate.

"Oh well, I hope you get a good placement," said Millie, before returning to Zanthred.

Callin ap Elsiren stared at her back from behind his scented handkerchief with murderous intent; no one upset *his* troth.

"You just made yourself some enemies," said Zanthred.

"It doesn't matter, if it's a question of only upsetting those I didn't respect anyway," said Millie. "Besides, she's a damn cunning one. I'd call that a draw. You see what kind of girl you've fallen for now?" She was looking at Zanthred, but she was aiming the remark at Hanuru as well.

"I see a girl with flaws. Show me one without?" said Zanthred. And Millie could make no reply.

"A wise person corrects their flaws when they are pointed out. They do not make theatre out of them," said Baytee. "I wondered how long it would take one of you to stand up to her." She smiled approvingly at Millie.

"Thank you for your endorsement," said Millie. "But why didn't you say something sooner?"

Baytee gave a hearty laugh that made her loose bosom jiggle.

"If I had to correct every young person's flaws that

came through these doors I'd have no time to eat or sleep! You young ones come to Chepsid to escape that kind of thing. No, it is much better that one learns 'correctness' in the company of one's peers."

There was a commotion over at Janistor's side of the room. She had risen from her state of dejection and made confident strides over to the palace messenger. She took the stylus from his hand.

"I, Janistor of Serra, will join the volunteer civic service," and she wrote her name down on the wax ledger without a word from the palace messenger.

A flurry of whispers whipped round the room. Zanthred, who had resigned his designs on Janistor as hopeless, was given a sudden boost of optimism; they would be in the same cohort, training and marching together.

Callin looked seized with purpose. He not only rose from his seat, but stood on top of one of the tables.

"I, Callin ap Elsiren, am of privileged birth and as such will be given the honour of riding in the war-cavalry, probably at the Emperor's own side. But I renounce that honour! I will gift my horses to some worthy person and join Janistor as volunteer under the banner of the Perched Sparrow!"

There was a great cheer, and other troths and would-be troths were climbing on tables to renounce their privileges in honour of Janistor. Suddenly the palace messenger was overwhelmed with volunteers.

Many thoughts rushed through Zanthred's head, but he was certain of one thing as he followed

Janistor's admiring gaze to Callin, standing on the table, one fist raised to the air, cheering the name of the Emperor and the Ban; Callin was the one who was going to get to take her home tonight.

* * * * * * *

Akai watched the drilling regiments from the roof of Tisenin's mansion. They were stunning to behold. Each man (and the volunteers were almost all males) wore a bright purple sash, carried a tall wicker shield and held a two metre long pole. Many of the poles still did not have spearheads; there simply were not enough bronze smiths in the city to cast them all. But that was alright, because Akai had a strong feeling they would not need to use them.

Each unisoned turn showed a different colour, like the glint of a school of fish. Their shouts in a thousand different voices became a crashing wave of sound. It was mesmeric.

Adrin ap Foras was the one drilling the troops. He walked up and down the lines with a pole twice as long as any mans' spear. When he thought he found a soldier out of place, he would level the staff against them and push them back until they made a dead straight line with their comrades.

"Just a step out of place and you open yourselves up! In Cathri they have a saying *'the men at your sides are your best shields'*, remember that!" barked Adrin.

When he was tired from drilling his troops he came over to the mansion, took off his lizard coat and carefully folded it over a hitching post. He took a jug of water from a mansion servant, drank a few swigs and then tipped what remained over his head.

"I never realised giving orders was such arduous work," came a woman's voice from inside the mansion. Dago strolled out. She was giving her full attention to the assembled troops and did not even make eye-contact with Adrin.

They were right below where Akai sat on the roof, but they did not see him. Akai would have moved to give them their due privacy, if only he were not so curious about Tisenin's two best friends.

"You should join us and find out. You know you have a place as an officer in this army, should you want it?" proposed Adrin.

It was phrased like an offer, but Dago clearly took it as an accusation of cowardice. She fixed Adrin with an icy stare. "Adrin, you know I am a mage."

"There is no reason why you can't be an officer and a mage. You are tall and haughty. In armour you would make a handsome soldier."

"Hmph! You would love to have me under your command, wouldn't you?" accused Dago.

Adrin grinned, "It would certainly be a pleasant novelty. You've been under me plenty of times, but I cannot remember once when it was at *my* command."

Dago scowled at the crude pun. "You sound better with rosy verses coming from your mouth than old barbs. Stick to the love poems."

"Aye, if only they had got me somewhere."

"Your wife does not appreciate them?" asked Dago. "Or do you find her wanting as a muse?"

Adrin looked away, uneasy with the question. "She is a loyal and adequate wife. She will be a superb mother to my son."

"It must be so nice to be married to someone *adequate*," mocked Dago.

"Well, I decided there was only so much time one could wait for that reluctant someone before it became obvious it was an expression of madness."

Dago clutched her blue cowry and set her face to stone, as if she were trying to stop overwhelming rage leaking through. But her feet said it all as she stormed back into the mansion. Adrin shock his head and wiped a single tear from his face. He looked like he was disgusted with himself for that last droplet of bitterness.

We most readily hurt those we love, sprang to Akai's mind. He knew it would take some strong emotions to get these two respected and mature nobles to share cross words.

Adrin put his lizard coat back on, picked up his pole and went back to drilling the synchronized soldiers.

"Did you hear anything worthwhile?" came Quinias's voice from behind Akai.

Akai twisted round in surprise. He had not heard Quinias approach.

"Uh..." Akai felt filled with shame for being found out. "Nothing I can repeat."

That seemed to amuse Quinias. There was a hint of twisted lip from beneath his hood. "A wise policy. Discretion is the most underused of the great virtues. But it never hurts to know something more about one's friends. That is more or less my personal mantra."

"Adrin will have no kind words for me if he knows what I just overheard," said Akai, urging Quinias to use his vaunted discretion.

"I'm sure. But who needs to spy on Adrin and Dago to know what passes between them. *Love and pride* are the two things which will always bring a cherno pain. Adrin suffers from both more than most. And Dago....?" Quinias shook his head dismissively as if words could not quite sum her up.

But Akai noticed Quinias's body language. As he said '*love and pride*' his right hand came to his balled left fist and unconsciously stroked it. Once again, his body seemed to be recalling something his mind ignored.

"I didn't come up here to spy, I was watching the troops," said Akai

"Ah, yes?"

"They're magnificent aren't they?" said Akai, sweeping his hand across the field filled with soldiers.

"It makes my heart swell with pride for our enterprise," declared Quinias.

"We won't even have to fight, not really. One look at our column of disciplined, dedicated volunteers and the people of Serra will give up any hope they have of resisting the change to the Ban."

"Hmm, one hopes," said Quinias, but he sounded less certain than Akai. "Anyway, I didn't come up here to spy either. I have a job for you Akai."

"Yes?"

Quinias held out a scroll.

"Copy this out twelve times and give the copies back to me. I don't want anyone else to see the contents."

"Certainly!" said Akai.

Akai took the scroll and went down to the room he had been using as a study, copying old maps of Quri and Jewasri. He laid the scroll out and read down the columns.

It was the names.

People of likely dissent. Black for possible anxieties, red for open opposition. The list was a lot longer now; Quinias had been doing a lot of research.

Akai spread out a sheet of parchment and began precisely transcribing names in two colours of ink. He had not progressed far when he came across one that knotted his throat.

Ashlaya ap Woodrin in bright blood red.

She had not stopped calling for her father. Every morning she came up to Tisenin's mansion and screamed for him until she was hoarse or she collapsed from exhaustion. There was not much they could do about her, other than carry her back down to her home when she no longer had the energy to move. Small crowds of people who had lost loved ones in the disappearances had started to come with her. And now her name was in red.

Akai hated being woken by her each morning. It reminded him of that moment in the galley when he saw the lock of black hair and had to choose what to do. Sometimes he thought that the idea he had helped cover up a murder was so absurd that he almost laughed with relief. What a fool he had been to feel so guilty! To worry so much! Other times it made him want to die.

He poised with quill hovering above paper, a red bead slowly coagulating at the end.

No Ashlaya, you deserve to scream all you want.

He put the red quill back and picked up the black one. He just hoped Quinias slept more soundly in the morning than himself.

Chapter 6

War Craft

The Magnolia Court. It was inevitable he should end up back here at some point. The flowers still bloomed, the cherry blossoms still fell and everyone looked upon him with reverence, but Kirrie's throne was uncomfortable in both the literal and metaphorical sense.

He needed to make things happen quickly. There was no time to develop a war office from scratch, so he had to work with the established social structures. And that meant wooing the guilds.

In front of him now were representatives from guilds covering every profession that was needed when raising an army; coopers, sail makers, rope makers, caulkers, carpenters, foresters, smiths, wheelwrights, ship builders, fletchers, cartographers, tanners, horse breeders, warehouse owners and rune crafters among others. The guilds were informal networks, only a little more advanced than a social club, which allowed like-minded individuals to share ideas, techniques and resources. But they were also the best way Duarma could get a large number of people organised and resources flowing into Serra quickly.

Thankfully most of the guilds had agreed to help him quite easily. They were dominated by the older generation who held the office of Emperor in the greatest respect and, whether or not they agreed with the Ban, held Tisenin's actions in horror.

There were only two guilds yet to agree to Duarma's requests; the Mages' Guild and the Shadow Guard.

"Who speaks for the Mages' Guild?" asked Duarma.

A huddle of the magic users briefly conversed. Whilst the other guilds had sent one or two people, the mages had sent ten venerable representatives. The meteomancer Mordhai stepped forwards.

"As you know my Emperor, the Mages' Guild is governed by a large council and our head, Pallah ap Foras, is infirm. So the council has asked myself, as the member most familiar with serving you, to speak on their behalf."

"That suits me perfectly Mordhai. What says your guild? Will you make the weather fair for our ships? Will you shelter my troops from arrows? Will you tell us where our enemy tries to hide? Will you strike fear into them with fiery bolts?"

"No, my Emperor."

"What?"

The other representatives echoed Duarma's indignation.

"You must understand my Emperor, there are some very strong feelings in our guild regarding the Ban. We both have the mages entrusted with ensuring the Ban is held firm, and the very people who stand to lose most. With my farsight, I can see the air currents eighty kilometres away. I can feel the weight of water that burdens every thimble full of sky. I can sense every molecule of breath rushing in and out of your lungs. The Ban will take that away from me. It is a lot to ask."

"Mordhai? Have you forgotten your mistress already!"

Mordhai looked shamed by the suggestion. "No my Emperor! I am *for* the Ban, and *for* intervention on the side of the Faithful! I simply seek to illustrate what a sacrifice we are being asked to make. And some of our number do not wish to be forced into it. Others worry that our magic will be used to a violent purpose, to our moral detriment and the benefit of Karlsha."

Karlsha. Duarma had not heard that name since he was a child and his mother would tell him not to push his cousins over because it was *'to the benefit of Karlsha.'* That faceless god from cherno history.

"You would abandon me because *some* of your number have reservations?"

"No, my Emperor, we have come to an accommodation. As per our charter, we will hold a vote on the matter and the whole guild will respect the outcome."

"That is acceptable. I have faith in your members. How soon can you make the vote?"

"...A month my Emperor. We have to give time for all the mages from the Inner Sea to gather. If it were just those members resident in Serra I'm afraid the results would not be accepted."

"A month! But Tisenin's army could already be in power by then."

"I-I'm sorry, my Emperor, this is what has been decided. In the meantime, we will continue to perform our normal duties. I will predict the weather and ensure the safe passage of your ships."

That was scant consolation.

"I could simply dissolve the guild and free up the loyal mages to join my cause," said Duarma.

"You could," agreed Mordhai.

But then I would not know how many mages I was gifting to Tisenin.

"Let your colleagues at the Mages' Guild know I am greatly angered by their reticence, but will indulge their desires out of respect for the venerable sages that reside in its halls."

"I thank my Emperor for your patience and wisdom."

Besides, I can always dissolve the guild if this voting takes too long. Duarma caught himself; that was the first sly thought he had entertained as Emperor. Did that mean he was growing into the role, or becoming jaded?

Next to Mordhai stood the Master of the Shadow

Guard. He was an elderly man, but every muscle in his body was so well defined that it looked like he had more than his allotted share of youth below the neck. He wore simple white cotton robes without any kind of adornment or embellishment, except for a leather sheath at his side. Up until this moment he had remained perfectly still, with barely even a heave of the chest to indicate he was breathing.

But suddenly he ripped his rune-etched sword from its sheath, held it high and sent it crashing blade first into the ground, with a crackle of blue sparks.

"I am ashamed to be pledged to protect the Mages' Guild! My master, and his master, and every master since the simurgh first split our seed from the humans, has pledged their life to safeguard the weavers of the Ban. Now I find our charges are not worthy of our blades!"

The sword quivered in the earth. It was a long bronze weapon, perhaps as old as the age of Elsiren, with a narrow waist and broad leaf-shaped tip to add weight to any blows. Along the spine the runes were glowing with dull heat and oozing a magical energy of rare intensity.

"I can only apologise to the Shadow Guard for our equivocation," said Mordhai.

The Shadow Guard Master looked to Duarma. "My Emperor, you have my weapon and that of all our brothers. Though were are small in number."

"How many?"

"A hundred. And some of them are out in the

human lands hunting the daemons which prey on our weak-minded progenitors."

"I am sure a hundred of your blades are worth a thousand of Tisenin's. But is there any way to increase your numbers?"

"In the dark days when the Ban was being erected, the mages were plagued by daemons which saw their end coming. We were many. Since the Ban, such creatures are thankfully rare and our numbers have declined accordingly. However, I see that a mortal foe who chooses to set themselves against the Ban is as rightfully our enemy as any daemon. Thus I will open our shrine's door to new recruits."

"That is good to hear. It buoys my heart."

"However, there are obstacles. We demand only the fittest initiates and they must take vows of chastity and poverty so their soul knows no temptation. But above that, our equipment is time-consuming to make and only a few expert smiths know the techniques."

"Very well. I shall make it known that anyone who joins the Shadow Guard is exempt from other forms of conscription or civic service. Any smith who services your guild will be exempt from the general ordinances. You will have their exclusive use."

"Thank you, my Emperor."

At least the Shadow Guard are easy to please, though Duarma. *Smiths and a foe.*

"There is one other thing. A palace guard by the name of Hesiad. I was unfair to him the day my wife died and I have not had the chance to apologise to him. I heard he was a former member of the Shadow Guard. Have you heard of his whereabouts?"

The Master looked thoughtful for a second. "Yes, Hesiad. A warrior of rare skill. He came to us rather broken, but proved his worth quickly. However, he left our guild over a hundred years ago and I have not heard from him since."

"Unfortunate. If you do hear news of him please find a way to convey it to me, or my apology to him," said Duarma.

"Consider it done, my Emperor."

Good, that was the matter of the guilds dealt with. Now he just had to figure out how to get hold of the other things the army would need; the bread, the salted fish, the pickled fruit, the clothes, sandals, rope, whet stones, wax, oil and all the things people normally made at home as they were needed.

* * * * * * *

The anger Zanthred had felt four days ago when he first heard that Tisenin was raising an army had subsided. He now had to think carefully and remind himself of that sensation in order to convince himself he was doing the right thing.

Perhaps the main reason was that this was *hard*.

They had been doing a marching drill for two days now. The first day all the volunteers from the Perched Sparrow had queued up ready to get their weapons and begin training. But all they had each been given was a sack of stones and a red number painted on their forehead. The number was their position in the company, written there so that everyone (but particularly the instructors) could clearly see if someone was out of place. The sack of stones was to inure them to the hardship of marching with all the equipment they would eventually have to carry.

The soldier in the centre of the front rank was given a pole to carry; what would eventually become their flag. They were supposed to remember their position in relation to the 'flag' and keep it no matter what. What helped more was to memorize who was in front, behind and to the side. Then a commander with a drum would issue beaten orders to the flag bearer and the company would march behind him trying to keep good order. Wheeling, reversing direction, breaking up, reforming, walking, double-speed, halting, extending the line, contracting the line. They practised it all day long, even through the midday sun. They were not even allowed to leave the company to get water. Instead they had to wait for an attendant to bring a jug over. Several people fainted on the first day. Many were in no condition to take part on the second. Luckily Zanthred was not one of them; he and Millie had made the long trek north from Icknel not long ago and were still in good shape. Janistor had been surprisingly stalwart, a fact Zanthred ascribed to her frequent exhausting hunting trips and Millie to the extra water she took from her admirers. Hanuru had barely made it though and Zanthred and Millie had been forced to carry her back to the Sparrow at the end of each day.

Their battle formation was only three people deep. Zanthred was in the front rank, with Mille and Hanuru directly behind him. Janistor was on the other side of the company protected by a wall of three of her troths, including Callin. That put an end to the vain romantic notions he had of saving her in the midst of battle.

Callin was the only one in the company who had a sword, even if it was of the old fashioned bronze variety. He had also managed to find himself a jerkin made of iron scales. It came down to his thighs, making him look like a kind of fish that clanked whenever he moved. Both were relics from his journeys to the spice colonies where he had fought the tribals and claimed the feather that now perched in Janistor's crown. The rest of them had begun to realise they would have to wait a long time to be given 'official weapons' and no one could find an axe or sword in the city market for any kind of favour. They came equipped with a motley assortment of clubs, kindling hatchets, sickles, fire pokers and long knives. Zanthred had whittled a club from a branch with a heavy knot at one end. In the evenings most people had started making themselves a protective gambeson by quilting together many layers of linen. The heat would be unbearable with one of them on, but it was preferable to being sliced open.

But today it was all changing. Today they had finally been given bows, five arrows each and told to go to the archery butts.

Zanthred regarded his unstrung bow sceptically.

"This is lemon wood, you don't make proper bows out of lemon wood. And it has knots. It could snap at any time."

"It's just for training, I'm sure," said Millie.

They lined up at one end of the butts in battle order. There were several ranks of straw targets laid out at different ranges. A man in a heavy woollen cape limped onto the field using a stick for support.

"I am Gargrace. I will teach you to shoot!" his voice boomed like a white lion's roar. "You will do exactly as you are told. You will shoot when I tell you to shoot and stop when I tell you to stop. To be an archer you need to shoot an arrow every ten seconds and you need to be able to keep that up for at least two minutes. If you can't do it, I'll make you practise harder. And if your fingers bleed, I'll know you're doing it right, and you can carry on until you can show me the bone."

Scary man, thought Zanthred.

The first thing Gargrace showed them was how to string and unstring their bow. Even Hanuru managed this easily; the bows they had been given were sports bows made for nothing more than target practise.

Next he taught them how to take aim properly with three fingers, always drawing the bow back so the knuckle of the thumb touched the same part of your face. Little of this was new to Zanthred. He had shot at hares regularly whilst tending his sheep in Icknel.

Gargrace allowed them all a few practise shots to

gauge the power of their bows, then started them aiming at targets. He called a range and they had to aim at that set of targets.

"Twenty-five metres!"

The first volley was a fine solid mass of arrows that thudded to ground with a satisfying 'whoomp,' although few of them actually hit the targets.

"Fifty metres!"

This time people struggled to re-nock their bows and only a few arrows were loosed at the command. A disorganized clatter of impacts lasted for several seconds. Zanthred was used to shooting, but not this fast. He misplaced the arrow several times in his panic, failing to slot the string into the nook of the arrow. But Gargrace did not slow down his calling pace for the slackers.

"One-hundred metres!"

Another dismal spray of arrows, few if any reaching their intended range. But Zanthred was a shot behind and something misaligned in his mind so 'fifty metres' and 'one-hundred metres' became 'one-hundred-fifty metres.'

He sent an arrow sailing clear over the hundred metre mark and watched it slam into the heart of the target beyond. It was by far the furthest out.

"Cease!" yelled Gargrace. "Who shot the arrow into the far target?"

Murmurs raced along the line of archers and people looked from left to right to see if anyone would own up. Zanthred felt the blood vessels in his face flush hot and his mouth dried up. No one would know if he stayed quiet; but that was not the cherno way.

A wise person corrects their flaws. Baytee's words came back to him.

Zanthred stepped forwards. "I shot the arrow," he announced with what he hoped was dignity and contrition tied together.

Gargrace limped over to him and Zanthred saw the deep lines over his face. He stood so close that his hot garlicky breath stung Zanthred's eyes. It took a conscious effort not to shrink away in disgust and fear. Gargrace plucked an arrow from the quiver on Zanthred's hip.

"Make that shot again."

Zanthred nodded, but dared not speak back. He took the arrow, made sure the shaft was straight and the feathers keen, then he nocked it on the string, one finger above, two below. He set his left arm ridged, just crooked enough that his wrist would not catch the string, and pulled back with the right so his knuckle grazed his ear. He took aim, pivoting from the waist so he was sending the arrow up at almost forty-five degrees. With a weak bow like this, a hundred-fifty metres was about the limit of its range. He held the shot for just a second to make sure the wind was low, then released.

It was a good shot; the release was smooth and the wobble on the arrow as it took flight was minimal. The wind stayed down as it made its majestic arc over the range. Zanthred could not breathe. The arrow slammed home into the border of the target.

A good shot, but not great.

"Humph. You have sound technique for an amateur. Easy to build on," said Gargrace. "You have no bow of your own? That surprises me."

"No, my teacher. I left it in Icknel. I planned to make myself another when I was settled here."

"Make?" Gargrace nodded sagely. "As every fine archer should! But for now, try this one."

He thrust his thick staff into Zanthred's hands. Zanthred thought he was joking; the staff had the dimensions of a club, not a bow. But then he saw the horn collars at the top and bottom and the notches to take the string. He turned the pole and saw the split between the dark yew heart wood and light, springy sap wood. It was definitely a bow, but its thickness was so immense that it looked like it belonged to a giant.

"This is too heavy for me," said Zanthred.

"Try it anyway. It's what we shoot with in Lansissari. Good yew, well frozen in the winter. A battle bow."

Zanthred braced it against his foot and tried to bend the top down. But try as he might his arm just did not have the strength to bring the string to the notch.

"No, no! Don't use your arms!" growled Gargrace. "Hold it with your arms and bend your back."

Zanthred did as he was ordered and just managed to loop the string on, turning the straight staff into a useable bow. He nocked an arrow and drew it back as far as he could, but his arm shook with strain and the string bit into his fingers like solid steel before he had touched his lips. He released early and the arrow wobbled hopelessly through the air. It missed the target, but to Zanthred's surprise, sailed clean over the top and finally fell another fifty metres beyond.

"It's too heavy for me, my teacher. I cannot draw it, let alone shoot every ten seconds."

"But you will! Practise every morning, every evening. Eat meat. Make your arms strong. Soon you will draw it to its full and make your arrows sigh as fast as I do." He leaned in and whispered the last line, "And if you learn to shoot as well as I think you can, I'll ignore the fact that you just shot at the wrong target."

Zanthred thanked Gargrace for his gift and the lesson for the company continued, although he barely managed to put half the arrows in the air that the others did.

At the end of practise Zanthred clutched his sore fingers and rubbed the blisters.

"Well done dear Zanthred, they say you are the best shot in the company."

Zanthred looked up and saw Janistor. He was almost too surprised to talk back.

"Umm...thank you. Although with fingers like this I doubt I'll be able to shoot too much more."

"Can I see?" Without waiting for a reply, she took his right hand and gently stretched out his digits with her delicate finger tips. She made a sympathetic grimace when she saw the injury. "Oh, poor you. I have something that might help." She pressed a small white leather patch into his good hand. It was a finger guard. "Doe skin. I'm told it's the best for archers. Supple and soft."

"Thank you, Janistor. But won't your fingers suffer?"

"No, I have another. Perhaps you could teach me to shoot sometime? I have only ever tried it from the saddle before."

"I'd like that."

She smiled coquettishly, then made her excuses and returned to her troths. For an instant Zanthred thought he might still have a chance with her. *But ever the hopeful heart turns an act of kindness into something more*, he thought, remembering how wrong he was before.

Millie was not far behind Janistor. "Well—" she began.

"...I know what you are going to say. 'Stay away from her, you're a fool,' and so on," said Zanthred.

"Actually I was going to say well done, that's the first thing you've done to restore your reputation since we got to Serra."

The company began traipsing back towards the Great River and the bridge to Chepsid. For the first time Zanthred and Millie did not have to carry Hanuru, although it was obvious her shoulders were in pain from all the shooting. But she did not complain.

"You'll feel it more tomorrow," said Zanthred.

"I know, I'm just glad we have another day of practise manoeuvring tomorrow. And I never thought I'd say that," said Hanuru.

The route took them round the outskirts of Serra where they could watch all the other companies practise their manoeuvres. There were companies from every guild and district in Serra, but the Perched Sparrow was the only one from Chepsid. Most were training to be archers, but a few were practising clashing shields and spears in a tightly packed melee. All of them from the Sparrow watched nervously; it was the crucial point of the battle they all feared. Kill or be killed. Plant your legs firm and push. And hack and stab until the enemy runs.

"I still don't know if I'll be able to kill someone whilst looking them in the eye," said Hanuru.

"It'll be okay. We're in the rear rank. We just have to make sure not to run," said Millie.

Zanthred did not have that luxury.

Not all the youths on civic service had volunteered for the army. Around the periphery of the city those youths who were too cowardly, committed to pacifism or sympathetic to the Sagacious cause (and there was a lot of public speculation on that point) were busy digging a defensive ditch and hauling the spoil up to make a rampart. They worked with antler picks, wooden shovels and leather buckets. It looked like extremely hard work. Older figures moved among them; any citizen with idle hours was coming together to defend their homes. Everyone from venerable elders who had earned the right not to work, to house servants who had been temporarily excused by their masters. The wooden palisade was taking longer to build. But then most of the forests around Serra had been exhausted many centuries ago. The wood had to come all the way from Lansissari.

However, by far the most spectacular sight was watching as the cavalry arrayed in two lines for a mock battle. Their hooves had thrown up clouds of billowing dust which were slowly blowing away as the lines stilled. But the horses were excited to be gathered in such large numbers and they tossed their heads and whinnied in glee.

"My, my. How many horses would you say are gathered there friend?"

Zanthred turned to the speaker. She was a tall woman with an unusually hooked nose. Zanthred did not recognise her, but that was nothing exceptional; once the word had spread that the Sparrow was forming its own company, many people volunteered who had only been to the Perched Sparrow once, or even who just felt a kindred spirit with the company of artists and poets.

"I don't know, maybe a thousand?" said Zanthred.

"Two-thousand-two-hundred-fifty," said Hanuru as if it were obvious.

Zanthred and the new woman looked at her incredulously.

"How can you possibly know that?" asked Zanthred.

"I counted," said Hanuru. Zanthred continued to

look at her in disbelief so she explained. "It's a mnemonics thing, group counting. It's really easy. But not usually useful."

"Thank you, my friend," said the woman with the hooked nose. "You are a credit to your teacher."

"But I taught myself," Hanuru whispered. Although no one heard her, not even Millie.

****

Haddra looked grimly at his cavalry force. He was in the middle of the two lines of battle with Duarma and a flag. The recruits, almost all Quri nobles, had yet to impress him.

"This mock battle will show me what you have learnt. Remember when to split and when to come together. Remember the turns and the pincers. Above all, listen to your unit's drums!" Haddra turned to Duarma. "My Emperor, do you want to do the honours?"

"I look forward to seeing the gleaming gem of your labours," said Duarma. Duarma took the flag from Haddra's hand and gave it a long flourish.

Immediately chaos erupted around them.

The two lines of cavalry charged towards each other. The ground physically trembled beneath the feet of so many running animals. The noise was every bit on par with a roll of thunder. The cavalry was supposed to move within bow shot and form a series of pincers to flank and trap pockets of the enemy horses; some would feign retreat, some would press the enemy and some would try and break through their formation, whittling away at their numbers until they panicked and fled the field. It was the Delfuri way of war.

What actually happened when they got within bow shot was that the two lines continued to close together. The riders tried to turn their mounts and form up into separate divisions, but the animals were so excited to be part of a herd that each just followed the animal next to it, ignoring their masters. The result was a giant crash of lines in the centre of the field, and then in the press of flesh the animals panicked. Some squealed and carried their riders off in directions of their own choosing, all semblance of formation gone. Others dived away from the press, forming a new herd that was a mixture of the two sides. These galloped away from the battlefield for the sheer joy of galloping.

"Is this supposed to happen?" asked Duarma.

"No, my Emperor, it is not." Haddra mentally uttered curses against the bloodline of all Quri horses and their breeders.

There were a few hundred riders on the flank nearest the city who had managed to control their beasts. They were doing their best to charge, retreat, then turn their horses and charge again. The manoeuvres were slow and sloppy; however, they were at least managing the basics. They repeated the sequence about five times, but then some of the horses refused to move at all, despite their owners liberally applying the whip. That kind of disobedience was a death sentence during a feigned retreat.

"My Emperor, I will be back soon."

Haddra urged his horse down to where the recruits were practising. They had all stopped now.

"Why have you stopped! The battle is not yet over. If this were the real thing you few soldiers might be the fulcrum of the battle!"

One of the soldiers trotted up to him. He was a young Quri noble on a tall dappled horse. He jabbed a javelin into the ground in frustration.

"This is pointless! All this back and forth manoeuvring. Our horses are tired! We could have closed with the enemy and finished this battle in a few seconds."

Haddra looked around. All the animals were panting. Their tongues lolled out of their mouths and traces of white sweat were visible on their flanks.

"Try closing with *my cavalry* and you'll be left looking at my horse's rear end with a dozen arrows in your chest!" said Haddra. "The cavalry archer is the king of the battlefield. Able to avoid any danger and attack at any point. Throwing that advantage away is nonsense." He picked the noble's javelin up and handed it back to him. "Now continue the practise, even if you have to walk your horses."

The noble reluctantly took his javelin then went over to his colleagues and spoke words Haddra did not hear. They regrouped and walked their horses a little way back to restart the mock combat.

But then they carried on walking. Haddra called them back.

"Not that far!"

Either they did not hear him or they did not listen. They were walking their horses over to where the spearmen were practising. Finally Haddra came to the conclusion that the nobles were giving up and walking away from the training. However, just as he settled on that thought, the recruits picked up their pace to a trot, heading straight for the tightly packed phalanx of spearmen. The spearmen were facing the cavalry, still and well formed. As the horses closed the distance and showed no sign of deviating or slowing, the infantry started looking nervous. The horses were not moving fast, only slightly above a man's walking pace, but they formed a solid wall of flesh that towered over the head of the footmen. Finally, only a few strides away from the solid thousand strong infantry block, the handful of cavalry lowered the points of thier javelins into menacing lances. The infantry panicked and in an instant the whole company disintegrated into a mass of running and shrieking fools.

The horses continued for a few hundred metres before coming to a halt, then they started heading back to Haddra. The noble on the dappled horse had a huge gloating smile on his face.

"How was that, my teacher? I think *my way* has some merit. The name's Copidius ap Ranra! Remember it, you're going to here it a lot, old man!"

Haddra snarled and was about to issue a retort about how easy it was to scatter allies during a practise, but Duarma led his horse up along his side.

"That looked very effective to me," said the Emperor. "We should talk about reforming our cavalry force."

* * * * * * *

That night, a tall woman with an unusually hooked nose slipped out of the Perched Sparrow whilst no one was particularly paying attention. She stole a small row boat and crossed the Great River from Chepsid to Serra without having to use the bridge. She found her way to a galley from Hern, leaving at night to catch the morning tide. The Captain of the galley had neglected to inform the Harbour Master of the ship's departure.

Chapter 7

Elsiren's Tomb

The news Quinias's spy brought had chilled the mood of the revolutionary Sagacious League. The old Serra nobility had installed Duarma as their new figurehead Emperor. They had discovered the League's intentions (despite the storm) and were now training their own army. It looked like there would be a fight after all.

The soldiers had covered their wicker shields in leather to give better protection from arrows. The smiths had been furiously casting and beating out bronze and iron helms. All the spear shafts now had deadly pointed heads. No one was relying on intimidation alone to win the day.

Akai, Quinias, Tisenin, Adrin and Dago stood on the quay of the harbour. The great storm that had raged for weeks was now dispersing.

"As soon as the sea is clam, I want you to sail out, Dago and Quinias." said Tisenin.

"Are you sure you don't want to wait a little longer? Paramount Janjula of Hern has raised a sizable troop. She can sail them here from White Bay in a matter of weeks," said Quinias.

"No, if it comes to a contest of size, they will win. We can never transport as many people as they can put in arms on their home ground. We have to attack now and hope our superior preparation sees us through. And this vote in the Mages' Guild plays firmly into our hand."

"You know my objection to the vote," warned Adrin. "We could be sending our mages to their deaths. We must assume Duarma's grief will win out over all the promises he has made. It certainly would mine."

"I see the risk," said Tisenin. "However, I know Duarma almost as well as I did Kirrie. At his core, he is honourable. If he says he will respect the Guild's decision, he will respect it. And can you see the Mages' Guild voting *for* the Ban?"

Dago smiled; she was a first rate mage with lots of sway in the Guild. "The vote is an absurdity, a foregone conclusion. The fact Duarma had to allow it is a sign of his weak position. They are still reeling, still trying to form an effective war council."

"Quite," said Tisenin. He took Dago's hands. "Dago, you are my most trusted mage. Take our members of the Guild and make sure the vote goes our way. When you have the Guild at your disposal, do everything you can to get them to quit the city and join our fleet. But beware. I trust Duarma, not everyone in Serra. If old Haddra now has as much influence as they say, he could be a maverick danger."

Dago momentarily squeezed Tisenin's hands, then touched two fingers to the tattoo of the tears under her eye. A sign of commitment. "Tisenin, it shall be done as you say."

Adrin hesitated in saying his farewells, then threw his caution away and enveloped his ex-lover in a tight embrace. "Stay safe, take no risks. It would break me to see you hurt, Dago."

Dago froze with what looked like loathing. She did not hug back. *"Please, be content with your wife!"* she whispered back just loud enough for Akai to hear.

Adrin released her, shame-faced. For a moment Akai felt very sorry for him; that hug looked like it stemmed from genuine concern rather than having any romantic meaning. But then Adrin whispered back a retort of equal venom.

"I'm sorry, I forgot just how very *proud* you like to play it."

Tisenin chose to ignore the personal insults his lieutenants were swapping. From what Akai knew about Tisenin, he would not care what his officers got up to in their private lives so long as it did not become a public embarrassment.

"Quinias, are you sure about our allies in the city?" asked Tisenin.

"Yes, as soon as the storm disperses, they will know about it in Serra and know we are coming. That is the signal they are waiting for," said Quinias.

"If you say it is so Quinias, then I consider the matter fact. Has there been any more word from the emissaries?" asked Tisenin.

"The city of Kelmor follows Serra, as it always has. But Sunnel and Icknel waver towards our cause, Icknel the most. Lord Roldern may be seduced. Across the waters our messengers must have reached Cathri by now and will soon be in Lansissari as well. Cathri is a hotbed of Ban haters and Archlord Kamil has no love for the Emperor in Serra, whoever that might be. We have the ear of several of his close entourage. We should cautiously count on his support. Archlord Serenus of Lansissari though? She is a different matter. We must do everything we can to woo her."

"Good. I shall bear that in mind," said Tisenin. "Now then, make the first conquest of the Sagacious League. Go to Adlan. We will follow with the full fleet tomorrow."

"Adlan? What's there?" asked Akai.

"A woman I have to see. Another maverick who might upset the balance," said Quinias.

* * * * * * *

It was good to sail on smooth, familiar seas once again. Akai had made this journey many times before and could navigate it without even looking at the horizon. Just the colours of the water were enough to tell him where he was. The island of Adlan was less than a day's journey from Efrandi and they frequently took pilgrims there on route to Serra. It was a rocky isle cut from the same black volcanic basalt as the cliffs under Efrandi. It had little in the way of its own produce, but one good harbour and a long black sand beach still gave ample comfort for a small town.

The island was famous for two reasons. Firstly, when Elsiren had forced the simurgh to transport the cherno to a new world away from the Ban, it was to Adlan that they were brought. His daughter, Geleda, was the first to set foot on the world of Haven and she became the cherno's first Emperor. Elsiren himself only made it to Haven when he was on the cusp of death; it had taken him his lifetime to gather the disparate cherno once they had scattered out of their desert prison. He was buried on the island in an elaborate tomb befitting the greatest hero of their people.

The second reason it was famous was because Elsiren's daughter had founded the cherno's first great temple to the god-creature Solrax.

Solrax, the entity at the centre of the Ban.

Solrax had been the master of the simurgh. It was she (as far as it was possible to assign the hermaphrodite simurgh a gender) who had conceived the idea of the Ban and been the architect of its construction. She who had selected the cherno to be the chosen slaves. She who had taught the mages the Great Song and led the chorus. But there had not been enough time; the daemons had discovered the prison veil being drawn over them and attacked. Solrax had to use her immense magic potential to physically translate her body into the magic realm and finish the spell with her soul.

The ultimate martyrdom.

Solrax would endure forever holding the Ban in place, keeping her children and perhaps all creation safe. The pittance she asked in return was for the cherno to occasionally turn their thoughts in her direction and lend her enough energy to sustain the Great Song.

Solrax and Elsiren were both domineering and acted without the permission of those their acts would affect, but their intentions were selfless and it was a great burden they took on for the ultimate good. For that altruism, Akai revered them both. He had no doubt he would one day be able to openly praise Tisenin in the same list. But what would become of Solrax?

"Will we still worship Solrax when we overthrow the Ban?" mused Akai.

"I should think so. If the re-alignment goes to plan the Ban will still exist, just not here. Solrax will still need us," said Quinias.

"And if it doesn't go to plan and the only way to stop the Ban is to destroy it?"

"Then...collectively we have some big decisions to make."

The ship skated on the surf and over the shallow green water where land met sea. They were coming into the harbour. The ship's crew had been supplemented with some of Adrin's soldiers, who were busy donning sword belts and helms. Once dressed they took up their wicker shields and tested the weight of their spears one last time.

Quinias addressed the crew, "Once we are in the harbour, we will go straight to the Temple of Solrax. As soon as that is secure, we will come back down and announce our presence in the town square. The soldiers and half the crew will come with me. The rest will remain here and guard the ship. But stow the mast. We want them to know we are here for good."

"Are you sure about the mast?" asked Akai. "Without it we won't be able to leave if there is trouble."

"That's my point," said Quinias. "Have you been to the temple before?"

"A few times."

"Then come with me. I may need a guide I can trust."

The crew drew in the sails, eased the ship into harbour, tied off on the quay and stowed the mast. Half the crew grabbed the few weapons that were available – short bows and hatchets mainly – and followed gingerly behind the soldiers. Akai had only his scrimshawing knife on him. Altogether, there were only thirty people in the expedition.

They skirted around the town. Plenty of people saw them, but no one dared to approach the armed group. Instead they just watched, gathering in ever greater numbers. The town must have had a population of a few hundred and it made Akai feel very vulnerable indeed.

The temple was situated on the top of a large cliff overlooking the sea. Akai had heard it was so that when the simurgh visited, they had good thermals to take wing on. Remembering that one little fact told Akai why they were here. The path up was steep and dusty. It forced them into single file and made Akai nervous about ambushes. But as they ascended, birds were scared out of pungent thyme bushes on the side of the road and that reassured him that they were the first to take the path for a few hours.

The way levelled out at the top of the cliff and suddenly the temple was before them. It was an imposing cyclopean structure built of huge blocks of white marble imported from Serra. Akai had once marvelled at the effort put into such an immense edifice by his ancestors, fresh to the world and not yet fully established. But someone had then reminded him that the temple was built before humans were exiled from the Hublands and it was essentially a product of human slave labour.

The temple had a single entrance, but the way was blocked by a group of twenty or more white robed cherno. They linked arms in a single chain. Akai could sense an above average level of magic emanating from them and knew some of them were in a magically linked chorus. Akai's own magic was paltry, but he could feel the strand of connection between them and that ineffable matrix of the Ban. They were devotees, still half in the trance that allowed them to infuse Solrax with part of their souls' energy.

One of the devotees spoke up, "Are you here representing Tisenin?"

Quinias prompted the soldiers to get into a battle formation before responding. "Yes, we come on the authority of the Sagacious League. I suggest you do not bar our way into the temple. Despite our weapons we have no desire to use them and no ill intent towards worshippers."

"We shall not move for enemies of the Ban. You will have to kill us to enter!"

Quinias bit his bottom lip.

"Your orders?" asked one of the soldiers.

"Do nothing yet," said Quinias. He turned to Akai and whispered. "They tie our hands. We cannot kill devotees, that would turn everyone in the Empire against us. But we cannot allow them to force us to wait. There are several hundred potentially hostile people in the town below us and one very dangerous woman in that temple."

"Are you sure she's in there?" asked Akai.

"Yes, I can feel her magic. Can't you?" said Quinias.

"Not past the devotees."

"We will have to work on your ether sight, it can come in immensely useful," said Quinias.

There was a thud behind them. Then another.

Akai looked up to see one of the devotees hurling sizable rocks at the soldiers. He was young, not even a hundred, and had unusually narrow lips that were curled into a snarl. Another rock thudded into the wall of wicker shields.

"Go back! Go back to your ships and leave us in peace!" shouted the youth. Another devotee broke the chain of linked arms and hoisted a stone to hurl.

One of the sailors nocked an arrow and half drew the bow.

"No!" screeched Akai, grabbing the sailor's wrist.

"That settles it, we cannot stay or retreat. We must advance," said Quinias. "Soldiers, keep a tight formation. Advance slowly. Use the butt of your spears and try only to hit their legs!"

As a single body the soldiers moved forwards, half a pace at a time. They had reversed their spears and held them high ready to strike. The devotees looked scared, but they were not about to flee. Instead they gripped each other even tighter and braced themselves with prayers.

"Stop this, my disciples." A woman's voice rang out clear and powerful from within the temple. A relatively young woman stood in the doorway.

"But teacher Feydrin! We cannot allow these traitors to hurt you!" implored one of the devotees.

"Let me worry about that. I will not see bloodshed on my behalf. Go home and continue to practise what I taught you. You need no temple to help spread the Ban." The devotees reluctantly unlinked their arms. Feydrin touched several of the indignant devotees on the shoulders. "Be at peace, go now."

The devotees cagily skirted round the armed troop and made their way down into the town. The youth that had thrown the stones gave Quinias a long angry stare as he passed.

"Soldiers, wait for me here. Akai, come with me," ordered Quinias.

Feydrin left the threshold, wordlessly inviting Quinias and Akai in behind her. Such was the scale of the temple, the interior was dark and heavy with smoke, despite a large hole in the roof to allow the full wingspan of a simurgh to gain entrance. The walls were covered in slate carvings of the simurgh; sinuous creatures like snakes covered with scales which half resembled those of a fish's and half the soft feathers of a bird. They had four powerful limbs and two leathery wings. Their heads were the most terrifying part; jaw as long as a cherno with teeth like daggers. Then there was the terrible poison gland that sat in the roof of their mouth. The artists had not even tried to represent it, just drawn a double headed trident at the tip of its tongue – the symbol of death.

"My good Feydrin, we have not come to kill you," said Quinias.

Feydrin threw her head back and laughed, "Ha! What makes you think you even could!"

Akai was suddenly confronted with a massive surge of magical energy. It was stronger than anything he had felt before, overwhelming all his senses, like looking into the sun. Feydrin opened her hand and blue sparks crackled between the finger tips. Akai had heard some powerful mages could throw lightning and he braced himself for the rush of pain.

Quinias half drew his sword.

Feydrin closed her hand and extinguished the blue energy. "No. You didn't come here to kill me and I have no intention of killing you. Speak frankly then. I have heard of Tisenin's deeds and the army he gathers."

"Tisenin has sent me to ask you one thing: Do nothing," said Quinias.

"Do nothing? Why how easily I can do that." She pulled a face full of disgust. "Go back to Tisenin and tell him I will stay silent. The simurgh come to me once every hundred years and I will not call them before they are due. But hope beyond hope that this rebellion of yours is done by that time."

"You have nothing to worry about. We will be done within the year," said Quinias.

Feydrin did not seem convinced. She turned her back and contemplated the stone carved simurgh reliefs.

Quinias seemed satisfied with her response. Such was the weight with which a respectable cherno's word was held. He put a hand on Akai's shoulder, "I am going down with the troops to deal with the townspeople. Watch Feydrin until I return."

Akai gulped at the responsibility of holding such a notable and powerful woman captive, if indeed that was what could be said were happening. "Of course, Master."

Quinias left and Akai heard him marshalling the troops back down the hill. There were several minutes of silence before Feydrin finally spoke, although she did not honour him by turning to face him.

"So, good warrior. To whom am I speaking?" asked Feydrin

"Akai of Efrandi, my ven-, goo...." Akai stumbled over his words.

That got her attention and she finally span around. "Why the hesitation?"

"Forgive me Feydrin, but I do not know how to address you. I always assumed the priest of Solrax would be venerable, but you are so young. And I was about to call you 'my good Lord,' but I do not know your blood or lands," said Akai.

Feydrin smiled at his clumsy social mishandling. "I am ap Lanlar, but no person's lord. Most people call me Teacher. Come, join me as I look upon the carvings."

Akai accepted her invitation and went and stood by her side. She was staring up at a picture of Solrax in her glory, flying high above the Great Desert of Earth.

"Tell me Akai, do the simurgh fill you with fear?"

"They do," said Akai.

"It is rightly so. When they are moved to anger...a handful could destroy our whole Empire. Reduce us to bands of scavengers living in holes in the ground. And that is just what I know they can do with their bodies. There is no telling what they could do with their magic. Consider, they managed to transport thousands of us across the stars!"

She paced around the room to a carving of the simurgh in the act of creating the cherno, as envisioned by an artist who could only dream and wonder at how it was done. The beast was infusing a human with desert sands and a heart full of magic. Akai suspected something much darker. There were stories of them forcing fathers to breed with their own daughters. Stories of them stealing away children with defects and clusters of tiny bones found in the desert. Stories which did not endear the simurgh to cherno ears.

Feydrin continued. "But they live in a trance for millions of years and our lives are like sparks to them. They come every hundred years to see me and ask if anything has changed. To which I reply 'no' and then they depart. To them that is considered a frequent annoyance. *Honour, freedom, dignity* and *gratitude* have no expression in the simurgh language and when I try to explain them, it just seems to cause boredom and confusion. The reason I am so young, is that it would confuse them further if they had to deal with a different venerable cherno every couple of visits. 'Priest' is a lifelong occupation starting as young as possible."

She looked very sternly into Akai's eyes. "You understand that the reason I will not summon the simurgh ahead of schedule is not due to respect for your cause or sympathy for the participants, it is because the simurgh will not care that we are killing each other over the Ban. When the Ban is in imminent danger and they do start caring, they may well carry out their ancient threat and kill us all. To their minds, that will be the most elegant solution."

"I understand your fears," said Akai. "But this will all be done before they next visit. We are the heirs of Elsiren and we will finish his work and preserve our species from the Ban and the simurgh."

"Oh? Heirs of Elsiren? Can you imagine Elsiren assassinating his own cousin to make a statement?" mocked Feydrin.

"Yes, if he had spent as long as Tisenin has trying to persuade with words alone. I was there, I saw the pain in his face. There was no other option."

"Did he weep?" asked Feydrin.

"Not openly," said Akai.

Feydrin sighed. "Come with me."

She led Akai out of the temple and up onto a nearby hillside. The path was worn down to the smooth bedrock – ancient and well trodden. The whole way was lined with marble and bronze sculptures, each piece of the same figure. Some were fresh, but most were thousands of years old with disintegrating features, the marble looking like melting snow and the bronze having turned green and flaky. At the peak they came to a small open sided shrine. Akai had not been here in years.

At the centre of the shrine was a sarcophagus. The lid was carved in the likeness of Elsiren as he was on the day he died. The sculptor had captured every detail of the ancient traveller's face; every wrinkle and pore set with the anima of still living flesh. Akai had to restrain himself from stroking the cheek. He felt a degree of love and awe for the man that he thought should be impossible for someone he had never met.

"You know that it will not end with the Emperor Kirrie?" said Feydrin. "More people will have to die."

"I understand that. I hate it, but for the greater good it is justified."

"Are you prepared to do the killing yourself?" asked Feydrin.

"I-I don't know," Akai hung his head. "I have no intellectual inhibition, but my heart tells me it is wrong. Childhood conditioning, I guess."

"Good, then there is hope for you. When Elsiren killed, and he killed many, he wept. Promise me one thing Akai. Promise me you will never stop weeping for those you kill. And never take an order from someone who has forgotten to weep for their foe. Promise me this."

"That is a promise it will be easy to keep."

"You think so? Many are the legends of Elsiren's heroism. Few are the stories we keep of Set's despotism or Ishtar's deceptions. Do not think a thousand years of peace has left us above the instincts of our past. Make me the promise."

Akai thought on her words for a long time. She was worried the violence would alter their racial mentality. As much as he wanted to, Akai could not entirely dismiss her fears. If a promise would help avoid that outcome, he would make it.

"I promise, my Teacher Feydrin." And he meant it solemnly.

She touched the back of his head. "That is all I ask."

"I'm glad you two are getting on so well," came a voice behind them. They turned around to see Quinias.

"How did it go in the town?" asked Akai.

"Well. The objectors agreed to ignore us. They will bring us no food and they will snub us in the street. But there are enough supporters amongst the townspeople that it need not concern us."

Feydrin looked relieved. "At least there will be no bloodshed."

"Yes. And the Sagacious League has its first conquest," grinned Quinias.

Chapter 8

The Mages

"I don't like it at all!" boomed Haddra. His horse sensed his uneasiness and shook its head nervously.

"Nevertheless, it is my decision," asserted Duarma. "We will let the mages come ashore for their vote."

A large Jewasri galley, the first to come for weeks, now sat in the harbour. It belligerently displayed the purple coat of arms of Tisenin. At Duarma's orders a gangplank was lowered for the mages. A tall, proud looking woman with teardrops tattooed under her eye was the first to disembark. Duarma had a vague memory of meeting her before, one of Tisenin's bosom friends.

"Dago ap Keldron?" asked Duarma.

"Yes. I thank you for your clemency," said Dago.

"I respect the Guild, not you or your coat of arms. Your father and mother were friends to Kirrie. It shames you to be in Tisenin's colours."

"With respect, if you know my parents at all, you should not be surprised that I stand with Tisenin. They have not attended the Magnolia Court for many years."

How isolated have we become? ran through Duarma's head.

"Go to the tower. My guards will escort you there and back. There will be no delay in your stay. You will not talk with anyone in the city, except within the confines of the Guild."

"I accept your terms." Dago indicated to the rest of the mages to come ashore.

Behind Duarma, Haddra growled with frustration. He turned his horse and whipped it away in protest.

Duarma could sympathize. Since the storm ceased everything had gone wrong. Rumours of war had spread wide throughout the land and a flood tide of refugees had poured into Serra. Every floor in the city was full and they had begun building a second city of tents outside the new ramparts (which were still far from complete). The Hot Season was just beginning and without good shade people would suffer.

More pressingly, he had already used the city's reserve of grain. This wave of refugees mostly came empty handed, thinking to rely on the kindness of strangers, as was the cherno way. This had not been helped by a spate of fires erupting all over the city. Two of the food stores had been incinerated and a potentially disastrous fire in the docks had been narrowly averted by a watchful Harbour Master. It was easy to spot the hand of saboteurs.

They were days away from mass starvation. He had sent urgent pleas to Kelmor, Sunnel and Icknel, but they would take weeks to respond. He was having to contemplate sending refugees away, or reserving what food there was for the soldiers.

He desperately did not want this information to reach Tisenin, but there was little hope of keeping it secret. The mages would no doubt talk within the Guild and even excepting that, there was no way to keep track of every person in the city.

He needed this war to end quickly.

* * * * * * *

"Oh no! It's already past noon!" cried Hanuru. "I have to be at the Mage's Guild for the vote!"

Millie went wide eyed and slapped a hand to her forehead. "Of course! I'm sorry, I forgot to watch the sun." She squeezed Hanuru's hand by way of an apology. "But you'll never make it now. The streets are choked with newcomers and you'll be like a gnat trying to push through them. Plus the sun is fierce. It will scorch you if you leave now."

"But I must! My vote might swing the Guild's decision! And if I don't turn up people might think I am a sympathiser with Tisenin!" Hanuru seemed on the verge of tears.

"Shh, shhh! It's okay. We can try. What you need is a big, strong soldier-man to barge you through the crowds. I know just such a man." Millie smiled devilishly and looked at Zanthred.

Zanthred was busy flexing his arms against the Lansissari war bow Gargrace had given him. He was glad for the chance to let his arms rest and give his burning muscles a minute to recuperate without looking feeble.

"Me? I don't think I'm big or strong yet," he said.

"You are compared to Hanuru," said Millie. "Besides, you owe me for getting you a new blue cowry."

Zanthred played with the little smooth shell at his throat. What choice did he have? "Very well, I shall play the escort."

Millie wrapped a white sheet over Hanuru's head to keep the worst of Quri's harsh sun off, then filled a skin of weak mead for her.

"You two go quickly...And keep her safe Zanthred," ordered Millie.

It was a challenge just squeezing out of the Perched Sparrow. The number of people staying there had doubled in the last week, and even more poured in at midday to escape the hottest arc of the sun.

The bridge to Serra was choked full by a constant stream of refugees trying to gain entrance to the city – Chepsid had no defences and anything south of the river was to be abandoned if Tisenin made it that far – so Zanthred took Hanuru to the ferries. One burly oarsman was willing to make a crossing before the day's heat reached its peak and when Zanthred explained their predicament, the other passengers were very willing to let them skip the queue.

When they were halfway across the river, Zanthred noticed Hanuru looking very agitated. She was fixated on the great Mages' tower looming over the city.

"So what kind of magic can you do?" asked Zanthred, thinking to distract her a little.

"Pure magic. I study how to control the ether," said Hanuru.

"So you couldn't make it rain or see through solid metal?"

"No, nothing useful like that. But I can see a gathering of mages like there's never been before. If all of them worked together they could move rivers or freeze the sea."

"I've never studied magic, but I've always liked the idea of controlling the wind," said Zanthred.

"That's what Millie said, that first night when she was drunk on your wine." Hanuru looked back from the tower to shyly glance at Zanthred. "You know, me and you are love rivals?"

Zanthred thought of her longing looks aimed at Janistor and the cruel rejections both of them had received. From a distance Zanthred could see there was a farcical humour to their longings, but underneath it really hurt.

"I don't think we need fear each other. She has twelve troths we should worry about first," said Zanthred.

"Twelve?" questioned Hanuru. "No, I don't mean Janistor! I mean Millie!"

Millie...? And there it was, the one emotional pain he felt more keenly than Janistor's rejection. *We don't talk about that*, said Zanthred in his head, remembering the very moment they managed to hurt each other more than every sling and arrow life had thrown at them since.

"She has no romantic feelings for me," he said flatly.

"I don't mean romance, silly!" Hanuru giggled, finally breaking her anxious demeanour. "I mean we both care for her so much, we are bound to come to resent the one that gets to spend all their time with her."

"Ah, I see," said Zanthred.

"But you'll win," said Hanuru, her face once more setting glumly. "She wants romance with me and you as a friend. And when things go sour, I'll have to run away and you will still be a friend."

"What makes you think things will go sour between you?" asked Zanthred.

"Don't they always, eventually? Plus she told me she wants children. That means next time she hits oestrus, she will drop me for a man."

"Ha ha! Is that all you are worried about Hanuru? There are ways around it! And even if she did couple with a man for a few weeks every hundred years, would you *have* to reject her?"

"No, I wouldn't mind. Not too much anyway..." She wrung her hands uncomfortably.

"You worry too much Hanuru. You have decades before that might be an issue. Some humans live their entire lives in that time! Worry about it when it happens. But for what it's worth, I've never seen her this way with anyone else before."

"Thank you, Zanthred. You are wiser than she gives you credit."

Zanthred gritted his teeth and swallowed the last line as a compliment.

Soon they were on the northern bank of the river and in the city of Serra. The streets were thronging with people and the press of bodies made it feel like the humid heat of midsummer. Some people were stretching sail cloth between the buildings so people would have some shade to rest in. Zanthred pressed through them, profusely apologising as he went. The people were not used to being jostled and they moved in a state of passive shock. Only the very young and very old offered him any angry remarks. Hanuru tripped and bumped close behind, looking a mixture of embarrassed, apologetic and exasperated.

When they got close to the great Mages' Tower the press of people became so intense that even pulling and pushing them away did no good. There was jeering and some people were prising up stones from the road surface to throw. Zanthred jumped as high as he could to see over their heads and caught a glimpse of soldiers flanking a group of people. Those in the middle were huddling tight together and shielding their heads with their arms. The soldiers were pushing the crowd back and slowly moving towards the tower.

"Are those mages right ahead of us?" Zanthred asked.

"Yes," said Hanuru, using her ether sight to see through the press of bodies.

"Let's get in behind them."

Zanthred pushed through the angry mob keeping a tight hold of Hanuru's arm. But as he got to the front, there was a surge from the crowd and a crush against the soldiers. Zanthred was thrown into their lines with Hanuru in tow. One of the soldiers raised his spear shaft to strike Zanthred, but a display of open palms and profuse pleading stayed his hand.

"Mages! Mages!" Zanthred begged, pulling Hanuru into view. "She is a mage, she needs to get to the tower."

The soldier seemed to understand. He took Hanuru's hand and pulled her into the soldier's protective lines. She looked back at Zanthred with fear in her eyes.

"Look after this one!" the soldier shouted and he passed her forwards to a comrade with a large shield.

Just out of Zanthred's earshot, Hanuru found herself next to a tall woman with tears tattooed on her cheek. The woman's magic potential was exceptional and made Hanuru feel entirely inadequate. The woman looked down on Hanuru and smiled.

"Welcome my young friend, you have made a good choice."

Hanuru felt her stomach churn at the idea people were mistaking her for a follower of Tisenin.

"I'm not a one of you," she whispered, but it was so quiet no one heard, not even the tattooed woman.

Zanthred tried to keep alongside the marching soldiers shouting 'Fidelis! Fidelis!' so people would know it was now a mixture of the Sagacious League and those faithful to the Emperor. It did not do much good. What is more, he was getting caught up in the crowd and slowly slipping behind Hanuru.

He stopped and gasped for breath. He would have to trust her safety to the soldier with the shield.

"Excuse me young stranger."

Zanthred looked up to see an old man addressing him. The man had a bent spine and withered muscles that left his skin loose and wrinkled. Both his eyes had gone milky. He was probably on the verge of blindness.

"Yes?"

"I hate to trouble one so exhausted, but you look strong and not given over to the hysteria the rest of the crowd has taken towards the Jewasri mages. Could you help me to the tower? I have business with the vote."

Zanthred was tired and hot, and he wanted to say 'no,' but his selfish core was fast beaten into bloody submission by force of habit.

"Of course, my venerable friend. Tell me if I go too fast for you."

Zanthred took the man's arm and together they

slowly picked their way to the tower. Zanthred no longer pushed people, but barked orders at them – 'make way!' – They complied as soon as they saw the elderly man on his arm.

They finally made it to the base of the tower. The tower was the tallest building anywhere on Haven. It was designed to help the Serra meteomancers gaze on distant weather patterns and make their magical predictions. At its top it was a gleaming white spire that every traveller to Serra knew (and many had called in favours to be allowed to climb it and see the capital city from above). It had managed to stand proud through earthquakes and hurricanes, making it one of the engineering marvels of the cherno world. But the lower levels of it were broad and housed a great library and audience hall where the mages of the Guild practised their arts.

There were throngs of crowds outside, eager to hear the results of the vote, but a line of guards kept them a good distance from the entrance. The guards nodded to the old man and let him through without any questions. Zanthred made to enter the building, but the old man pulled back.

"Oh no, not in there, not yet."

"But won't you miss the vote if you don't go now?" asked Zanthred.

"No, no, not at all. There will be a debate before the vote and everyone who wants to will get a chance to speak. Can you imagine anything more dull?"

Zanthred had no reply. The old man led Zanthred

round the corner to a small side door. Opening it revealed stone steps down into a basement. Zanthred careful helped him down, almost lifting his feet from the floor.

"Decran! Decran! Give this poor man some help with me!" shouted the old man.

A young boy, half Zanthred's height, emerged from the gloom and did his best to help Zanthred lift the old man down the steps and into a chair. The boy immediately took a candle and began lighting oil lamps around the room. When he was done he sat it back down next to an open book he had been reading.

"This is Decran, my grand nephew," croaked the old man. "Only thirty years old. I am teaching him magic. But for now I think I would like to rest before they make me ascend the stairs to the meeting hall. I take it you have no magic?"

"No," replied Zanthred. "But I have often thought about learning."

"Do so! It is an important skill. I can recommend a few good teachers if you like?"

"I am not at liberty at the moment. I must do my civic service," said Zanthred.

"Ah, being useful with your hands before being useful with your mind, eh? Well, nature does seem to bless us in that order," the old man took a few deep breaths with his eyes shut. When he opened them he seemed much more relaxed. "Where do you stand on the Ban?" he asked.

"I hate Tisenin," said Zanthred.

"I didn't ask you about Tisenin. I asked you about the Ban."

"Then, I guess I'm not sure. I don't know much about the Ban at all."

"Don't know about the Ban!" the old man scoffed. "To think one could go around in days such as these and be ignorant of the Ban." He paused for a while, then began struggling to get up. "Come, I will show you the Ban."

The old man was on his feet again and he hobbled into the adjoining room. Zanthred followed perplexed. This room was cut from rock and was blissfully cool. Old frescoes of famous mages filled the walls, but the plaster was loose and some overwork details had faded. It pained Zanthred to see great art in a state of decay.

"I wish I had the time to freshen up these frescoes for you. They shouldn't be left with such shabby patches," said Zanthred.

"Bah! It makes no difference with my eyes!" dismissed the old man. "Though if you do ever come here to study, let them know you have my permission to do what you like with decor."

Zanthred quickly found the reason why the room was so cool and why the plaster was mouldering; a trickling spring tinkled in a corner of the room and filled a large pool cut into the rock itself. The edges were encrusted with flowstone and some kind of green brass mechanism was visible beneath the dark water.

"Decran! I'm showing him the ether-pool, make yourself useful!" shouted the old man.

The boy got up from his book with a sigh and grabbed a shiny brass handle projecting from the wheel next to the pool. The wheel seemed to be connected to the mechanism in the pool by a series of cogs.

"Now then, my young ignoramus. The ether is like this pool. It infuses the mind of every sentient creature. In fact, every creature. But the intelligent ones like cherno and humans most of all. For a heart to operate, it needs blood. For a mind to operate it needs ether." He plucked a small pebble from a basket. "This is one of your thoughts, throw it into the ether and tell me what happens."

Zanthred took the pebble and cast it in. There was a plop and some ripples glinted in the lamp light.

"It caused ripples," Zanthred announced, slightly perplexed by the simplicity of the task.

"Precisely!" said the old man. "Our thoughts and feelings cause ripples in the ether. We change it as we use it. The essence of magic is manipulating that ripple we cause to have an effect in the physical world." He now took an armful of stones from the basket. "These represent the thoughts and feelings of you and everyone else around you. Throw them into the ether."

Zanthred threw all the stones into the centre of the pool and water splashed upwards. A large ripple shot to the sides of the pool and overtopped the edge, spilling water over Zanthred's feet, then it rebounded and continued to make chaotic patterns on the water's surface.

"The stones splashed and made a large wave," said Zanthred.

"Correct again, you're a surprisingly straight-thinker!"

"That's twice today someone's declared I am not *so* dull-witted as they had cause fear. Perhaps I have found my niche as muscle for cerebral mages?"

The old man tittered and then carried on his explanation,

"When lots of creatures think and feel the same thing, their 'ether ripples' combine and make something much larger. And what are the thoughts and emotions that are universal to all creatures. Fear? Pain? Anger? Hunger? Unfortunately it is the negative emotions we all share. Sometimes, the ripple becomes self-perpetuating, maintaining the essence of the thought that created it."

"*Karlsha*. A daemon," said Zanthred, seeing where this was going.

"Yes, a daemon. The ripple becomes an eddy. The eddy takes on the appearance and will of our fears. Normally these cannot harm us. They stay in the ether, barely noticeable to any but the most subtly attuned mages. But occasionally, the volume of thoughts and feelings give such strength to the 'ripples' that they overspill and the daemons are given the strength to manipulate the physical world – become *manifest*. Wars, famines and plagues all carry that risk."

Zanthred had a cold shock of fear when the old man mentioned wars. The old man seemed to note Zanthred's reaction and nodded approvingly before continuing.

"But the real danger is when there is enough life in the galaxy that the daemons can manifest at will. This has happened twice in the history of the simurgh. A daemonic incursion. The simurgh call it the Great Dying. Their species barely survived. Most life did not. So they bred our species and wove the Ban to stop it happening again." The old man motioned to his grand-nephew. "Okay Decran, you can begin."

The young boy heaved on the wheel and slowly, creakily, it began to turn. Zanthred could make out small prongs in the water beginning to turn in unison. As the wheel gained pace, the prongs turned faster and they caused scores of small whirlpools to appear on the surface.

The old man held up one final pebble. "Now, take this and tell me what difference you see."

Zanthred cast it into the water and this time it simply sank; there were no waves.

"There were no ripples. The swirling water absorbed them?" speculated Zanthred.

"Cleaver man! Yes, the interference caused by the artificial eddies stop the ripples spreading out. And such it is with the Ban. The Ban is a disturbance created in the ether, designed to spread and strengthen exponentially from its centre on Earth. It stops one being's thoughts from combining with those of another, stopping the generation of daemons. The only downside is it means we cannot use magic. Of course, the Ban (unlike my pool) does not need a small boy turning a wheel to power it. It needs the mental energies of the cherno, humans, simurgh and their other engineered races turned towards Solrax to supply its power. If we keep her in mind, it might last millions of years."

"But what about Tisenin's claim? Is it possible to create a bubble in it where we can still use magic, but the galaxy is safe from one of these *incursions*?" asked Zanthred.

"It might be. Or unravelling one corner of the Ban may slowly cause the whole thing to disintegrate, like pulling a thread on a tapestry. Whatever anyone says, there is no way we can know until it is tried. The simurgh understand the ether far better than us and the idea seems so dangerous to them that they would be willing to annihilate us to stop it happening. Trust me, if you had gazed into the ether like I have and seen the daemons who dwell there, you would not even think about subverting the Ban."

The boy stopped turning the wheel. He was panting with exertion.

"Thank you Decran. You may return to your studies. But remember to be ready for our excursion tonight." He turned to Zanthred. "I must now go to the gathering hall. Unfortunately I have to ask you to wait in the courtyard. The other mages will not like that I have asked a stranger into the building during so delicate a time. Thank you for your help today young man. What do I call you if our paths cross again?"

"I am Zanthred, of Icknel. Thank you for your lesson. Whom should I say taught me when I impress my mage friends with my knowledge of the Ban?"

"I am Pallah ap Foras. And now I must bid you farewell."

I know that name, thought Zanthred, but he did not have time to muse on the matter. He bowed and left. It was only when he was outside that he realised he had been talking to the head of the Mages' Guild.

* * * * * * *

Zanthred waited for hours outside the Guild, as did a huge crowd of people. Helpful residents took it upon themselves to bring jugs full of cool water to keep the crowd fresh in the heat. The rowdiness from before had left them; now there was mostly silence and a keen sense of anticipation. Those that could even find space to sit down.

Finally, late in the afternoon there was a ruckus from above them and many baying voices. Something had happened to cause a commotion within the Mages' Tower. The noise of many voices continued from within the Guild for a long while.

The first person Zanthred saw emerge was the young boy Decran. He was leading an old grey nag laden to the point of collapse with packs and a hooded rider.

As they neared, Zanthred could clearly see the rider was Pallah ap Foras, trying to disguise his face.

"My venerable Pallah! Forgive me, I did not know who you were before. What is happening in the debating hall?"

"Shh, not so loud young Zanthred. I am trying to leave without being stopped by every person I pass. I am simply an old mage who found the heat of the debating hall too much to bear."

"Where are you going in disguise?" asked Zanthred.

"Into retirement. I have my desires set on a hermitage in the Dividing Range. A beautiful place I once saw, far from the usual travellers' ways so no one will idly bother me, but close enough to the head of the Great River and the mountain pass that it will be easy for Decran to come down for supplies."

The old man motioned for Decran to continue leading the horse.

"But what about the vote?" asked Zanthred.

"Terrible!" said Pallah as he retreated. Then he turned in the saddle as best he could. "But, I suppose, not as bad as it could have been."

A few minutes after Pallah made his escape, the grand doors to the Guild opened and mages began pouring out. Some were smiling and others were in tears. They tumbled into the crowd and the whole place was filled with a cacophony of voices as everyone at once struggled to ask the result. Zanthred could make no sense of who was saying what. Then he saw

Hanuru and plucked her from the throng before she got mixed up in the crowd.

"How did it go?" he asked.

"Wonderful!" said Hanuru, throwing her arms around him in celebration. "There were a lot of mages wavering and we didn't know which way it was going to go and I was really worried, but then Pallah ap Foras appeared and gave this really stunning speech about our duty and almost all the waverers came over!" she was running one word into another.

"Whoa, slow down. What was the result?" asked Zanthred.

"A landslide to uphold the Ban. We are going to fight for the Emperor!"

Ah, that is what Pallah thought was so terrible. He'd have wanted the Guild to abstain from the fight altogether, thought Zanthred.

"A few mages resigned from the Guild, but most are being honourable and sticking with the decision," added Hanuru.

"Good, let's get back to tell Millie. You'll never guess what happened to me whilst I was waiting."

* * * * * * *

Haddra watched above the crowd from the saddle of his horse. A smug smile came to his face as he saw the Sagacious mages looking grim and downtrodden within their escort of guards.

"Haddra! How goes it with you?" Jandor clopped up beside Haddra on his own mare.

"Better, now the Mages' Guild has come to its

senses. What brings you down to the docks? Come to gloat with the mob?"

"No. I heard you had taken your steed and your sword and feared you were planning something," said Jandor.

"So you came to stop me?" Haddra grunted. It was a grudging acknowledgment of Jandor's intuition. "Well I *am* planning something, but I doubt you'll disapprove."

He waited until the escorted group was level with him, about to embark their galley. Then he stood in his saddle and boomed over the bustle of the crowd.

"DAGO AP KELDRON!" Dago stopped and looked up at Haddra. Haddra drew his sword and thrust it into the sky. "A MESSAGE FROM HADDRA AP WOODRIN. WHEN YOU SEE TISENIN, TELL HIM HE'LL DIE WITH MY SWORD UP HIS ARSE!"

Dago snarled back, but said nothing.

Haddra re-seated himself and turned to Jandor. "Well, do you think I went too far?"

"No," said Jandor. "I think you struck just about the right tone."

Chapter 9

Invasion

Tisenin could already tell things had not gone well from the stern look on Dago's face and the precious few mages on the deck of her ship. It was fewer than she had left with. She jumped across the gangplank between their vessels to deliver the news. Adrin offered his hand to stabilise her, but she did not take it.

"Was it bad?" asked Adrin, ignoring the rebuff.

Dago did not answer, but aloofly pushed past Adrin and fell to her knees in front of Tisenin. She threw her arms around his waist.

"I'm sorry Archlord! I did my best but we were defeated in the vote. I was hardly able to persuade anyone to join us. I thought we had such a strong hand."

"Get up, dear Dago. I don't doubt you did all you could." He waited for Dago to rise. "This is a setback, yes. But we will not be stopped. Is there anything else you discovered whilst you were there?"

Dago related as much as she had found out about the internal politics of Serra, carefully spelling out just how close to starvation the defecting mages believed the city was. She ended with Haddra's personal insult.

Tisenin looked greatly angered, but he kept his speech cool and measured. "We will see how confident he is soon enough."

* * * * * * *

On the following morning Mordhai the meteomancer was the first to spot the Sagacious fleet from the top of the Mages' Tower. The call to arms went out and within a few hours Serra's fleet of merchant ships was at sea, blocking the entrance to the harbour. Serra's carracks and caravels were many times larger than the Sagacious galleys and it was pretty certain that their tall sides would tip any battle in Serra's favour, but the small galleys were frustratingly manoeuvrable and could not be brought to fight against their will. So the Serra fleet sat across the estuary of the great river and weighed their stone anchors. By nightfall Tisenin's fleet had made no progress and they could be seen floating on the sea as a new firmament of stars. Each vessel had a lantern in its prow so it would not run into its colleagues in the dark.

Duarma watched all this from his vantage in the palace, along with Haddra, Jandor, Gargrace and Mordhai.

"They must come to shore soon," said Gargrace. "They have a lot of mouths, their water barrels must be as dry as a drunkard's tongue the morning after an orgy. The question is, will they try and land to the north or south?"

"As soon as we see them move, I will take my fastest cavalry and oppose their landing. That will be our best chance to strike," said Haddra.

"Can you conjure us some weather to scatter their fleet, Mordhai?" asked Duarma.

"No, my Emperor. Not from here. Their mages are making a small but significant disruption to all our meteorological efforts. But perhaps if we got closer to their ships, we might be able to overpower them locally."

"Gather your best mages, at dawn tomorrow I will send you out against them," said Duarma.

* * * * * * *

The next dawn Mordhai found his old and aching body being helped onto a caravel. He was the last of the mages to board. He looked over the faces; he had taught most them at some point in his life. It was not difficult to tell mage from sailor. The sailors were all naked; their standard summer dress. Whilst other professions hid from the midday sun, confining their activities to the cool of dusk and dawn, sailors spent all day on deck doing hard physical tasks and considered all clothing a burden.

Mordhai needed to be at the front of the fighting if his meteomancers were to have a chance of disrupting the enemy. The wind was against them, but they drew in the sails and allowed the flow of the Great

River to push them out to sea. Mordhai could see the Sagacious galleys forming up into a column; now the wind was behind them they were going to try to force through the estuary blockade.

Once the Captain began to tack towards the Sagacious column, Mordhai settled into a chorus with the mages on his ship. He felt their minds slipping into a synchronous unit and mana flowing from their souls into his. They had been trained to do this to deflect hurricanes from the city and now it was as natural as holding hands with a lover. It was an exhilarating feeling.

Mordhai was dimly aware of the lines of archers and javelineers who watched them from friendly vessels as they passed by, but now his attention was focused on the flow of molecules around the enemy galleys. He could also feel the aura of the Sagacious mages forming a protective bubble around their ships. One in particular he recognised – Dago – the woman who led the rebel mages during the vote. It felt like lead and tasted sharp like citrus.

You will not stop us anymore. Every metre they closed, his chorus's power became greater than the resistance that could be mustered against it and soon their chorus would be invincible.

But something was wrong. Four of the galleys had moved far ahead of the main column of Sagacious ships. What was more, two of the lead ships seemed to have no crew; they were being towed. Mordhai did not recognise the threat until he saw the first flames rise.

Fire ships.

They were planning to let the ships drift into their lines, setting the Serra fleet aflame and forcing them to scatter away from the blockade. The lead vessels cut their tow ropes and the fire ships drifted free, leaving Mordhai's chorus of mages as the only thing between the Serra lines and disaster. There was nothing for it but to act.

Mordhai was not used to using his abilities in haste. He usually had tens of kilometres to act over and days or hours to effect his change. But there was one time he remembered, on a voyage to Cormarace, he had watched three waves press into each other and swell into something that had towered over their vessel. He could see a good wind and three such waves beginning to form not far from the two fire ships. *Very well, it shall be a rogue wave*, he thought.

Compress.

Speed up.

He reached out and forced the patterns of air and water to bend to his will. He felt them flow forcefully through his mind's grasp. It was so easy with the elite of the Serra mages fuelling his designs. He saw the push of water as the three waves squashed close together and knew he could do better than imitate a natural event. He felt like he could conjure a tsunami if he wanted! So he added a fourth wave to his matrix. The roiling cone of water rose up like a cliff face. Drunk on power, he wanted to add another, to make a mountain. But he restrained himself; it was taking too long. He could see the two fire ships getting closer and he would have to release the wave soon.

The last twist of the ether finished it and a huge wave as high as the galleys' masts rose from the water and swamped the two fire ships. One ship was instantly pitched on its side and smashed to pieces leaving only a scatter of charred timbers as evidence it had existed. The other, amazingly, managed to rise with the wave and smacked back down, only briefly plunging its prow under water. It was not enough to stop the vessel's progress or douse the flames. But the wave did not stop; it ploughed through the fire ships and kept going. Too late Mordhai realised it was about to hit his ship as well.

The wave struck and the caravel rocked violently from side to side, sending mages and sailors sprawling across the deck. Mordhai felt his hip crunch as he hit the rough planks and knew he had cracked his old bones. He did not feel pain through, not at first. He was too terrified about sliding off the edge of the ship as it rolled along powerlessly.

When the ship finally came to a halt and he realised he was safe, then the pain shot through his leg. He tried to re-establish the chorus, but now few minds were open and he could not focus on it through the agony.

But the fire ship was still heading towards the Serra lines. From his prone position Mordhai looked back to the estuary and saw the Serra fleet beginning to scramble out of the fire ship's way. It was disorderly and in their panic several captains had crashed their ships into the sides of others, bursting planks, breaking keels and casting their decks full of militia into the water. The fire ship had to be stopped quickly to prevent full scale chaos.

There was no time for a chorus to form and the fire ship was still being protected by the Sagacious mages; more than Mordhai could handle by himself. There was only once choice, although Mordhai hesitated to make it on everyone's behalf.

"Captain, can you ram the fire ship?" asked Mordhai.

The Captain regarded him gravely, but seemed to understand what was being asked. "We can try, but I doubt we'll turn in time."

"Try anyway. I'll make sure we succeed," said Mordhai.

The Captain issued orders and the sailors began to bring the caravel round in a big loop. The Captain was right, it was taking too long and the fire ship was going to inch passed them. Mordhai set to work. This time he only had his own mana to work with, but that was all he needed. He felt the flow of air around the ship and shifted one current so it pushed only the prow and another so it caught the sails at the right angle. The ship twisted faster, listing heavily to the side.

The last few metres to the fire ship closed with painful slowness and everyone on deck braced themselves for the impact.

Crunch

Timbers shattered and the fire ship began to drift off course. Mordhai smiled; he thought he had done enough. But as the first tongues of flame licked up against his ship and he watched the Sagacious fleet breaking off from their attack run, he noticed something.

He noticed there were not as many galleys as there had been the day before.

Well done Tisenin, this second round goes to you.

* * * * * * *

Duarma watched in horror as Mordhai collided with the fiery ship. The sailors were throwing themselves in the water and a small sloop had broken from the Serra lines to go and rescue them. He hoped it would make it in time for the old man.

"A noble sacrifice," said Haddra.

"Let us hope it is only the vessel we are sacrificing," said Duarma.

"Indeed," agreed Haddra. But his tone made it obvious he did not hold out much hope for the old man.

A messenger announced himself at the door. "My Emperor Duarma, I bring news from the south of Serra. An army has been discharging from a fleet of galleys since dawn. I rode here as hard as I could. It might be a day's walk on foot."

"What! But how?" Duarma blurted. "Their ships have been watched since they arrived. None have split off and no ship has reported seeing a second fleet."

Jandor and Gargrace rushed to the window and

began counting ships. Eventually Jandor sighed in exasperation. "The messenger is right," he said. "There are fewer galleys now than there were before."

Gargrace half smiled out of respect for Tisenin's tactics. "Tisenin has taken us for fools, such an obvious manoeuvre. Last night he lit the lanterns on the galleys so we *would* count them, then moved the lanterns from one vessel to another so they could slip away unnoticed...Any idea who his general is?"

"No, but from what I saw in Jewasri he was practising Cathri infantry tactics," said Haddra. "There are a few sympathisers it might be. Although I have a feeling Tisenin is cunning and bold enough as it is."

Duarma paced up and down the room, words he dared not speak on the tip of his tongue. The others could see his anxiety and were silent until he found the words he needed. "We still have had no word from Kamil," said Duarma.

Jandor read what was not stated. "Are you thinking that Hilsi's disappearance might not have been due to youthful fear?" he asked.

"I don't know what I'm thinking. But it is odd that he has not even sent condolences," said Duarma.

"Do we not have enough traitors to deal with?" growled Haddra. "We can save the speculation for later. I need to take my cavalry south immediately. Gargrace can follow as soon as his infantry is ready."

Duarma was about to give Haddra his blessing, but Gargrace forcefully interjected.

"That is an amateur's mistake, Haddra! The cavalry

run off, get defeated and then they retreat into the infantry, spread panic and the infantry get defeated as well."

"I may be an amateur with infantry, but my cavalry *will not* be defeated!" retorted Haddra.

Gargrace shook his head dismissively, as if he were talking to a child. "We are facing a wily opponent, as they have already demonstrated. Victory is never certain. Your cavalry should deploy behind the infantry so we march as one. Only a handful of scouts should range ahead."

Haddra ground his teeth together and looked to Duarma for a decision. Duarma was minded to go with Haddra's plan; his instincts told him speed was important. But one look at Haddra showed that he was so pent up with frustration that if he found an enemy he would instantly fall on them with fury, and that might cause disaster.

"We will go with Gargrace's marching order," said Duarma. "This time," he quickly added.

Haddra did not like the response, and he bowed very stiffly with his tongue pressed against his teeth. He stamped off down the stairs of the tower to gather his cavalry.

Gargrace bowed to Duarma, "I apologise my Emperor, I can lack tact when the situation is critical."

"Do not worry, only win this war for me. Go now and muster your troops south of Chepsid. Do everything in your power to bring a favourable battle as soon as possible," said Duarma.

"I understand," said Gargrace and he hobbled away down the stairs.

When Gargrace was out of earshot, Duarma turned to Jandor.

"I worry about Haddra," said Duarma.

"Don't," said Jandor. "He may seem resentful, but that is only because he knows the stakes of this war and, *rightly*, thinks his experience should count for something. In his heart, I am sure you will find he is your staunchest ally."

"If only he didn't think he had something to prove," said Duarma.

"If he thought he had nothing to prove, he would make a very meek soldier."

* * * * * * *

The patrons of the Perched Sparrow were the closest to the muster field south of Chepsid and were the first company to assemble. Most, like Zanthred, had few preparations to make. They grabbed their linen gambesons, bows and whatever else they had for weapons and marched out. The sensible ones also took a skin of water and whatever they could beg in the way of food.

Whilst they waited for the other companies to march across the bridge from Serra, they sat on the parched earth and watched Callin spar with another of Janistor's troths, Malichar ap Sunnar. Janistor managed to be dazzling even when dressed for war. She had chosen to wear an elegant white silk dress which left her whole left side bare from her shoulder to her hip.

A yellow undershirt prevented a view of her bosom from the side. It was a battle dress, made for her so she could shoot a bow and not get the sleeve caught in the string. A narrow bracer tied with braided silver wire sat on her forearm, protecting the bare skin from grazes. Everyone else in the company just wore their normal loose robes, but had bound the left sleeve at the wrist.

Callin had a permanent grin on his face as he mock-fought; whilst most people were feeling a knot of apprehension at the news Tisenin's army was at hand, Callin seemed to be relishing the opportunity to prove his worth. He swung his long sword in big, dramatic arcs as he cycled through the forms and stances of a duellist. He liked reminding people he had fought before in an expedition to the spice colonies. He was deliberately just slow enough so his hard-pressed opponent could parry each blow.

A clang of metal on metal rang out and Malichar stumbled backwards onto his rump.

"Ha ha, you see! Even if your opponent does block this move it leaves them off balance!" boasted Callin, clearly tailoring his commentary to Janistor.

Janistor clapped her hands in delight, "Oh Callin, you look almost ready for the Shadow Guard!"

Callin bowed. "My dearest troth, but that would mean I would have to take a vow of chastity..."

Janistor giggled. "Callin! You shall scandalise me in front of my peers!"

The cherno thought nothing of two troths sharing

a bed, but expected the matter to stay private. Having the matter expressed so bluntly in front of Zanthred gave him an awkward feeling. It must have shown on his face, because Millie saw fit to comment.

"The biggest scandal she's going to face is what she looks like in a gambeson. What's the point in commissioning an elegant battle dress like that when there's a wedge of quilted armour as thick as your fist over the top?" said Millie.

"I'd love a dress like that," Hanuru mused idly. Then she caught the look of contempt Millie shot her way and glanced down in shame.

"With all of her noble troths, I think they will find her something stiffer than quilted linen," said Zanthred.

Hanuru shrugged. She opened up her pack and took out some of the cold mutton they had been given the previous night. She munched heartily. "Ummm, this is so nice after weeks of nothing but bread and salted fish."

"Don't eat it all," warned Millie, "I doubt they'll bring us much in the field."

"They can't be as short on rations as the rumours say," said Zanthred. "Not if they're feeding us fresh meat."

Millie leaned from her reclined position and slapped Zanthred's foot, "It means they are worse!" she said. "If they are killing the wool stock to feed us, then things are really desperate. Tomorrow there might only be boiled bones and blood left."

Hanuru stopped chewing and looked thoughtful for a second. "...The meat won't keep in the sun, so we may as well eat it whilst it's good," she said, then resumed sucking on a clot of fat.

A shadow fell over the three of them. Zanthred looked up to see Gargrace's creased face leering down. Zanthred instinctively scrambled to his feet. Gargrace smiled. He seemed pleased that he commanded such respect and terror in his star pupil.

"The young girl has the right idea. Eat and sleep when you can, you might be marching all day. And don't worry about the food. Killing sheep is nothing. Worry when they start killing the horses," said Gargrace.

Millie shielded her eyes from the sun and looked upwards, "And let me guess, we have to eat all the dogs before we get to the horses?"

Gargrace grinned, "That's the idea." He placed a rough hand on Zanthred's shoulder. "And now my student, show me how you have been getting on with my war bow."

Zanthred took out the bow and braced it against his foot. It took all his weight and the rigid knots of muscle in his stomach to bend it down so the string would loop over the horn at the end. He was glad he managed it first time in front of Gargrace; it did not always happen like that.

"Strung as soundly as a goose's neck! Now shoot that tree over there," commanded Gargrace.

It was a small shrubby walnut tree at least two

hundred metres away. One of the branches had been broken off (probably by a deer relieving its itches), which gave a clear view of the tree's trunk. Zanthred took a single deep breath, slipped on the white leather finger guard Janistor had given him and took his best-fletched arrow out of its quiver. He notched it on the waxy string and drew it back with three fingers, until the flights tickled the thin whiskers of his face. His muscles still ached with practise, but it was so much easier than the first time he had drawn it. He let fly and the arrow sailed cleanly on target. Then, almost as the arrow struck home, a gust of wind picked up and the arrow pitched to one side, sticking in the earth to the side of the trunk.

Zanthred let out a deflated sigh.

"Not bad. One can't account for the wind every time. You've started to put your whole body into the stretch, that's good. You'll have the arrow by your ear soon enough." Gargrace held up Zanthred's right hand. "But what is with this finger guard? It's too thick. It'll slow you down. Save it for the sports field, rely on your calluses if you want to be true war archer."

Gargrace made to slip the patch of white leather off Zanthred's hand, but Zanthred instinctively made a fist, stopping him. Gargrace raised an eyebrow.

"Oh?"

"It was a gift," said Zanthred.

Gargrace clearly understood *'it was a gift from a woman,'* because he looked carefully at Millie and Hanuru to see if he could guess which one had given the favour. When all he got back were blank stares, he gave up and shrugged his shoulders.

"Do as you will then. But I don't give advice for the sake of hearing my own voice," said Gargrace.

Gargrace hobbled out to the front of the crowd and addressed them in his booming drill-master voice. "You good soldiers of the Sparrow Company are the first to muster, so I will give you the honour of marching at the head of our column. When we get to the field, you will be at the centre of our line. Now let us do what we have practised. Form up! And await the rest of the army!"

The Perched Sparrow patrons shuffled to their feet and started forming a column.

"What does being at the centre mean? Is that a good place?" whispered Hanuru.

"I don't know, but if we are at the front, then it means we are the first to get into any trouble," whispered back Millie, as they moved to assume their correct positions.

* * * * * * *

The column from Serra marched most of the hot day and only stopped when they saw scattered clouds of dust in the valleys in front of them.

"Foraging," Gargrace and Haddra announced in unison.

They looked at each other, a mutual respect for the other's experience passing wordlessly.

"Night is near, but I can take my horses down and try to capture some of the foraging parties," volunteered Haddra. "What say you? They'll be by the streams. It's thirsty work rowing from Efrandi."

"If we were up against a bunch of humans, then I'd let you run right up to their camp. But Tisenin has some sense and he knows we are coming for him. If I were him, I'd have set up some ambushes to catch us out," said Gargrace. We should camp on this ridge where it'll be difficult to attack in the night. Just before dawn, we'll march out. That low hill where the bend in the stream cuts across our east flank will be ideal."

"Fair enough. Should I have the scouts investigate his camp?" asked Haddra

"Have them survey the land between us and make a map for me. But tell them not to get within a bowshot of the camp or foraging parties. I'll have my infantry dig a ditch surrounding the camp as insurance against any unexpected attacks."

* * * * * * *

Zanthred sweated digging a perimeter ditch whilst Millie and Hanuru went out foraging for firewood and filled their leather skins with water. Zanthred's length of the ditch was the first to be started and the first to be finished. He went and sat in the camp, under the Perched Sparrow's company banner to check his arrows' fletching and await Millie's return.

"Zanthred, I see we are the first finished."

Zanthred looked up and saw Janistor smiling down. He felt a little awkward being pushed into making small talk with her.

"I thought you were busy foraging," he stammered.

"I was, but I am done now."

Janistor dumped an armful of small twigs beside Zanthred. It would be enough kindling to get a fire started, but not much more. He could see other women down the hill hauling up big loads of branches on their backs to keep fires burning through the night.

Janistor rolled her shoulder in its socket, "Ooh, my neck hurts from all the marching with packs today. Could you give it a massage Zanthred?"

Without waiting for a response, she knelt in front of him and slipped her robe from her shoulders, holding it loosely just above her breasts. Zanthred stared in awe at the curve of her soft brown shoulders and the gentle arc up to her long neck.

Those shoulders! Now Millie had armed him with the knowledge of his own weakness, he could feel the naked skin working its effect on him.

"Y-yes, of course," he said.

His hands actually shook as he reached out to touch her. He began to slide his fingers over her soft skin and delicate bones. He could feel the heat of her body against his face and every twitch of her long black hair filled his nostrils with the delicate perfume she had been given by the Emperor. She gave a sub-audible moan of pleasure.

It was too much for Zanthred. Although he thought himself a man in control of his body, one very minor part of him began to disagree. He did at least retain enough shrewdness to hide his bulging robe behind her back.

Surely she must know the effect this would have on me? She is enticing me, said his lustful side. *She is selfish and I am the only one in the camp,* said his pessimistic side.

"So Zanthred, what do you think of the banner Baytee has made us?" said Janistor, indicating the large flag fluttering above them.

Zanthred looked up. The Perched Sparrow's banner had been woven under the watchful eye of Baytee and depicted their namesake on a thorny bramble, with mouth open in song. Around it were moths fluttering in the wind. It was a reference to Janistor's elegy, reminding them why they fought. At the bottom of the banner – in fact at the bottom of every banner in the Serra army – was written the word FIDELIS. They were the faithful. The banner made Zanthred feel proud about his company of poets and artists. Although none felt prouder upon seeing it than Janistor, because it confirmed in her mind what everyone already knew. It was not really Baytee's company or Gargrace's honour guard, it was Janistor's.

"She has captured our spirit perfectly and served us well," said Zanthred.

Janistor smiled, glad that Zanthred agreed with the subtext. "Ooh, just a bit to the left...that's it," she ordered. She held up her wrist and thumbed the grey goose feather that hung among so many others. "So Zanthred, you have been my sworn friend for a while now and yet I cannot remember us taking the time to get to know one another. Tell me about yourself. What is it like where you are from?"

"Icknel? It's a hilly country, deep valleys and steep hills on a small peninsula. But cool, for the south. The hotter the plains are across the water, the stronger the wind blows. Makes it quite pleasant in the Hot Season. The town is nowhere near as big as Serra, but it has its own small version of the Mages' Tower to warn us of hurricanes. They like their houses more colourful than in Serra. Everyone paints a new fresco on the front of their house when the Storm Season is done. I did my share of them around the town. I used to enjoy my trips there to trade sheep and wool."

"And you never wanted to go anywhere else or do anything but herd sheep, for a *hundred years*?" asked Janistor.

"There is nothing wrong with herding sheep. They are fine creatures, if you know how to treat them. They will give you cheese and wool in abundance and meat when they are too old to birth anymore. Wax and daub too, if you know how. You can even burn their droppings on a cold night."

"Ha ha, Zanthred, you sound *so* provincial! There is one thing that they cannot provide a man with (at least I hope not). I hear the girls in Icknel have the shapeliest calves on account of all the hills. Did you have any hot romances there?"

We do not speak about that.

"...I would rather not talk about it," said Zanthred.

"Oh, you don't mean...?"

We do not speak about that.

"-I'd just rather not talk about it," cut in Zanthred. "It is bad etiquette in front of one to whom I gave a feather."

"Of course, I understand. But one might also say it is bad etiquette to give a woman a feather and then ignore her, dear Zanthred."

"I apologise. But I would not cause strife with Callin. He has made his feelings towards me quite clear."

"Callin?" Janistor laughed out loud. "Pay him no regard, he talks angrily but has pride, not malice, in his heart. Are you sure it is not Millie that seals your mouth around me? You talk quite freely now, when she is not here."

Ah, so this is it, his pessimistic side concluded. *She would entice to drive a wedge between me and Millie. This is an act of revenge.*

"Millie is, and always will be my best friend. She has only good advice for me," said Zanthred.

"Hmm, that may be, but I fear whilst she is around we can never get to know one another better." There was a long painful silence between them as the softly worded ultimatum sank in. "Did you at least attend Lord Roldern's parties?" Janistor asked at last.

"What, Lord Roldern ap Sunnar? No, I saw him a few times, but never spoke to him. It was only visiting nobles who went to his estate," said Zanthred.

"That is a shame, his events are of some renown. I

thought you might be able to provide an introduction. Would you mind moving to my feet?"

Zanthred looked down. The robe he was wearing did nothing to hide the anatomical issue he was having. He could not kneel in front of her without her noticing it.

"Err, I think not." Zanthred reluctantly took his hands from her shoulders. "I must attend to other things."

"Humph, very well." Janistor shrugged her robe back onto her shoulders.

Zanthred quickly spun around so she would not notice his predicament and span right into Callin. Zanthred did not know if he was lucky or not that Callin was staring fixedly into his eyes. He had obviously seen something of what passed between Zanthred and Janistor, because his fingers twitched nervously on the hilt of his sword.

"Ah, Callin, I think Janistor could use your assistance," Zanthred managed to stammer.

"Callin!" Janistor grinned up at him. "I could do with your special touch."

Callin's fingers stilled and he pushed past Zanthred, refusing to even acknowledge him with words.

Pride is dangerous enough, thought Zanthred.

Zanthred began building a small fire and waited for Millie and Hanuru to return from the foraging. They took a very long time. When they finally came back and threw down their bundles, Zanthred saw they each had a black crow feather in their hair. They had become troths.

They did not say anything about it. Zanthred did not say anything. He just hugged them both tight to his chest.

The sun went low and the smell of aromatic wood smoke filled the camp. Everyone knew this sundering would be resolved within the next few hours, but the bravado of earlier in the day had left them. A low cheerless song picked up through the camp. It was about solidarity, not merriness. No one had brought tents, so they lay on the bare earth and wrapped themselves in cloaks. If they had not been so exhausted, they would not have been able to sleep at all.

Zanthred looked over the camp and saw tens of thousands of bodies tightly packed on the floor. Pickets silhouetted in the firelight wandered up and down the ditch, keeping watch for saboteurs. The only noise was crackling kindling and the neighing of horses.

Then he saw Janistor curled on the ground in Callin's arms and felt an enormous pang of jealously. Her face was serene and her body yielding and soft. Then he realised through the flickering firelight Callin was looking straight back at him. Jealousy turned to shame and he turned away quickly.

Millie was spooning Hanuru. Zanthred had innocently shared an open air bed with Millie on many occasions, but he thought they deserved their first night as troths alone, so he curled up by himself and made a pillow of his sleeve. The heat of the land was flowing out to sea, causing a steady cool breeze. Zanthred shivered alone.

He felt a small hand curl around his wrist.

"Don't be silly," said Millie, and she pulled his arm around her and Hanuru both.

"Thank you," said Zanthred, slotting his body into the warmth of Millie's back.

But what he meant was, *'Come tomorrow, I'm going to do everything I can to keep you safe.'*

Chapter 10

The Battle for Serra

During the night several hundred soldiers silently made their way from the Serra camp to the Sagacious army and declared their allegiance for Tisenin. He interrogated them at length about the enemy force. Most of what he learnt corroborated the information his spies had managed to sneak to him over the last few weeks.

When the arrival of the deserters became known, spirits soared in the camp. The soldiers were even happier to learn that almost a third of the Fidelis forces were women; it made the slight advantage they had in numbers seem insignificant. Not only in terms of strength, but because it spoke to the fact the Duarma's defenders had been impressed from every walk of life, whereas Tisenin's followers were all volunteers, ready to give their all for the fight.

Just before daybreak Tisenin's scouts announced that the enemy was moving, so he called his troops to battle order and took his lieutenants out to survey the field.

The enemy had picked a low hill overlooking a level flood plain. The plain was bounded to the west by steep hills and to the east by a stream which bowed into the plain just under where the hill began to rise. It made a minor pinch in the line of advance, but nothing his captains could not manoeuvre around. It was just about perfect ground for a pitched battle.

"Why have they not taken the higher ground?" asked Dago.

"They *want* this fight," said Tisenin. "The deserters said their last meal was roast mutton. That means they are almost out of food. If they don't fight today, they begin to starve. If they had picked a good defensive spot, they worry that we might have been too timid to attack. They are giving us just enough of an opportunity for victory to tempt us."

"But then why fight?" asked Adrin. "If they are close to starvation, let them starve. We might break Serra without ever having to fight. Not that I am shy! But starvation is always more sure than the sword."

Tisenin shook his head. "No, Duarma will never surrender without a fight. He will send the refugees away and kill the horses before letting us across the

Great River. We need to smash his army to show them they have no hope of victory. Then they will surrender. Besides, if we put siege to Serra and all the innocents die, it will hardly help our cause in the rest of the Empire."

The Serra battle line was arrayed in three great crescents like the horns of three bulls standing shoulder to shoulder. The 'horn' portion of each crescent was made of archers, with a small solid core of spearmen making the 'skull.' Adrin did a quick estimation of the number of troops on the hill.

"Twenty-thousand infantry. But only a thousand cavalry," he pronounced.

"Then if what the deserters said is true, they're hiding their main body of cavalry," said Tisenin. "I will send in the horses and light infantry ahead to break up their ranks, then withdraw and hold them in reserve to deal with any cavalry that tries for the flanks. It's a shame their cavalry didn't fall into our ambush last night. But I do not know if that means they are timid or wise."

"Haddra ap Woodrin is not timid," said Dago.

"But neither, I dare say, is he wise," said Adrin.

"Then you underestimate him. His war record is...intimidating," said Tisenin, with the first note of worry his friends had seen on his face since he killed Kirrie.

"Humans don't count," said Adrin. "Trust me, I've killed my share."

"They have the advantage of ground and numbers,"

cautioned Dago. "Are we sure we want to commit to this?"

Tisenin whirled his pony around to head back towards his troops. "Numbers mean nothing. We have the better morale and better preparation." He spurred the horse on. "Let us advance!"

* * * * * * *

Zanthred stood in the front row of the Serra line, feeling very exposed. Gargrace stood next to him, which added to his nervousness. They sat more or less at the centre of the battle line, supported by some experienced colonial spearmen to the east and the Shadow Guard to the west. The prodigious horns of archers projected forwards beyond them.

Zanthred had been right about Janistor's troths commissioning some better armour than the thick quilted gambesons. They had arranged for her to have a sleek corselet made of silk stiffened with rabbit glue. It was elegant and second only to Callin's iron fish scales in the protection it would provide. While the nerves showed on virtually every other face in the company, she seemed perfectly composed, secure behind her line of troths. Then Zanthred noticed the sheen of sweat on her fingertips as she warmed up her bow; she was as nervous as anyone, just better at hiding it.

In contrast with the rank and file, Gargrace seemed eager to get things started. He was sucking at an ulcer on his lip as he swept the field with eyes of deep comprehension. The way he acted was almost blasé to the danger. He had even forgone armour, trusting luck and his own skill.

The first moment Zanthred saw the enemy cavalry moving, his heart quailed and he felt his guts turn to water.

"Ready bows!" shouted Gargrace, and the drummer beat out his order for the whole battle line.

Zanthred strung his bow and slipped the white finger guard on.

The cavalry advanced down the centre of the field in a thin line that encompassed the whole front of the Serra forces. But then they suddenly bolted west, massing into a spear of living flesh and aimed at the outermost horn of archers, seeking to break the flank of the Serra line. A sprinkling of arrows came from their ranks and fell among the infantry. With a uniform *whoosh*, the cavalry were met by a terrific return volley. It was literally a rain of metal spikes. Around a hundred horses fell and almost immediately their captain signalled a halt and tried to lead his cavalry back. The overwhelmed cavalry had severely underestimated the Serra archers and needed no extra urging to spin their horses and gallop away. Only a few stopped to pick up the riders who had been pitched to the ground when their mounts were shot.

Haddra saw his chance and led his vastly greater force of cavalry archers down the mild slope to catch the retreating force in the rear. As the thousand-strong body of cavalry moved, so did the earth. It sounded louder than thunder and kicked up more dust than an earthquake. The two forces of cavalry archers met in a running whirl. As one horse chased another and the chaos spread out, they raced away from both battle lines and struck a course which led off into the distance, beyond the sight of either side.

Gargrace gritted his teeth as he watched. "That more or less plays into Tisenin's hands. His small force of cavalry archers just neutralized our larger body, even if it was by accident. The battle will be over by the time Haddra stops the pursuit, re-organises the troop and makes his way back."

Tisenin's cavalry had kicked up a huge quantity of dust on their approach, and now as it settled it was possible to see a loose line of infantry advancing in their wake. They were armed with a variety of weighted darts, slings and short bows. It was a motley assortment of weapons that represented what the people of Efrandi could get their hands on at the time of departure. As soon as they were in range they began to loose their weapons haphazardly. The Fidelis archers responded in kind with thick volleys that momentarily turned the sky black with each humming release. Zanthred joined them, shooting his bow for the first time at fellow cherno. *May I live to find forgiveness.* But he could not follow his arrow through the air to see if it hit, not among the black storm.

What followed next should have been bloody slaughter on both sides. The near defenceless Fidelis archers should have been impaled on darts and had their bones broken by heavy lead sling shot. But a strong wind suddenly picked up and forced all the enemy missiles to fall short whilst the Serra arrows were carried right on to the enemy.

It was the mages.

Volunteers from the Mages' Guild peppered the Serra ranks and their magic rendered the Sagacious weapons null. And even though most of the volleys of Serra arrows landed in between the skirmishing light infantry or were caught on their shields, it was obvious it was a one-sided fight and they fell back. Even the slingers, who had counted on having a longer range than the archers, were sharply surprised by the magic and retired from the lethal hail.

Finally, the main body of the Sagacious army came forwards. Zanthred had been feeling a little more confident after seeing the first two waves turned aside by their arrows, but that evaporated when he saw the last. They were packed tightly together like a pulsing river of black and silver. All the spearmen held large rectangular shields and the first two ranks seemed to gleam and shimmer with each step. Zanthred recognised it as the kind of scale mail Callin was wearing, only bigger and heavier. The coats were made of hundreds of tiny iron fish scales that overlapped into a long robe from shoulder to ankle. It was clear what the blacksmiths of Efrandi had spent their months of preparation doing.

"How are we supposed to hurt them?" Zanthred found himself saying aloud.

"Don't worry about the armour, just focus on shooting," said Gargrace.

The line of heavy infantry advanced steadily. It did not matter that there were less of them; to Zanthred they looked like a slow tide of death with bronze spears jutting from the morass at every angle. The whole Serra line fell silent, awaiting the signal to attack. When they were two hundred and fifty metres away, Gargrace nocked an arrow.

"Watch this," he said. He pulled his thick war bow back like it was a mere twig. With a *thuck*, he released the arrow and it sailed straight for the general's banner bearer in the middle of the front rank. The bearer saw it coming and ducked behind his shield. But the arrow was too high and passed right over his head, embedding in the crossbar of the banner he held. The crossbar swung loose and collapsed to the floor, taking the general's banner with it; the arrow had passed right through its binding.

"That was phenomenal!" gasped Zanthred.

"Eh, I used a touch of magic," said Gargrace with a wink.

At the sight of the enemy's banner falling a cheer went through the Serra ranks. It was a good omen. But it did not stop the Sagacious march. There was barely a moment of consternation before someone managed to re-lash the banner to the pole and it was aloft again.

Finally, when the Sagacious troops were a hundred and fifty metres away, Gargrace gave the order.

"Loose!"

A uniform rattle of flexing bows and whooshing arrows surrounded Zanthred. The black cloud shot forth and landed among the Sagacious warriors. It did not seem to do much; a few people screamed and fell out of rank, becoming consumed in the advancing morass, but mostly it just caused the pace to slow as those at the front huddled behind their shields.

"Loose!"

Ten seconds later and another volley was called. Another whoosh of black. This continued for almost a minute whilst the Sagacious forces closed in. Time after time Zanthred pulled his arm back and loosed just a millisecond after the rest of the company. When the Sagacious troops had just about drawn parallel with the bowing stream at the foot of the hill, they were close enough for the front rank of archers to shoot directly forwards and not have to angle their bows. Zanthred began to pick out his targets. Faces, feet and gaps in the shield wall.

Suddenly there was a change. The companies on the east flank where the river bowed in got compressed by the narrowing stream and stumbled into each other, deforming their neat ranks. At the same time, the very eastern horn of archers was placed to shoot into the flank of the broken line. There were screams and the advance ground to a halt. Panic seemed to spread through the Sagacious line and their neatly ordered regiments broke up in to nothing more than a tight mass of frightened men.

"What's going on?" asked Zanthred.

Gargrace made his bitter smile. "You shoot from the left, from the right and from the front. A thick volley of arrows and even a soldier with a shield tries to move away from the source. The enemy's left flank presses right to avoid the arrows. The right flank presses left, and the front rank presses back. Meanwhile, those at the back don't know what all the fuss is about and keep trying to press forwards. The result? Those in the middle get crushed from all sides. Trampled. Suffocated on their feet sometimes. The narrowing at the bottom of the hill and the direct fire from the flanks make this the perfect spot." Gargrace loosed another arrow. "Don't forget to shoot Zanthred! Every shot should count now."

The enemy was close enough to make out every detail of their face. They had an anguished look as their own colleagues' bodies became the instrument of their suffering. The Sagacious drums beat orders frantically, but nothing seemed to happen with any coherency. Zanthred poured arrows into the mass of men, very few of which were on target. But he was surprised to see his over-powered arrows pass right through their wicker shields and knew that at this range he could not fail to do some hurt. Some of the men at the front abandoned their stagnant regiments and rushed forwards to close the tantalizingly small gap with the archers. The normal soldiers out in front were cut down easily – stuck from every side with arrows – but the armoured ones seemed almost impervious to the shafts. An armoured soldier pointed his spear right at Zanthred and charged point first.

Zanthred made to nock an arrow, but the leather finger guard flopped the wrong way over the string and he was unable to release the shot. He kept hold of the arrow and shook his grip, but it did not work. The man was barely two metres away and snarling with anger. Zanthred thought his silent promise to Hanuru and Millie was going to be a very hollow one indeed.

At the last second, he switched from a three-fingered grip to using his thumb and index finger; the leather patch flopped back from in front of the string and the arrow ripped from his weak grip, taking a layer of skin with it. It shot faster than his eye could follow and embedded in the armoured man's naked neck. His spear went wide and he flopped into Zanthred's arms, gargling blood.

Things were too fast; Zanthred had no thoughts about the mortally injured man as he pushed his body away. Still, some cruelly alert part of his brain said *'you will remember this'*.

In other places down the line, spearmen were haphazardly making contact with the archers. The slow pressure on the Serra line was building as more Sagacious warriors freed themselves from the mass crush at the bottom of the hill and fell into the melee. The archers were quickly pushed back, distorting their careful triple-horned formation.

Zanthred extricated himself from the limp body

of his armoured opponent only to be bashed in the face by the shield of a warrior coming up behind. The spearman put all his weight behind the thrust, trying to force Zanthred over and free up space to use his spear.

Kill or be killed. Plant your legs firm and push. And hack and stab until the enemy runs.

The rules of the melee came back to Zanthred and he knew he must give no ground. But he could feel himself being bent with nothing he could do to stop himself losing his feet.

Then a small shoulder pressed into his spine.

"Don't worry Zanthred, I've got you!" urged Millie.

It was just enough to keep him upright. The Sagacious soldier seemed angered by the fact he could push Zanthred no further and he tried to withdraw his spear to switch to a shorter, handier grip. But the spear was stuck and if Zanthred could have seen behind himself, he would have seen both of Millie's hands desperately holding the shaft firm.

Zanthred and the soldier were locked together, his shield between them. The soldier stared at Zanthred for a few seconds and suddenly Zanthred became aware of his opponent's ether presence flaring into overdrive; a vortex of mana was flowing from him. Zanthred instinctively yelped in pain before he realised what the cause was. He looked down to the source of anguish at his ankles and was alarmed to see flames licking up from the ground and taking root on the material around his legs.

Zanthred could not possibly have withstood more than two seconds of the magical flames, but a second source of mana resonated strongly within the ether and smoothed out the ripples caused by his opponent. The flames evaporated like shadows before a candle. The soothing ripples felt familiar, imminent.

Hanuru.

The soldier was frustrated enough to scream in rage. But now Zanthred had a chance to seize some initiative. He yanked the knotty wooden club from his belt and levered his opponent's shield away with his other hand. That little space to act was all he needed. He felt the weight of the club in his fist and brought it down on the soldier's face. The spearman dropped his arms and stumbled back, bloody and misshapen. Zanthred glared at the wounded man, eager to finish him off but too frightened to leave the shelter of his comrades by even a pace to do so.

Down the line things were not going well. The spearmen were pressing hard on the archers and things seemed grave. However, there were islands of firmness in the centre of the horns where the Fidelis army's own spearmen had enough cohesion to fight back effectively. The only part of the line where the Serra army was bulging forwards was around the Shadow Guard, who seemed to fell an enemy with every stroke of their mighty enchanted weapons.

Gargrace's face was fixed in a grim snarl. Although his leg injury rooted him to the spot, he knew how to get past the enemies' shields, slashing at their feet and hamstrings whenever they came close. A little further on, Callin looked like he was locked in a desperate plight. His long sword was wedged halfway into his opponent's shield, whilst he held the man's spear-wrist tight.

There was a roll of drums from behind the Serra army. The thunderous charge of horses began again. The larger portion of the Serra cavalry rode forwards from their hiding place on the opposite side of the ridgeline. The young noble Copidius ap Ranra was at their head, making the best of the command Duarma had given him. They moved much more slowly than Haddra's cavalry had; the horses and the riders were similarly clad in the heaviest armour they could find. The cavalry wing slowly rounded the westernmost horn of archers.

It was obvious what was going to happen. The Sagacious drums beat out new orders and their light infantry went running over to the west flank to block the cavalry's attempt at envelopment. They hurled darts, sling stones and arrows at them, expecting to turn aside the charge as easily as their own cavalry had been arrested.

But Gargrace had been right. *A few archers don't make the difference of a piss against an enemy intent on closing with you.* There were not enough of them and their missiles clattered off the horses' armour. The tide of cavalry continued to close and even before they had come within a hundred metres, the Sagacious infantry could see the inevitable and began to panic. They broke and fled.

The cavalry burst into a canter and poured down on top of them. The infantry was swamped, disappearing between the bodies of horses. Some were cut down from behind and many more fell to the floor begging for mercy. But it did not stop the armoured cavalry. They continued on and smashed into the back of the spearmen. As the charge rolled west to east along the Sagacious line, the spearmen fractured, panicked and ran.

What followed was complete collapse. Previously stalwart warriors gave in to the herd mentality and ran, throwing down their spears and shields behind them. Zanthred was so relieved to see his opponent turn around and run, that he fell to his knees and gasped for air to still his pounding heart. But some of the Serra archers were taken by a blood fury and tried to chase the Sagacious soldiers down, hacking at their heads from behind. Gargrace ordered a drum roll: *Stand your ground.*

"This is one of the most dangerous parts," Gargrace explained to Zanthred. If our army disintegrates in the chase we might be ambushed by hidden reinforcements or isolated by their rallying forces."

A few pockets of brave men held out, determined to fight to the death for their ideals. But these were quickly surrounded and thrust with stolen spears from a safe distance. The armoured cavalry who had precipitated the rout did not pursue the fleeing troops, but milled about allowing their horses to recover from the furious thrust through the light infantry. Zanthred gazed out on the field of destruction and saw the enemy escaping. But then he saw the cloud of dust between the retreating force and their ships. Gargrace was staring at it as well.

"Let Haddra do what they do best in Delfuri. Herd sheep," said Gargrace.

* * * * * * *

Haddra had to hand it to his young Serra nobles; they might not have been good cavalry archers, but they certainly knew how to hunt. He saw a group of Sagacious soldiers hiding in a copse of walnut trees and made an ululating noise at the back of this throat to draw his comrades' attention. Instantly a group of them took up positions all around the copse. Two riders plunged in and the foot soldiers bolted in the opposite direction, right into the circle of waiting horsemen. The horsemen closed in and the foot soldiers threw themselves on the floor in surrender.

This was how they hunted deer in Serra. It was even easier with people.

Haddra was impressed that Gargrace had managed to cause such a major rout. He had envisioned having to return to the battlefield and harry the Sagacious infantry so the Serra troops could regroup and try again. But as it happened, his furious pursuit of the Sagacious cavalry had left them in the perfect position to cut off the retreat.

Haddra was not so bothered with the ordinary rank and file. Any fool could take them. He was after Tisenin. He knew he must be making a dash for the ships, but he could not simply burn them and be done with it; the traitor had been possessed with enough sense to leave a strong reserve and dig an entrenchment round his beachhead. So instead Haddra was trying to catch them in flight.

In the distance he spied two riders coming up to a man on foot. They stopped. One man got off the horse, knelt in acquiescence and helped the foot-bound fleer on to the saddle in his place. The second rider took the reins of the newcomer's horse and led both their mounts towards the ships.

Got him!

Those were acts of profound respect. Haddra ululated and urged his mare in pursuit. Only two riders heard his call, but that was all he needed. They ignored the dismounted man, instead cutting a path that would intercept the two Sagacious riders before they reached the ships. When the two Sagacious riders saw Haddra was going to block their way, they split up and veered off into the countryside. Haddra's mare was still full of stamina, whereas his companions' were flagging and near exhaustion. He shouted for them to follow the slower of the two escapees. He smiled, guessing that Tisenin would have been given the fresher, faster horse. A little vain part of him wanted to face Tisenin alone; anything to give him a better excuse *not* to take the man alive.

The parched ground tumbled underneath his horse's nimble hooves and he made up the distance to his target quickly. The fleeing man led his horse into rough ground in an attempt to get away; over ditches, through thickets and down steep slopes. But Haddra was easily able to follow. His mare was trained for all kinds of tricky terrain and responded to his every command with perfect discipline.

When he thought he was close enough, he drew his bow from his shoulder and nocked an arrow. He squinted; the man seemed to have a strange, ragged cloak. Without slowing the horse, he stood in his stirrups and let the arrow fly...

For a second it looked like it hit the man square in the back: But he spun the horse and came to a halt, looking none the worse.

Damn, always so hard to hit at a gallop.

Haddra drew up to him so there was only twenty metres between them. It was obvious now that this was not Tisenin. He did not recognise the man. But the man seemed to recognise him.

"Haddra ap Woodrin! You are getting too old for battle, your eyesight must be failing!" he mocked. The man spread out his coat so the hole ripped in it by the arrow was obvious. It seemed to be the skin of some kind of reptile. "You damaged my lovely cape."

"Not so old I can't skewer a man in the saddle!" he growled. "Where is Tisenin?"

"Ha! Last time I saw him, he was giving me his horse."

It hit Haddra like a lead weight. He felt like an idiot for falling for another of Tisenin's tricks.

He contemplated riding back for him, but knew after this lengthy pursuit Tisenin would already have found his way back to the heavily defended ships.

Haddra regarded the man in front of him darkly. "I commend you for your commitment to your master, but I hope you realise I will be taking your life in his place. What name do I give to your family?"

"My name is Adrin ap Foras. And I am not so sure you will." Adrin drew an iron long sword from his belt and held it like he knew how to use it. "You know I learnt to fight in Cathri. The Ofhan Mountains is where I slew this beast I wear on my back. The clans there are said to be the fiercest of all humans. They're vicious, quick, crafty. You had to have the reflexes of a cobra to take them on. I got quite good at it. They say the humans of Delfuri are puppies by comparison."

Haddra reached behind his saddle and drew a javelin from its sheath. "Don't brag about killing humans. They're all just one of the simurgh's failures at making a slave race."

They charged at each other, each with their weapon raised for the killing blow. As their horses crossed paths, Adrin brought his huge sword down in a killing arc that would have caught Haddra in the belly. But whilst they were talking Haddra had unhooked his feet from the stirrups and a moment before the blow landed he slid down the side of the horse so his saddle was empty and he was holding on with the mane and one foot on the rump. The blow cut through thin air, throwing Adrin off balance in his saddle.

As soon as Adrin's blow was passed, Haddra struck backwards with the butt of the javelin, catching Adrin in the head. Adrin was pitched from the saddle and his horse galloped off. The cocky general lay prone and weapon-less on the floor. Haddra trotted over, javelin point at Adrin's neck.

"Do you yield?" asked Haddra.

Adrin coughed before replying, winded by his fall. "No."

"A choice I admire. I will make sure people know you died well."

He drew back the javelin to strike.

Then a screech caught his attention. Haddra looked up to see the second rider thundering towards him. Evidently she (because he could tell it was a woman now) had escaped her pursuers. Before he had a chance to do anything else, a ball of fire erupted from her fingertips and struck him in the face. He screamed in pain and the horse whinnied and tossed below him, terrified of the flames. It bolted in a direction he could not see. He grabbed the animal's neck and through the pain spoke calmly to it until the animal stopped panicking. Only then did he examine his face with his fingertips and dare to open his eyes. He was not burnt badly, just singed.

Once he got his bearings he looked back and saw the woman (he now hazily recognised as Dago ap Keldron) helping Adrin onto her horse and the two of them cantering off towards the coast. Haddra unslung his bow from his shoulder; he could still hit them at this range, even with eyes full of water.

But something made him stop. Perhaps the rush of pain had taken the fight out of him. Perhaps he considered himself to be in Dago's debt because she had not finished him off when he was blind. Whatever it was, he let them go and take their chances with the rest of the Sagacious forces trying to get back to their galleys.

"Come on girl, let's see this thing through," he said to the horse.

Haddra walked his mare back to the fight feeling very old, tired and full of aches.

Chapter 11

Aftermath

When Zanthred had finally calmed his racing heart, he stood and surveyed the battlefield. There were surprisingly few dead people, friend or foe, where the melee had taken place. There were far more at the bottom of the hill where Gargrace's crushing trap had come together. The sounds of pounding feet had retreated and that let him hear the cries of the wounded. It brought his mind to Millie and Hanuru.

Were they alright?

He turned around and found them patiently waiting behind him. He threw his arms around Millie.

"You're not hurt are you?" he asked.

"No. I'm fine," she replied. Then she pressed him away. "Let go Zanthred! You're hugging me too tight! And you're wet..."

Zanthred let go and looked down. There was a sodden patch on the lower half of his robes. From the smell it could only have been urine, but he had no idea if it was his own or his opponent's. He opened his mouth to apologise, but Millie cut him short.

"It's okay, you did a good job keeping me safe," she said.

"I tried..." he said.

But Zanthred knew how close he had come to being spiked by that first Sagacious spearmen. He could feel a large red blood blister rising on his thumb where he had been forced to change his grip on the bow. Gargrace had warned him the finger guard was too thick, but he had chosen to ignore him for the sake of comfort. It had nearly cost him, and perhaps Millie, their lives.

He knew if he wanted to protect her and Hanuru he needed to stop merely playing at being a soldier, he needed to get stronger.

Zanthred took the white leather tag off his hand and searched for Janistor. She and Callin were crouched over someone on the floor. It was Malichar. He had a narrow puncture wound in his chest that had soaked his whole gambeson in blood. Janistor was in tears. She took the long red feather from her hair and placed it on his chest.

She sobbed only barely coherently, "I never wanted to see one of my troths die! I was so happy when he gave me that eagle feather...He was so handsome and brave."

Callin looked vacant, in shock, and had no reply. He

was clutching a broken sword in his hand. He glanced up when he noticed Zanthred standing over him.

"It was too long...I couldn't swing it in the press," said Callin. "Then when I managed to stab at him with it, it caught in his shield. He would have killed me, I thought I was dead. But the sword broke in two and I managed to slice him with what's left. Damn sword breaking saved me."

"How's Janistor?" Zanthred asked.

Callin glanced over at her and seemed to notice her distress for the first time.

"He was so brave...so brave," she was still sobbing.

Callin put a hand on her shoulder and pulled her away from Malichar's body. "Then and now. We will carry his body home and give him a good funeral so everyone remembers his deeds."

Janistor nodded and allowed herself to be drawn away. Malichar's blood had seeped into the hem of her dress and she seemed very perturbed by this. She took a small antler handled knife from her belt and tried to saw at the fabric. But in her agitated state she was making a terrible job of it, simply fraying the weave.

Zanthred could stand by no longer. He put a hand on her shoulder to get her attention and held the finger guard out.

"Thank you for the gift, and I know this probably isn't the right time. But I don't need it anymore, so I think it's better that you have it back." He dropped the finger guard in her lap.

She stared at him not comprehending the words or the action, but he could not deal with it at the time, so he turned his back and returned to his post.

The guilt and imperative to guard Millie and Hanuru was so strong that he did not stop to think that perhaps the three of them did a good job at guarding each other.

What he did stop to think about was how lucky Malichar was, because he had been blessed with a quick death. The screams and sobs of the wounded were like a grim dawn chorus. He knew many he passed on the way back to his post would take a day or two to die from their wounds, and even more would have a thousand year lifetime to live with their maimed bodies. It did not feel like a good victory.

* * * * * * *

Once the message got out that Gargrace and Haddra had won, Duarma made his way to the battlefield by swift horse. It was late afternoon when he and Jandor arrived. The soldiers were busy collecting weapons from the battlefield, tending the wounded and cooking the food they had found in the enemy camp.

Gargrace and Haddra looked very pleased with themselves. For the first time, they were smiling in each other's presence.

"What's the news?" asked Duarma.

"The battle went as planned," said Gargrace. "Although it was in the balance until we were saved by Copidius and his armoured cavalry. Haddra pursued the enemy to their ships."

"And what of Tisenin?" asked Duarma.

"Unfortunately, the wretch escaped," said Haddra. "They had reserves who stopped me putting fire to the galleys. They have castoff. I watched for a while and they were heading north-west, back to Efrandi."

Duarma sighed deeply. It seemed every chance they had bring him to justice slipped by.

"How many did we lose, and how many does he have left?" asked Duarma.

"A quick head count and we have lost around two-thousand commoners and fifty-six nobles. We killed three-thousand of them and have taken six-thousand prisoner, seven-hundred of whom are noble," Gargrace replied.

"Which begs the question," prompted Haddra, "what to do with the curs?"

"Take me to them," ordered Duarma. There was a venom in his command that he had been trying to keep in his breast.

Haddra led him and his horse away from the main camp to the banks of a stream where thousands of men had been stripped of their weapons and now sat together guarded by a ring of Haddra's cavalry. They looked broken and morose. Duarma felt no sympathy for them, only anger.

Duarma opened his throat wide so the whole mass could hear him.

"I am Duarma, Emperor of all cherno by assent of the Magnolia Court. You have followed the traitor Tisenin who murdered my wife, tried to seize power with arms and seeks to overthrow the sacred Ban. Does anyone deny they came here with Tisenin?"

There was silence.

"Does anyone claim they were brought here by force or coercion?"

Again there was silence. Then one voice shouted out from the ground.

"No! We all volunteered for this fight, made necessary by the obstinacy of the Emperor Kirrie and now you!"

Duarma looked deep in his heart and found only a rage and coldness that he had been suppressing since Kirrie's death.

"Then I find it self-evident that you are guilty of one of the most terrible crimes in our race's history. I sentence you all to death."

A commotion erupted from within the prisoners; some cried and begged for their lives, whilst others shouted angrily and began to fruitlessly wrangle with their armed guards.

Jandor quickly came up by Duarma's side. "My Emperor! I Implore you, Elsiren forgave his enemies. Please follow his example!" begged Jandor.

"Elsiren forgave his enemies who in defeat were willing to walk through the gate from Earth to Haven. I have no such gate," said Duarma. "We do not even have enough food for ourselves, let alone the prisoners. And how am I to restrain them all? Such are their numbers that if I sent them to the colonies to do penitence, they may overpower their wardens and sail right back to Tisenin. Death is the only way we will have security."

Haddra assented slowly and gravely. "It is a hard decision my Emperor, but I believe you have made the right one," he said.

Duarma nodded in thanks, then looked at Gargrace, "Well, do you have an opinion as well, general?"

"No my Emperor. I fight battles. I'll leave what we do after them to you," answered Gargrace.

"Find volunteers who are willing to perform the executions," said Duarma.

"I will do," assured Haddra.

"We should follow up this success and chase Tisenin down. We should start moving the army to Efrandi from tomorrow," said Duarma.

Haddra and Gargrace looked at each other, then shook their heads.

"My Emperor, that is impossible," said Haddra. "We have no food. Any army we sent to Efrandi would starve. By the time we have enough supplies, it will be the Hurricane Season and no one will dare set sail then. I hate to say this, but we must wait."

"You're saying I must let Tisenin stew and lick his wounds for eight months until I can get at him? That's simply unacceptable!"

"Alas, a hard fact of resources to hand, my Emperor. But we can use those eight months to good effect," said Haddra. "Build a real army, train it, equip it, supply it. I will go back to Delfuri and raise a great host of veteran cavalry. We will return at the first opportunity. Your breast will swell with their magnificence when you see them. Until then, I believe we have saved Serra."

"I am already eternally grateful for what you have done Haddra. I am even more in your debt for your offer of troops. I will make ships ready for your journey," said Duarma.

"I too will write to my mother Serenus and request some veteran soldiers from Lansissari. But before that, the people of Efrandi may surrender now their army has been defeated. You should send an envoy to them and offer an amnesty if they lay down their arms and give up Tisenin," said Jandor.

"I will do as you suggest. Although it galls me to know traitors will go free, reluctantly, it seems *expedient* to bring about a swift end to the conflict," said Duarma. "Jandor, you are among one of the most reasonable and well spoken ambassadors I know. Will you go to Tisenin's court and persuade him or his people to capitulate?"

"Gladly my Emperor."

Gargrace stroked the scars on the side of his face. "We are unfit to chance an attack on Efrandi, but we can send troops to Adlan and start building a forward camp. Plus, if they left Feydrin ap Lanlar unharmed, she will make a fine insurance policy for us."

Haddra looked alarmed at the prospect of calling the simurgh for assistance. "We will *not* need the priest Feydrin," he asserted.

"Most likely not, but in war nothing is certain," said Gargrace.

"Do you think Serra will be safe?" ask Duarma.

"Yes. It will be immensely difficult for Tisenin to raise another army and resupply them before the weather closes in," said Gargrace.

"Good, then take as many troops as you need and go to Adlan," said Duarma.

"I will only need a hundred. Those damn lethal Shadow Guard and a few archers," said Gargrace. "I've never seen soldiers like them."

"Then the only thing that is left is the imminent food crisis. I will send the refugees away now there is no longer danger. They will have to find food further afield. I'll thin out the militia and set them to the fields." Duarma gazed once more over the faces of all the men he was condemning to death. "Hopefully this will be the last major drama until Tisenin joins his followers here today."

* * * * * * *

They had to spend a second night in the camp. Now it stank of their own effluence, which they had been depositing in the perimeter ditch. The buzz of flies had become incessant, drawn by their shit and the fast decaying dead. The camp was a whole mixture of emotions now. There was some celebration for the victory and some commiseration for the dead. The prevailing wisdom was that it was all over. Tisenin's surrender could not be far off.

The Sparrow Company sat in a circle around a large fire, sharing tales of their members who had died. Janistor was unusually silent and paid no attention to the dynamic of the discussion or any attempt at flattery. Hanuru was also very quiet, content to rest her head on Millie's lap. When they were done with reminiscing, the stories turned to tales of narrow escapes and unexpected happenings on the battlefield. No one was vulgar enough to directly brag about their kills.

Gargrace hobbled over to them and the conversations ended.

"I'm looking for volunteers to take this fight to the enemy," he said.

"Efrandi?" Callin asked.

"Not yet, but eventually."

Hanuru raised her head from Millie's lap. Her face flushed with tears. "I can't do it!" wailed Hanuru. "I can't hold a bow in my hands and shoot people again! It felt horrible, it was madness." She broke into open sobs and Mille had to try and comfort her.

"Good," said Gargrace. "I don't want you shooting for me."

Hanuru stopped crying and looked up with surprise. She had expected to be berated for her cowardice. Gargrace reached down to the slim lemonwood bow in her pack. He snapped it in two without showing a hint of effort.

"I don't need a part time militia fighting with these toy weapons. I'm looking for people who are willing to become real soldiers. Real weapons, real strength, real discipline." Gargrace scratched his crevice-ridden face. "But that's not all I'm looking for, Hanuru."

Hanuru was a little surprised he remembered her name, given the number of soldier's at his command.

"Yes?" she asked.

"I saw what you did with the magic today. As strong as we are, we're going to need someone who is skilled with mana to keep us safe. If you stayed with me you wouldn't be killing people, only protecting your friends. What do you say?"

"No...I mean...I don't know," Hanuru dithered.

He spied the black feathers in her and Millie's hair. "You can even bring your troth. I need a few drummers. She wouldn't have to fight either."

"I-" Millie began to answer, clearly angry that her troth was being pressured, but Zanthred cut her off.

"...I will follow you!" he pronounced.

Millie looked at him wide-eyed. The expression said, '*You really should run these things by me,*' but not in such polite language.

But Zanthred *had* thought it through. If the war did not end quickly then they might have to do this all over again next year, or the one after that. By speeding an end to the conflict, he was reducing the chances Millie and Hanuru would have to fight to protect Serra again.

Gargrace clapped his hands together. "Good! I was hoping I could count on you, Zanthred. But I can see there are those among you who must discuss this request, so I will leave you to deliberate tonight. Tomorrow, I will come and find you at dawn for your responses. We leave for Adlan soon." Gargrace began shuffling away towards the next company, but then he looked like he remembered something and turned back. "Oh, I promised to spread the word. Haddra ap Woodrin is looking for people willing to execute the prisoners."

"They're killing some of the prisoners?" asked Millie, obviously alarmed.

"They're killing them *all*," corrected Gargrace.

"No! They can't, that's ghastly!" blurted Hanuru.

"It makes no sense, the battle was bad enough!" added Millie.

Janistor was suddenly roused from her reverie. She stood bolt upright.

"Where can I find Haddra ap Woodrin?" she demanded.

Gargrace raised an eyebrow at the seducer suddenly moved to action. "Down to the southeast, by the stream."

"They killed my troth. I will have my vengeance," said Janistor.

She began walking away from the circle. Millie scrambled after her and threw herself at Janistor's feet, hugging her legs in the act of surrender. Janistor was pinned and had to listen to her pleas.

"Janistor, I've not been a friend to you and you haven't been one to me. But I beg you to listen to me now. This act is monstrous. This rage you are feeling now is temporary, but the guilt you will feel if you take part in it will last for your lifetime. It will be bad for you and all Fidelis if it goes ahead. *It is only to the benefit of Karlsha.*"

Janistor tried to struggle free, but she did not have Millie's strength. "Let go! You are not my moral guardian!"

Hanuru now went over and somewhat more tentatively fell to her knees and wrapped her arms around Janistor's waist. "This is horrid, absolutely horrid. Do not be a part of it, for my sake."

Janistor's eyes began to water. "Callin! Get these two off me. I must avenge Malichar."

Callin rose to his feet, looking a little unsure of what to do. After a long heavy pause he finally spoke. "Janistor, I am your troth and I see it as my duty to do the things which are a burden to you. If you want vengeance for Malichar, I am obliged to go and execute the prisoners in your name whilst these two women keep you safely here."

Janistor's watery eyes turned to full tears and she gave up the struggle. She allowed herself to tumble limply into Callin's arms.

"Thank you Callin," said Millie.

Callin pulled a snarl. "If Janistor was in her right mind, I would gladly have killed you for her." Callin helped Janistor back to her seat at the fire side.

Millie shook off the shock of the outburst and addressed the whole crowd,

"Who will come with me and beg for the lives of

the captives? They can't refuse us if we all act as one." Blank faces stared back at her, united only in nervous silence. "Come on, one avoidable death started this, don't let us compound it...Zanthred?"

"Millie, I-" But he found it hard to express in words. "...Justice must be done somehow."

It was like a blow to her. She grabbed Hanuru's hand and together they wandered through the camp trying to find enough support to buy the prisoner's lives.

Gargrace silently slipped into the dark whilst the two young women began their quest of mercy. Inwardly he smiled. He admired the young ones' spirit; all that righteous energy, but still too young to realise that they could not make a difference in the affairs of state or affairs of the heart.

Chapter 12

Hidden Mercy

Whilst Hanuru morally supported Millie's quest, and Millie's enthusiasm was even admirable, it was far outside of her comfort zone to be dragged around thousands of people trying to rally objectors to the Emperor's proclamations. They were met with blank stares wherever they went. By the time they had worked their way to Haddra, they had only gathered around a hundred people. Millie strode at the head of them like an angry prophet leading her cult.

Haddra was in the saddle talking to a handsome, but weaponless, young noble. Hanuru had seen the young man at Kirrie's funeral and thought he was Jandor, the son of Archlord Serenus. Haddra passed Jandor a piece of parchment and Hanuru caught what was scribbled on it; a list of several hundred noble names. It was those of note who had already been executed.

Haddra had decided to have the prisoners executed in small groups away from where they were being held so they would not try a mass breakout and they would have enough time to record all the names. He was busy organizing the prisoners into parties to be sent out to the place of execution – six armed horsemen to twenty prisoners – but he stopped when he saw the delegation.

He saw the mixture of determined and terrified looks in their eyes. "You're not volunteers are you?" he surmised.

Millie knelt down on the floor in front of him. She bowed her head in supplication, but her voice was strong and resolute.

"Haddra ap Woodrin, I am Millie of Icknel. We come to you to beg for the lives of the prisoners. Executing them will be a great sin. It will bring pain where there could be peace. It will compound their evil with ours. Please, stay your hand," begged Millie.

"And is this the feeling of you all?" asked Haddra. The crowd assented and Haddra shook his head in indignation. "Millie, how many wars have you fought in?"

"This is my first," she admitted.

"I have lost count of the number I have borne arms in. Do not presume to dictate to me how they should be conducted."

Millie looked directly up at him with fire in her eyes, "You have my full respect Archlord, but this is not a matter of conduct, but of morality. And there I would say neither of us has precedence."

"That may be, but better moralists than you or I have already had this argument and the Emperor has decided between them. I cannot, would not and will not change his orders."

Millie saw Haddra's head was unmovable, so she tried to affect his heart. She let the emotions of the day well up and tears streamed down her face.

"I am begging you Archlord Haddra! Do not follow the orders of any man or woman that you would not confidently issue yourself," Millie pleaded.

Haddra turned his back on her; he considered the matter settled. Jandor looked sombre and reluctantly also turned away. There was a sigh of exasperation from Millie's cohort. Some of them shed a tear, some of them hugged and others just shrugged their shoulders. They began a slow wander back to the camp.

Haddra spoke to a mounted warrior and another six-guard, twenty-prisoner group began the walk to the execution site. Hanuru sympathetically hugged Millie as her bold lover desperately sieved her mind for a solution. Finally she hugged Hanuru back tightly.

"I have a plan." Millie whispered so quietly that Hanuru could barely hear the words. "We can free *some* of the prisoners at least...but it will be by duplicity and open betrayal. Go now with the others if you wish to remain innocent."

What she said, and the way she said it, made it

sound dangerous. Even more dangerous than the battle they had just lived through. Hanuru did not know if she had the strength to push herself more.

"Millie, I don't think I can,"

"Then go quickly Hanuru, I will meet back up with you when...if...I can."

If! If! That little word felt like a small death. At least if she were with Millie whatever they would suffer they would suffer together.

"Oh, Mille, I'll go with you," said Hanuru.

Millie again hugged her tight. "Thank you Hanuru, first we need permission to follow the execution party out into the woods."

Hanuru did not have to think hard how that might be accomplished.

"Archlord Haddra!" Hanuru shouted. Haddra turned around looking angry at being disturbed once again. "Archlord Haddra, I am Hanuru of Serra. Please let us go with the prisoners and record their last messages for their loved ones."

"Record their last messages? You have enough paper and ink on you?" asked Haddra. He looked sceptical.

"No, I am a mnemonics master," declared Hanuru. Haddra continued to look at her sceptically, so she began to reel off names.

By the fiftieth name, Jandor called a halt, waving the parchment Haddra had given him in the air. "Alright, alright! Haddra, the girl has memorized the list perfectly."

Now Haddra looked amazed, "But you can only have seen that list for a fraction of a second as it passed between our hands!"

"As I said, I am a mnemonics master," said Hanuru. "I can memorize several hundred confessions and transcribe them later. I am yet to find my limit."

Haddra nodded gently, "Very well. I am a practical man, not a cruel one. You two can go with the executioners and give the traitors a little comfort before they die. If you go quickly, you can catch the party that just left. The condemned tend to drag their feet. Remind me not to handle secret orders around you, Hanuru of Serra."

Privately Millie squeezed Hanuru's hand. "Hanuru, your mind continues to astonish me."

Her lover's praise revived Hanuru's spirit. "What now?" she asked.

"Now you stab me."

* * * * * * *

"Aaaargh!"

In the gloom of the night, close to the execution site, the guards were startled by Millie's screams. They halted the prisoner's progress and looked apprehensively in every direction.

Millie shakily waddled towards them supported by Hanuru. She had blood gushing from a shallow stab wound on her shoulder.

"Help us, help us!" Millie shouted.

One of the guards rode over to them. With his dowdy riding trousers and several war bows pinned to the horses tack, he looked like a seasoned warrior from Delfuri.

"What's this, what's happened?" he asked.

"Sagacious soldiers! Two of them wearing the purple armbands. We stumbled into them in some woodland and they stabbed me," said Millie.

"Over there," said Hanuru, pointing to the silhouette of a tree line on a nearby ridge.

"Go and get them! They were running when we saw them last!" implored Millie.

There was no question of belief or identity. The guards had seen the prisoners and knew that the Sagacious forces contained scarcely any women.

The one who had ridden out to meet them turned to the rest of his troop and picked four of them. "We shall go and cut off their escape route before they can get far."

"But what about the prisoners?" one of the guards asked.

"It does not take more than one soldier to be warden to bound men!" he barked.

The opposition was silenced and five of the guards rode off towards the woodland. The last guard took up position looking over the prisoners and toward the point his comrades had headed for. He had his back to Millie and Hanuru.

Millie silently drew the little bloody knife that they had used to make the gash on her arm. Hanuru knew she could never have stabbed Millie; Millie had merely rolled her eyes and inflicted the injury on herself.

That did not seem to faze her at all. Hanuru could only admire that strength.

But now she looked determined and frightened in equal measure.

"Are you sure about this? It is not too late yet," pressed Hanuru.

Millie stared at the oblivious back of the horseman.

"I just have to hope that with my blade to his throat, his heart quails and he delivers himself into our power," said Millie.

"But what if he doesn't?" asked Hanuru. "He may yet overpower us both. Or are you prepared to swap the life of one ally for twenty foes?"

Millie did not answer; she just sweatily readjusted her grip on the knife and began her advance on the lone guard.

All of a sudden there was the sound of tumbling hooves racing towards them. All three of them looked around in time to see a masked man on a white pony plunge next to the guard with a dagger raised in his fist. The knife came down and went into the rump of the guard's horse. The horse whinnied in pain and bolted away, tossing the guard from side to side as he desperately clung on.

The masked man brought his pony to a halt and stared directly at Millie and Hanuru. The scarf around his mouth meant they could only see a pair of intense eyes glaring at them.

"I know what you are planning to do. It is written all over your faces," he said. Millie and Hanuru fidgeted in fear, intensely aware that they only had one small knife between themselves should the newcomer decide to attack. But instead he looked away, wistfully up to the sky. "Is it so wrong to countermand an order that you know was conceived in bankrupt hatred? My mother always taught me to be open and pure in all my actions." Whatever thoughts were going through his mind, he did not look like he had resolved them by the time he again fixed them with that intense glare. "You know they will kill you if they catch you?"

"We know," said Millie.

"Then be quick in what you are doing. I will lead them away," said the stranger.

"But then they will kill you!" said Millie.

"Have no fear, I know little of weapons and war, but there is no better horseman in the forests," said the stranger. As he said this, he held up the knife and – with a tingle through the ether – its lifeless wooden hilt erupted in tiny green barbed thorns.

"What is your name, dear stranger, so I know who to thank should we ever cross paths again?" asked Millie.

The stranger whipped his horse around, ready to depart. "My name is Nohwan," he shouted as he dug the spurs in and galloped off.

"That's a very strange name," said Millie.

"Not really," said Hanuru, but then of course, she recognised the man's horse, his eyes and the crumpled scarf pulled up over his face which could only have shown a tree blooming in the winter, were it to be stretched out.

Thank you, my Lansissari prince.

* * * * * * *

It took them just moments to cut the bonds of the Sagacious troops. The last man stretched out his hands to allow Millie to saw through the rope. He had a beautiful, almost feminine smile and the kind of silky voice that made young women quiver with excitement. Most young women.

"Dear comrade, I thank you most deeply. You are a true credit to that Sagacious cause. I will speak of this to Tisenin's ear directly."

Millie met his eyes, but did not stop the cutting. "I am no comrade and I hate Tisenin with every part of my being. I do this only as an act of mercy in the face of unnecessary death."

The bonds came loose and the man rubbed his sore wrists.

"Well that may be, but I still owe you my life. It is quite something to be saved by one so beautiful. I am Killwa of Efrandi, Captain of my cohort."

Millie did not even acknowledge the flattery, "Then have your men take off any purple or Jewasri style clothing. We have to walk right past the Fidelis camp and the only way we will manage it is if you can all pass for Serra soldiers."

"Of course. And what shall I call my saviour?" asked Killwa.

"I am Millie of Icknel." She nodded to Hanuru, "And that is Hanuru, my troth."

"Ah!" he said, as if the gender of her lover explained why she seemed immune to his usual charms. It was almost as if he considered the huge ideological chasm between them as an irrelevance.

Another one of the soldiers came and put his hand on Killwa's shoulder. He looked about a hundred years older and all together more serious. His arms were thick with muscle and his head was shaved, making him look quite intimidating. This was only exaggerated by the fact one of his eyes had been left milky-white and pupil-less by some past trauma.

"My brother, should we trust them? They are soldiers, they have the calluses of archers. This morning they were trying to kill us! What would stop them betraying us at the first sign of danger? We would be better off making our escape by ourselves."

Killwa patted the man's hand, "Looshan, have no fear. We do not know these parts or their forces' ways. We are better off with guides. And I doubt that one who risked her life to save me would be of such low integrity to abandon us when things looked difficult." He turned to Millie, "I apologise for my brother's suspicion. These have been trying and unknown times."

"I will not force anyone to come who does not want to, but decide now because we have to move very quickly," said Millie.

In the end, twelve of the twenty opted to go their own way. Many of them had injuries that made quick flight impossible and others simply thought they had a better chance moving individually than as a group. Hanuru had every expectation that the injured ones would be caught and executed soon after daybreak, but she tried not to feel guilty that their plan could not accommodate everyone; it was not as if the remaining eight they intended to lead to safety were in a much better position.

Although Looshan made some hasty and strong words about following Millie, Killwa did not take long to persuade his older brother.

Mille had everyone gather some armfuls of wood and then taught them one of the popular songs they had sung on the march from Serra. It was a light tune which poked fun at Efrandi and its archlord's fastidious habits.

In Serra they say the food is bad,
Never a meal to make you glad,
But soon we'll get our wish,
When we serve a dish of the Celibate Fish!

In Kelmor they say the folk are tight,
Instead of a meal you'll get a flea bite,
But our belts we won't have to squish,
When we serve a dish of the Celibate Fish!

In this manner, they looked just like a foraging party come down from the camp to gather fuel. Looshan was unhappy about singing a song which disrespected Tisenin, but conceded the necessity. He half-heartedly carried the tune.

They were approaching another group of foragers, which was the key part of Millie's plan.

"More gusto, Looshan! Sing like you've just won a battle!" commanded Millie.

"Quite so, Looshan!" agreed Killwa, who started to belt out the song in rich and deep tones that slipped into you like velvet. Hanuru was impressed; her mind was filled with a wealth of new melodies and words that she could use that voice to carry.

They merged in with the second foraging party and Millie made some polite small talk whilst the men sang. The song caught on and soon both groups were warbling along like old friends as they climbed back towards the camp. Killwa seemed intent on flirting with the women in the new party (with apparent success), which made Looshan visibly angry.

Noting the anger in his brother's eyes, Killwa just shrugged.

"Let him," Millie whispered to Looshan. "It seems more natural."

As she spoke, there was the sound of fast moving hooves behind them. The party stopped and turned to see two of Haddra's horse archers bearing down on them. They called their horses to a halt as they reached the party.

"You there, which company are you with?" barked one of the horse warriors.

"We're from Sparrow Company," replied Millie.

"And we're from Vintner Company," said one of the women from the other group.

"Some Sagacious prisoners have escaped. Have you seen anyone suspicious whilst foraging?" asked the horse archer.

The foragers muttered to each other and shook their heads in consternation. The two horse archers carefully scanned the group, but the kindling in arms, patriotic songs and mixture of sexes all suggested they were nothing more than what they first seemed. Frustrated and keen to move on ahead of the escapees, they spurred their horses on to the next group of foragers.

Propriety demanded that they continue on to the edge of the Fidelis camp where they parted with the vintners and dumped their kindling. They picked up some water skins and made it look like they were going back out to gather some more. Only they headed out west. West towards the coast.

They walked down to the stream and filled their skins with fresh water. The Sagacious prisoners guzzled water straight from the stream. Most had not had anything to drink since before the battle that morning. Then they pressed on west, just hoping no one was watching them.

They reached the coast soon after that and found themselves on a sandy beach with crumbling cliffs. The tide was in, but just receding, so Millie made them all wade through the surf so their tracks would be wiped clean within a matter of minutes.

The cliffs had a thousand fractures and crevices. Trying to pick just one to hide in was mind boggling.

"You're a Serra native Hanuru. Does this look familiar to you?" asked Millie.

"No, I hate the sea. I never come here. Sorry," said Hanuru.

"Hated the sea?" Killwa prodded Hanuru jovially, "Just checking you're a real cherno and not a human trying to pass yourself off."

Hanuru did not like it, but she said nothing in her defence.

"Then I guess we take any cave not visible from the beach...." said Millie, but then she paused and looked pensively out to sea. "...That's odd."

"What?" asked Hanuru.

Millie pointed to where she was looking. The moon had just broken the black cloud and something white and luminous was visible not too far away. It slowly solidified in Hanuru's eyes to be a high-sided grey ship with a huge painted sail. The image of a vast courting swan hovered above stylized deep blue waves. In the moonlight it looked like the ghostly bird was watching their movements.

"We are doomed!" whispered Looshan. "They have seen us and are coming to shore!"

"Don't be silly Looshan, it could not possibly have made us out from the swishing surf at that distance. We must look like rocks or seals. And besides, it is turning away from us," said Killwa.

Hanuru could see he was correct. With all the

slowness and grace of its totem, the vessel was turning northwest, away from them and away from Serra.

"I recognise that sail," said Millie. "It was on a ship in the harbour at Icknel when I set out with Zanthred earlier this year. It was an ornate, big-bellied carrack. Every plank of wood had been carved into something beautiful. Not the kind of ship you bring to a warzone. I wonder what it is doing here?"

"When you round the Emerald Peninsula on a night like this, with cloud instead of stars, you must follow the land east until you come in sight of the lights of Serra. Only then can you plot your course. Otherwise you risk running into the rocky shores of Adlan," explained Killwa.

Millie bit her lip and began chewing it nervously, but Hanuru could not quite reason why. She seemed every bit as brooding as when she had held the knife ready to attack the guard earlier on that evening. As far as Hanuru was concerned, one ship was much like another and the fact it was moving away meant they were in no danger.

"I should ask Zanthred," said Millie "He was always in town helping to paint frescos. He would know the artist that painted the sail and probably who owned the ship. Only, I rather wouldn't speak to him right now..."

"My dear Millie, any man who has upset you cannot possibly be worth worrying one peck about!" said Killwa.

Millie shook her head in exasperation. "Never mind, that can wait. Let's hunt for a hiding place."

Once they began searching for a hiding spot, they quickly found a small fissure in a headland, only visible from a few metres away. The entrance was a narrow squeeze that chafed the shoulders and hips, but it widened out towards the back, so the eight escapees could comfortably rest lying down. The top was open to the elements, but leafy plants had grown over creating some good shade. It smelt of rotting meat; a lonely sheep had stumbled in from the top and died some months ago.

"I'm sorry, we're going to have to leave you here for the moment. I wouldn't dare build a fire or forage during the day. And you'll have to survive with the water you've got, so be careful," warned Millie. "We should be back with a boat in two days, or thereabout."

"Thank you kind Millie, I hope you have a smooth and fast journey so I may see your fine face all the sooner," said Killwa as he bowed a little too deeply to be taken seriously.

Millie nodded gravely; her head was already full of the task ahead. Rescue was by no means sure yet.

When they had squeezed back out of the crevasse, Hanuru turned to Millie.

"Millie, where are we going to get a boat?"

"We beg."

* * * * * * *

They crept back into the camp late that night. Zanthred was already asleep, curled up by himself and resting a little fitfully. Millie told Hanuru not to disturb him, although Hanuru suspected it had more to do with the unfriendly exchange they had earlier in the evening rather than anything else. Hanuru found some clean strips of cloth and bound Millie's arm. They found the leftovers of the evening's meal (predictably a thin mutton soup) and then set down for the night. Hanuru's anxiety was so high that she could not have slept without Millie's arms around her. It was all still new enough to be exhilarating and comfortable enough that they could have been married for five decades already.

They had just a few hours sleep before Millie woke and insisted that they get moving. It was still dark. It was faster walking individually than with the army and they were back in Chepsid before the sun reached its peak. They went straight to the Perched Sparrow.

The inn was empty; the majority of its residents were still on the battlefield. However, there were sporadic clatters of pots and tuneful humming coming from the kitchen.

"Baytee?" called Millie. "Baytee, it is Millie and Hanuru."

The humming stopped and Baytee emerged, looking surprised and glad. She had a big apron on and her sleeves tied back to the elbow with silver clasps.

"Well good day to you, my young shepherd and poet! I did not expect you back until this evening at least," said Baytee.

Millie managed a weak smile, "We won."

"So I heard! The messengers have already been round all the streets proclaiming it." Baytee clasped Millie in her big arms.

Millie winced where Baytee's hug caught the gash on her arm. Baytee looked down and saw the bloody bandages.

"Why you're hurt! Let me take a look at that," it was a command not a request. Baytee had rolled up Millie's sleeve and begun to unpick the bandages before she could reply.

"It is just a small war wound, nothing to worry about," insisted Millie.

Baytee tutted, "This needs more than bandages, I'll put some stitches in for you. I don't know who you showed it to!" said Baytee.

Hanuru shuffled her feet guiltily.

In a moment, Baytee had Millie sitting at a table and was drawing a needle with a silk thread through the wound. She was delicate and thorough, but offered Millie no relief for the pain.

"So..." Baytee steeled herself for the big question, "is everyone alright?"

"Malichar ap Sunnar was killed. But otherwise...ouch!...just minor injuries like this one," said Millie.

"Hmm, a noble young man, in both senses of the word. He has relatives in the city that I will send my condolences to. To be honest, I feared more deaths," said Baytee.

"As did I," said Millie. "...Baytee, there is a reason we are back early. We have a big favour to ask."

Baytee finished the stitching and let Millie's arm rest on the table. She regarded Millie with habitual cynicism; she was used to young people getting themselves in trouble and turning to her to get them out.

"Oh?" Baytee questioned.

"We need a boat, big enough for say, eight people? And we need it urgently," said Millie.

"A boat? Of all the things! What do you want a boat for? And what in Haven makes you think I have one!" exclaimed Baytee.

"I know *you* don't have one, but I thought with your connections and the respect you command you might be able to find one for us. Even the Emperor speaks fondly of you." Millie clutched Baytee's hand, "I know how big a favour this is and I know I have done nothing to earn your respect, but please know this is extremely important. I cannot tell you why we need it, but I would not be asking if it were not grave."

Baytee looked over Millie's face then turned her intense scrutiny to Hanuru, making her feel hot and uncomfortable. Finally, she pronounced judgement.

"I have always regarded you two as essentially honest. Therefore, I believe you when you say this is a potentially grave matter. And what a strange world it would be if one person did not give without first expecting some kind of payment. I know an old fisherman with a boat who might be willing to gift it to me. You shall have your boat, if it is within my power."

"Oh thank you so much Baytee! Truly it will take me a century or more to pay you back for this kindness," said Millie.

"Of all my current residents, I have the most hope for you two. Do not betray my trust. I will not be happy if I hear this is somehow related to...*mischief*," warned Baytee.

It was no idle warning; she was making sure that they knew this was the kind of reputation-wrecking affair that made Zanthred's gaffs look like chaff in the wind.

"Don't worry, you will not hear of it," assured Millie.

Baytee saw they were tired and let them sleep in their beds during the hot midday whilst she wrapped herself in cool linen and went out to find the fisherman. She woke them at dusk with plates of fresh grilled fish, stale bread soaked in olive oil, some weak mead and the news that a ten-person boat with oars and nets was waiting for them under the bridge to Serra. They ate quickly and thanked Baytee profusely. Before they left for the boat, Baytee just had one final thing to whisper to Millie, but Hanuru did not hear it. They both glanced at Hanuru and then Millie whispered something back. Hanuru was too nervous to ask them what it was about.

When they found the boat Millie jumped right in and picked up an oar. It rocked unsteadily beneath her feet, but she did not even flinch.

"Millie....I...I," stammered Hanuru.

"What is it Hanuru?"

"I can't swim. I'm afraid!" Hanuru squeaked.

"You can't swim! Killwa was right, are you even a cherno?" jibed Millie.

"I don't like moving water." Hanuru's eyes began to moisten. She did not like being a burden.

"It's alright, it's alright!" soothed Millie. "It doesn't matter. I promise this thing isn't going to capsize. You won't even have to get wet."

Hanuru nodded gingerly and Millie held her hands out. Hanuru took them and tentatively put one foot into the rocking boat. It was reasonably firm, but when she put her second foot in the weight made the boat lurch violently. She gave a little squeal and Millie pushed her to her knees so she was not in any danger of losing her footing.

Hanuru was okay when the boat stopped moving. Millie put an oar in her hands.

"Alright, this isn't going to be easy, but we need to get back as soon as possible. Row in time with me and we'll get there soon enough," said Millie.

They sat astride the centre of the boat and pushed off. It took them a few strokes to get in rhythm, but once they had found their pace, the river's current made it easy going.

"Millie, what did Baytee whisper to you as we were leaving?" asked Hanuru.

Millie smiled, "She said she was glad we had become

troths and that I should do all I could to get you out of your shell. I said, *why would I try and change her?*"

Hanuru felt blood rush to her cheeks at the praise. *Oh Millie, you've already done more than anyone to get me out of my comfort zone.*

When they got to the sea the rowing became tougher. It was a big boat, difficult for two small women to move. The swell of waves relentlessly pushed the prow off course. It took most of the night to row the boat back to the beach where they had hidden the escapees. They were already exhausted from two days of marching with little food, but they were near collapsing when the headland finally came into view. They beached the boat and staggered ashore.

"Killwa! Killwa, we have returned!" Millie hoarsely called into the crevice.

There was a long pause and then Killwa slowly emerged from the narrow fissure. He came towards the women, looking cautiously around for signs of a trap. When he could see none, he called to his fellow soldiers.

"It's alright! They're alone!" he shouted.

One by one, the escapees came out from hiding until all eight were assembled on the beach. Killwa bowed in front of Millie and Hanuru.

"I knew I could rely on you, yet even so I find that your return is the most beautiful sight ever to grace my eyes," he said.

"Are you all alright?" asked Millie.

"Yes, we heard horses come by at one time, but

they did not investigate. After that Looshan was brave enough to venture out and discovered a small fresh stream, so we have had enough water, though our bellies rumble," said Killwa.

"Sorry I can't help with the food. But we brought enough fresh water for at least a day. The boat has no sail, so you will have to row. I suggest that you either follow the coast west to the Emerald Horn and across the narrow channel to Jewasri, or travel by night north along the Red Coast until you can secure a sail," said Millie.

"In defeat, I do not trust our lives to anyone except Tisenin. We could easily be ransomed for favour with the new Emperor. Therefore, I do not like the idea of trying to cross the Emerald Strait in such a small vessel. We could be sucked south by the current and end up further away from Efrandi. I think we will head north. Between us we have some skill with woodcraft so it would not be ever so difficult to put a sail in a sturdy vessel like this."

"Very well, that is your choice. There is a net and tackle in the boat, so you can fish for food, but you'll have to eat it raw."

Killwa shrugged, "One must do as one must do at times like this. Could we at least take that knife of yours so we can cut it up and do not have to tear it with our mouths?"

"Of course," said Millie, holding out the small blade. "I only ask this. We have shown you great kindness, risking our lives to save you. Please do not forget that.

When you get back to Efrandi tell this story to your leaders so they may see the common cause between our factions and entreat for peace."

Killwa took the knife. "I promise to do all that you say. You have been our saviours...which is why I hope you will forgive us for what we must do next."

Before either of the two women had the time to digest Killwa's words, he had grabbed Millie's arm and twisted it round her back so the knife now rested at her throat. Hanuru began to shout, but suddenly Looshan's meaty arms were around her mouth and her waist. She could not run or scream.

What treachery is this!

"As I say, I hope you will understand," said Killwa. "I was right to trust our survival to you, Millie, but there is no telling who we shall meet as we try to return home. We need a guarantee of safe passage if we are discovered and I think two Fidelis soldiers as hostages will do nicely. Be comforted, that once we reach Efrandi I will make sure you are treated with due honour. You may wear the wrong colours, but for rescuing eight Sagacious soldiers, you will still be held as heroes by my people."

Millie's face burned with rage and fear, but her words came out level, "You should know simply by the fact I volunteered to fight, that I would rather die than see a traitor victorious."

Killwa smiled, "I realise that, but I think you will not throw away life when it does not have to be spent. And your lover may have different priorities."

Looshan squeezed Hanuru with all his might. Hanuru gave a muffled cry of pain.

"Alright! You do not have to blackmail me further! I will consent to be your prisoner," said Millie.

"Good, dear Millie, I knew I could count on you to make the rational choice." Then Killwa shouted to his men, "Get some ropes from the boat, bind these women's arms!"

Before long, Millie and Hanuru were tethered and powerless in a boat heading for Efrandi.

Chapter 13

Flotsam

Tisenin had never been in the company of men looking so forlorn. The soldiers sat on deck listless and without purpose. He wanted to enthuse them with vigour and assure them that the Sagacious League was not broken.

But it was hard to say that when all his promises lay shattered before them.

Oars crashed and the tiller creaked as they turned into another tack. The wind was against them, flowing to the east, which forced them into a slow, awkward series of manoeuvres to make it back to Efrandi. The sail luffed and flapped as the ship passed the midway point.

Around half his men had made it back to the ships, mostly without weapons or equipment. It was likely Tisenin himself would have been one of the captives if Adrin had not volunteered to switch places with him on the horse. The one good thing about the retreat had been seeing him and Dago rush into the camp at the head of a mob of pursuers just as the last galley was being loaded. Now Adrin sat with a needle and thread trying to mend the hole in his precious lizard skin cloak. Dago was busy meditating. She had some fresh parallel cuts on her upper arms and Tisenin did not think they were inflicted by any opponent. However, Tisenin would not compromise her intense privacy by prying.

"When I killed this lizard, I copied how the humans of the mountains did it," said Adrin. "You had to wait until the beast leapt and then make sure your spear was where you were when its feet left the ground... I think that's what Haddra did to me, only from the saddle."

"So the humans have some cunning then?" asked Tisenin. Although it was merely politeness. The distant clans of Cathri held no amusement for him when things were so dire.

"Cunning? I guess. But they were like most humans. Cunning, bravery and blind stupidity all valued equally. Difficult to predict, but easy to goad."

They were interrupted by an urgent shout from the ship's watch.

"Sails to the west! At least twenty!"

"Twenty?" Adrin repeated incredulously. It was a significant number. There were only a hundred galleys in the whole Efrandi fleet.

"What's the configuration?" asked Tisenin. He

whispered aside to Adrin, "If it's galleys and long ships, then Paramount Janjula is sending us some unexpected reinforcements from Hern. If it is carracks and caravels, then the Fidelis forces have managed to put a fleet to sea without us noticing."

"Junks!" said the lookout.

Tisenin and Adrin glanced at each other with incongruity. *What were Cathri junks doing all the way out here in the Inner Sea?*

"What's their heading?" asked Tisenin.

"They are heading straight for us," said the lookout.

Dago was roused from her meditation and joined them on the galley's prow. "Are they friend or foe?" she mused. "What are our options?"

"They have the wind behind them. We can either turn east and waste time in a chase that will leave us further from Efrandi and with scarcely enough water, or we can continue west and hope that they mean us no harm," said Tisenin.

"I say greet them then," said Adrin. "Cathri has deep sympathies in our favour. Those ships could be full of iron ingots and volunteers who have come to support the Sagacious cause."

"I am much inclined to agree. They must see our fleet is stronger and they cannot possibly know of our defeat, yet they show no fear," said Tisenin.

Tisenin gave orders for the fleet to maintain its course and soon the junks came into view from the deck. At first it was just their unusual trapezoid sails, ribbed like a whalebone corset. Then their huge square bodies loomed over the horizon. The junks were many times larger than a galley, bigger even than a carrack. The Cathri traders used them to transport huge cargos over the long voyage from Wettan to Serra. They had broad keelless bottoms so they could easily pass up shallower rivers and hulls strong enough to survive all but the most treacherous storm. Their only design flaw was their ponderous bulk, which made them sluggish in any conditions.

True to type, they closed with aching slowness. Tisenin told some of his men to arm, but to remain below decks, in case of scaring a potential ally. The few hundred men that had weapons were the ones he had posted as a rearguard; the ones who had managed to hold off Haddra's horse archers from the ships. Of all the men in the fleet, they were the only ones who still trusted their own skill with arms.

Tisenin had his galley moved to the front of the fleet and one of the junks made for him. They both drew in their sails and came up alongside one another. The sides of the junk were like a wall of wood and Tisenin had to crane his neck up to see the man and woman leaning down over the rail. They were silhouetted against the sky.

"To whom am I addressing myself?" Tisenin shouted up.

"Kamil ap Hexin, Archlord of Cathri," the man boomed down.

Kamil! It was too good to be true.

"My dear Kamil, I am Tisenin ap Elsiren. We have much to discuss!"

The faces withdrew over the side for a second, presumably to confer. Then they reappeared for only a moment.

"No Tisenin, I don't think we do."

The ridge of the rail was now filled with many faces, each peering over the cross of some mechanical device highlighted with fire.

No! It can't be!

"Down!" screamed Tisenin, as he threw himself behind a large coil of ropes.

The Cathri crossbows were released with a single uniform twang, sending a volley of flaming bolts into the deck of the galley. Two great chain grapnels were dropped onto the deck, catching in the woodwork and preventing their galley's escape.

"To arms! To arms!" Tisenin shouted. "Get some axes on the grapnels, cut us free!"

Men poured out of the hold with what few weapons they had. They tossed javelins up over the wall of wood without being able to see their targets. In response the junk's crew threw down large ballast stones they had hauled up from the belly of their ship.

Adrin was the first to grab an axe and attack the grapnels. He cut woodwork away with furious chops that were neither pretty nor precise, but they did the job. The grapnel he was working on fell loose and the junk's crew started to take it back on board to be cast again.

"Push off!" shouted Tisenin, determined to get away before they became trapped again.

The order was relayed to the oarsmen below him and they used their long oars like poles to push the vessels apart. However, before they could get away, two long crane arms swung out over the side of the junk. At the end of each was attached a smoking ceramic pot. The pots dropped onto the deck and cracked open, scattering smouldering charcoal in every direction. When the charcoal met the air it burst into flame.

"Get this ship moving! Get those fires out!" Tisenin desperately ordered, not sure which one was the most pressing.

The oarsmen started to pump and the sails were let down. All the soldiers who were weapon-less began hauling leather buckets of sea water up from the side of the ship and pouring them over the many fires which were erupting. It was a deadly dance, dodging thumping bolts and tumbling stones to put out fires.

Tisenin pulled several of the flaming bolts from the deck around him before realising that there was more than his one vessel at stake. The junks were formed up in a double column and his ship was about to pass down the middle of the line. He looked back over his galleys and did some quick mental calculations. There was only one simple order that would save them: *Maintain course.* He spoke to the Captain and the order was relayed to the rest of the fleet via torches.

Adrin saw the torches being erected and grabbed Tisenin. "Are you mad!" he blurted. "You want to take us straight *through* them?"

"Yes! If we turn, they catch us and chase what's left. If we keep going we pass them as quickly as possible and they can't turn into the wind like our galleys can."

The order was relayed backwards, but clearly some of the captains were thinking along the same lines as Adrin. Individual ships broke formation and tried to turn away from the looming Cathri junks. It caused chaos; they clashed oars with nearby ships and tore planks where they scraped past hull-to-hull.

But for those who followed them, Tisenin's orders had an elegance. The junks were so large and slow to handle that they did not dare deviate from their battle formation to attack a ship in their midst; if they had, the same kind of clashes that were going on in the Sagacious fleet would have been inevitable, only scaled up. It did not stop their burning crossbow bolts or hurled stones though, which peppered Tisenin's crew as they passed each vessel. Passing between them was like trying to sail between twenty erupting volcanoes.

Tisenin was aware of something dark moving in him. His icy mind tapped into something long repressed. Callous, bitter hatred. Wrecked pride. Stolen glory. He was so angry at Kamil and the Cathri sailors that he was already thinking forward to the chance he would get to inflict his vengeance. Far from confusing his thoughts, he found it put new vitality into his limbs. He hurled orders at dithering sailors, pressed wounded soldiers to continue the fight and bravely led by example in the thick of the chaos. He knew he would have been shot down many times over if his men had not desperately hurled javelins to protect him in his moment of bravado; but that was the power of inspiration.

With some hard panicked rowing, Tisenin's galley was almost out of the junk formation. But there was one junk at the rear that had no worries about glancing into friendly ships around it if it deviated course. It angled directly for Tisenin's galley and a collision looked inevitable; a collision which would probably crush Tisenin's ship and not even slow the junk. He ordered a hard turn and simply hoped.

Dago had other ideas though. She leapt onto the prow of the galley and pressed her palms together in an intense mana welling stance. A green ball of energy slowly grew between her hands and whined at a pitch only just audible. Tisenin stared open-mouthed; he had never seen a kind of magic like it. He could see the mana flowing through her and mixing in an altogether new way. When the ball was the size of a grapefruit, she released it in a streak towards the closing junk.

The ball exploded with a phenomenal boom, louder than any crash of thunder, and the whole crew of the galley covered their ears and eyes. When they looked up they saw the huge main mast of the junk falling across its deck and a large chunk of the hull torn open. Without its main sail, the junk was just moving on inertia and it looked like their galley could sneak past. The soldiers on the junk gave them no problem as the galley cruised by; they were in shock at having their floating fortress wrecked in a single blow.

"What was that?" exclaimed Tisenin.

Dago slumped to the floor with a huge smile of post-orgasmic satisfaction on her face. Magic could set every nerve afire like nothing else. But she held her hands up shaking; the skin of her palms was charred and blistered.

"A spell I have been working on. Never had the chance to test it for real," she confessed. "I call it my *ultima*."

Adrin gently scooped her up from the floor. Dago opened her mouth to object at being manhandled, but Adrin cut her off. "Ah, quiet now! That's twice you've saved my life. No protesting until I have you bandaged up."

The sternness drained from Dago's face. "Alright, but take me below so the crew cannot watch me wince."

Adrin complied and deftly carried her down the ladder to the ship's kitchen, shutting the door behind them. They were down there a little too long for just a few bandages and not all the moans seemed to come from Dago, but however they chose to make up their recent differences, and however bad the timing, Tisenin thought it was their own business.

It was as valid a response to the disaster as any Tisenin could think of.

He looked back at his ships. Most of the vessels which had followed him through the junks were now safe, although one or two had been engulfed in flame. But the captains who had tried to turn around were at the mercy of the Cathri fleet. Kamil had picked them off as they slowed to turn and ensnared them with the iron grapples. Flames jumped from one galley to another, fanned over the fleet by the strong breeze. It looked like over half the fleet had been caught in the carnage.

"I fear, I may have failed," said Tisenin.

* * * * * * *

Mordhai did not know where he was. He was aware that until a moment ago he had been asleep and that the room he awoke in was dark and smelt of salt and rotting seaweed. Quickly he determined that the 'room' was in fact a cave with dark gnarled sides where waves had eroded a cleft leaving knots of harder rock standing proud. But there were signs of habitation; the smoking embers of a fire, a pile of shells and fish bone, a heap of rope strands that must have been gathered as flotsam from the beach, and a straw mat, where he now lay.

"Ah, you're up," said a man hovering by the fire. "*Again.*"

"*Again?*" questioned Mordhai.

"You've been drifting in and out of consciousness for a day now, ever since I found you on the beach. But you managed to ask a question, so perhaps this time you will stay awake."

The battle returned to Mordhai's memory. After they rammed the fire ship, he had jumped into the water, where he had tried to grab a loose timber to float on, but it had been rolled by a wave and struck him in the head. He had no idea how he had managed to stay afloat long enough to be washed ashore.

The man dropped a pile of worn grey driftwood next to the fire.

"Forgive me, I must tend to the fire. It is easier to keep it going than get it re-lit. This close to Serra there is plenty of shipping waste that washes my way on a high tide, but it is a devil to dry."

"*How did the battle go?*" Mordhai asked urgently.

"Battle?" the man sounded genuinely perplexed and concerned.

"Tisenin's army? Did we stop it?" asked Mordhai.

The man abandoned his attempt to rekindle the fire and came and sat by Mordhai.

"I had no idea there was a battle. I have not spoken to anyone since….since Tisenin's last atrocity."

Now he was close, Mordhai looked carefully at his nurse; his clothes were ragged and dirty, his hands covered in scrapes and his face was deeply grooved by worry lines.

"I know you!" said Mordhai, astonished. "You were at the Magnolia Court!"

"Yes, you know me," said Hesiad the bodyguard. "And I know you, Mordhai, famed meteomancer."

"You have been living as a hermit ever since that day?" asked Mordhai.

"You are the first person I have talked to in...what?...three months? I wandered the beach until I came to a point where I could see no villages and then I found this cave."

"But you have to come back! The Emperor Duarma has made it known he wishes to apologise to you in person. He does not blame you for what happened to Kirrie."

"But he should," said Hesiad. "I failed."

Mordhai saw the deep melancholy in Hesiad's eyes and knew from eight-hundred years of experience that artful words would not shift the burden he was feeling. It went beyond any single incident.

"The Shadow Guard would have you back as well," said Mordhai. "They are fighting Tisenin."

That got Hesiad's attention. He looked pensive, gripped by a moment of hope; then he shook his head.

"No, I have been a Shadow Warrior. The last thing I want is to endlessly repeat my life... Has Tisenin really raised an army?"

"Yes, they say twenty-thousand strong, and we as many. It will be a catastrophe," said Mordhai.

"That Tisenin does not deserve to live!" growled Hesiad.

There was silence between them until Mordhai tried to move to his feet and the motion made him go dizzy and vomit up something yellow.

"Easy now!" commanded Hesiad. "You should rest some more. I will make a stretcher and take you to the nearest village."

Mordhai did as he was told and lay down watching Hesiad cut some poles to length and make a frame using nothing but a knife and the discarded ships' tackle.

"How have you managed to survive out here by yourself?" asked Mordhai.

Hesiad shrugged as if it were no great problem. "There are plenty of shellfish and seaweeds to gather. When it is calm I spear fish in the shallows, or take birds if I can surprise them. The leftovers I use to bait a shark line. My favourite is the eggs from the cliff face, but I need to climb high for them and the gulls can be vicious."

"That sounds lonely," said Mordhai.

Hesiad looked absently into the distant horizon. "When I was young, not yet in my hundredth year, I went diving for pearls in the Peril Isles. I swam away from my friends on their boat and I was suddenly gripped by cramp. I was too far away to shout to them, let alone swim back. But I saw some rocks nearby and thought if I could rest there, I could regain my strength and swim back. So I paddled my way over and planted my feet and hands on the closest rock. Only, the rocks were like razor blades. My hands and feet were sliced open and I shrieked in surprise. I tried to push away, but the waves were big and they forced me right back onto the rocks, smashing my chest against it. Every bit of me that touched it was cut. I fought the waves with all my might, pushing myself to arms length every time they receded, but I was losing the battle. No person is stronger than the sea and every wave thumped me back into the rock and shredded me more. I could see my blood float away. I held on like that for a few minutes, then despairing, I gave up and hugged myself against the rock with what little energy I had left. My chest pressed tight, wound to razorblade. But you know what I found? The waves rolled right over me. No more battering. There were no new cuts and slowly the pain ebbed out of me. Clutched like that, I regained my energy and was able to swim back to my friends. You know what all that taught me?"

"What?" asked Mordhai.

"Sometimes you have to embrace the source of your pain to make it disappear."

Mordhai took his time digesting this piece of philosophy. It filled him with sorrow for the plight of this man he barely knew.

"When I am recovered, may I come and see you?" asked Mordhai.

"No. By the time you are recovered it will be the Hurricane Season and I will have moved on. This cave will be flooded," said Hesiad. "I would appreciate it if you did not mention you met me here. I am not yet ready to be part of society again."

"Of course, my friend. Do you have any idea what you will do when the Hurricane Season comes?"

Hesiad again looked out of the cave, where foam hissed on the beach and across the western sea where gulls flew without care.

"Yes," Hesiad said, "I have some idea."

Chapter 14

The Battle for Adlan

There had been little to do on Adlan for the past few days. Normally Akai would have spent the landward time in the local cafes, striking up debates with old intellectuals and telling stories to gossip hungry socialites. But not here. The locals' eyes met his with scorn, or worse still, did not meet his at all. *Ostracization*; the worst punishment of the cherno, reserved for hooligans, oath-breakers, braggarts, sluggards and misers.

Akai was perturbed by the strong reaction, both of the residents to him and him to their scorn. He had known the League's actions would be controversial, but he also knew he had nursed a naive fantasy that they would be hailed as liberators and heroes. It was painful to have that taken away.

So instead of playing games in the parlours, Akai

had found a discarded piece of whalebone in the harbour and, using his little scrimshawing knife, began to carve it like one of the simurgh on the temple walls. He did this whilst 'guarding' Feydrin, although she showed no sign of attempting to escape or organising resistance.

On the twelfth day, Quinias called Akai outside the temple to the cliff overlooking the harbour. Akai hastily pocketed his knife and little simurgh figure, and joined him. They were expecting word from Serra. From the cliff top looking out to sea they could see a carrack approaching them. It was still in the distance, but unmistakably bore the colours of the Emperor Kirrie, presumably now adopted by her husband.

"We should be getting word from Tisenin, not Duarma," said Quinias. "I can only conclude something has gone wrong."

"We lost?" asked Akai.

"Maybe." Quinias stood on the very edges of the cliff and looked down. "There is a cove below with a shingle beach. It should be invisible from the harbour. To be safe, I want to quickly move the galley to it. If they overwhelm us in the town, we can retreat here and scale the cliff to make our escape. There are ropes aplenty on the ship and a narrow path they must tread to reach us," said Quinias.

"Shall I go now?"

"No Akai, I will tell the sailors in the harbour to go myself. There are people I must talk with in the town, final orders to be given. Take the sailors here and do what you can to build some kind of defence across the path," Quinias ordered.

Akai nodded, but he had no idea what kind of defence Quinias envisioned. As soon as he was gone, he turned to his sailors garrisoned on the hill and asked,

"Any ideas?"

They had hatchets, but the hill had no trees. The only abundant resource present was a parched hillside of stunted thyme shrubs. After some debate, the only thing Akai could think of was something very sacrilegious.

It did not take them long to build. They carried the marble statues from the tomb of Elsiren and stacked them together at the narrowest point of the path, leaving a small gap for Quinias and his men which could easily be filled when he was passed. At one point Akai found himself manhandling a statue with what might be called a 'heroic' phallus and wedging it into the armpit of another petrified sentinel.

"*My apologies to the honoured ancestors*," he muttered under his breath.

Between the statues they sandwiched some thorny shrubs, thinking it might also make some good tinder in a pinch. The part of him that appreciated fine art hoped it would not come to that.

They watched the galley leave the harbour and round the island. They had one good rope with them, so Akai had them securely tie it off and get ready for a hasty retreat if necessary.

* * * * * *

Quinias knew he only had a handful of soldiers and they would scarcely be enough to hold off the crew of a carrack in a fair fight. However, he reasoned that even this few – ten spearmen and ten sailors – could put up enough of a fight to stop the carrack's crew from disembarking. And if they managed that, the carrack would either have to leave or they would burn it.

Quinias's men stood patiently on the quayside, shields and spears ready. The carrack eased in its sails as it entered the harbour and edged towards them on inertia alone. The crew must have been able to clearly see his soldiers, but that did not seem to make a difference. Lassos flew from the deck, catching poles on the quay and began drawing the ship in. There was no attempt to parley, no attempt to dislodge his soldiers from the quay with arrows. They were clearly resigned to a fight. That made Quinias very suspicious.

Quinias carefully scanned the vessel with his ether sight. *Good.* There were no powerful mages, just a cluster of low-level practitioners. But there was something odd. Small 'nodules' of energy like knotted ropes. Frozen spells, as dormant as a glacier.

Runes.

There were a hundred of them. Quinias had never seen so many clustered together. The last time he had seen one was on an ancient sword from before the exodus that a member of the Shadow Guard had shown him.

Shadow Guard.

The name tumbled into his mind like a slow moving avalanche. Inevitable and tragic.

"Men, run quickly and without cease!" Quinias shouted. "Fast now, to the temple!"

* * * * * * *

Zanthred looked around at the Shadow Guard warriors. They were all mature men who had spent centuries perfecting the physical and mental arts of combat. Their bodies were bulging with lean muscle and popping veins. Zanthred was intimidated by their intense physicality, which went beyond mere athleticism. He was also intimidated by their intense personalities; they had none of the usual cherno humour, only stillness, quiet and profound focus. Zanthred's jokes had been left hanging amid a dour silence several times now and he was struggling to find a way to connect. He needed Millie's help with these people.

Millie. She and Hanuru had disappeared from the camp without saying goodbye and he knew there was no reason for it except that he had angered her. He had thought they would be able to smooth out the cross words before leaving with Gargrace, but apparently not.

The carrack rocked as it gently nudged into the quay. The small force of Sagacious soldiers were already running away. But they kept their weapons. They were ready to fight, just not here. Zanthred gripped his bow tightly, waiting for the order to give battle.

"Sensible men, it seems," said Gargrace. "Alright then, let's take back this island, but be careful of ambushes. Don't get split up."

Even before Zanthred could nock an arrow, the Shadow Guard warriors were leaping over the side of the vessel and chasing after the Sagacious soldiers. Zanthred only dared follow when the ramp was lowered.

The Sagacious warriors had a good head start, but when they came to a narrow path leading up the side of the cliff, they bunched up. Those at the back, the heaviest armed ones with spears and shields, were forced to turn around and defend themselves from the Shadow Guard warriors. They braced their shields, raised their spears and...

...And they did not even get a chance to attack back. The Shadow Guard warriors swung their two-handed leaf blades with such force and speed that they cleaved the spear shafts and shields in half before the spearmen could react. The enchanted swords treated wicker, flesh and bone like paper. In bloody moments they had hacked the spearmen to death.

But they did not pursue the remaining Sagacious soldiers up the hill. They could see it was a precipitous path and Gargrace's warning about ambushes still rang loud in their ears. They waited for their hobbling general to catch up with them.

* * * * * * *

Akai heard a few sharp blood-chilling screams then nothing. Quinias came running up the slope and paused momentarily to inspect Akai's handiwork with the statue barricade.

"It's unique Akai, I'll give you that," panted Quinias.

"Best I could do I'm afraid," said Akai.

Quinias put a hand on the statues either side of him and squeezed himself through the gap they had left. Akai was surprised to see Quinias use his left hand, open and tightly gripping a marble limb: It was not palsied at all. Rather, the two smallest fingers were missing below the second knuckle.

He has gone to quite some length to hide that mutilation. He must be terribly ashamed of his imperfection. But Akai did not have time to think of it further.

"Your barricade will serve, Akai. Close it up once the sailors are through, the enemy will be upon us any moment." The sailors filtered through the narrow gap one-by-one in Quinias's wake. "I must be the first down the ropes. I hate to insist on this, I know I am in command and should go last, but there are matters of significance that I *must* bring back to Tisenin…"

"-I understand," cut in Akai. "I will go last in your stead."

Quinias squeezed Akai's shoulder, "Thank you." He began to run for the cliff top.

"What about your spearmen?" asked Akai.

Quinias spun on his heels whilst still running. "All dead, don't wait for them."

Akai went ashen for a moment. But only a moment. He knew that was going to be one of the injuries he would have to store at the back of his mind and deal with at a time of leisure. Things were too pressing now.

As soon as the last sailor was through, they piled up a few of the remaining statues in the narrow gap and set light to the spiny shrubs they had woven in between. The shrubs began to smoulder and crackle, producing more smoke than heat. But it was the best they could do.

Akai and his building crew went back to the temple at the top of the hill. The sailors that had escaped the harbour were tying off extra ropes and beginning their climb down the cliff face. It would take a few minutes for all of them to filter away to safety. Quinias was already gone.

Good, though Akai, *if I have done nothing else, I have ensured the safety of my master.*

"Go smoothly now," Akai told his men. "Don't risk a fall on the way down." It was lucky they were all nimble and young.

As Akai patiently waited his turn, he looked around the landscape. There was more smoke than he expected coming from the barricade. Then there were flickers of flame on the plateau. He realised his fiery barricade has started a small bushfire. Small bushfires did not stay small long; soon it would engulf the whole hillside. It did not matter to Akai – shortly he would be away down the cliff face – but the priest Feydrin was still in her temple and would soon be trapped.

Akai did not think his men needed him standing

around above them, and it would only take a moment to warn the priest, so he jogged over to the temple doors and began weaving his way through the dull interior to find Feydrin. She was sitting meditating in a dark corner, that ineffable thread of mana reaching out into the part of void occupied by Solrax.

"My teacher Feydrin," Akai whispered in reverence.

Feydrin's eyes flickered and she slowly began coming round, stiffening her joints, as if recovering from a swoon.

"Akai? What is it?" she muttered half dreamily.

"The hillside is on fire and the temple will soon be amidst flames. We are escaping down ropes to the shore below. You should come. I can lower you if you are unable to climb."

"Silly boy," she slurred. "The hillside often has wildfires and not once in the thousands of years the temple has been here has it hurt an occupant or cracked a stone. We have vaults that protect us from the smoke."

Akai did not like being called a 'boy' by someone barely a older than himself and especially did not like being called 'silly,' but he could not argue with her. Wildfires were common in the arid Hot Season of the Hublands when every piece of vegetation was tinder. He should have guessed the temple had been through a few.

"I am sorry for intruding," said Akai.

"That is alright, I thank you for your concern. But

you should go now back to your comrades. They will worry for us both if you become stuck in the temple," said Feydrin.

Akai bowed and hurried back to the entrance.

He was just about to leave when he heard a noise behind him like footsteps. He span around, thinking the priest had changed her mind, but did not even make it half way before he felt a hard blow in the back of his head and his world went black.

When Akai opened his eyes, he was on the floor and the young devotee who had hurled stones at them was standing over him. The youth's thin lips were in a snarl again. In his hand was a bloody brass incense burner. It must have been mere milliseconds that Akai was unconscious for.

"You deserve to die for trying to destroy the Ban. I'm just sorry I only got one of you."

Akai tried to speak, but the crushing pain in the back of his head began to make itself known in strobing waves that distorted his words to nothing more than drool and spittle. A watery image of the youth advanced to deliver the final blow.

Akai autonomously felt the short scrimshawing knife in his hand and thrust it up. Up and up again. He just wanted to live. He wanted to live more than he wanted to be good.

* * * * * * *

Zanthred and the Shadow Guard warriors waited patiently for Gargrace to reach them and give them some new orders. But not only did he take a long while to hobble over, he stopped to talk to some of the townspeople along the way. Most of them seemed ecstatic to meet their liberator, but all the same they kept away from the scene of slaughter at the bottom of the hill. Gargrace was grinning when he finally arrived.

"Good work," said Gargrace. "The people tell me that there are no more soldiers on the island, just a few sailors who are guarding Feydrin ap Lanlar at the temple. Their ship has already left, so my guess is they are going to meet up at another portage and escape the island. I'm inclined to let them. But the problem is they might take Feydrin with them or try and kill her first, so we need to get up that hill and make sure she is safe. Let's go single file, some archers at the front and a big gap between each man. That'll mean that even if they do have something nasty prepared for us, they can only kill a few at a time."

Archers at the front.

In the shuffle Zanthred found himself in pole position.

Drat!

Zanthred wanted to be a true soldier, but he did not yet have the heroic reserves of courage that he hoped for. Still, in the face of shame he resolved to hide his unease as best he could. They advanced up the slim rocky path cautiously. Zanthred had an arrow nocked, but not pulled tight.

Before they got far they saw smoke rising ahead of them and soon found the way blocked by a smouldering heap of stonework. They were statues, but in the soot and smoke looked like a tangled heap of charred bodies. The slopes to either side were made of crumbly dry mud with plant roots poking through. One side was too steep to climb and the other offered a plunge down to the sharp sea-carved rocks below. However, Zanthred tested the temperature of the statues and found the uppermost surfaces still to be cool. He tore the hem off his robe and wrapped it around his hands and ankles, then poured some water on.

"Give me a boost," he said to the man behind him. "I think we can climb over without getting hurt if we are quick about it."

The archer behind cupped his hands to give Zanthred a foothold and raised him up. Zanthred put a foot on the head of a statue and nimbly danced across the barricade, one head or raised arm at a time. He knew one misstep would plunge him between the statues and trap him in the heat. And it was *hot*. The rising smoke was threatening to scorch his skin and he knew he could not stop for even a second. He had almost made it across when one of the heaped statues lurched to the side under his weight.

Zanthred leapt to solid earth before he lost purchase and rolled along the ground. But the statue fell on the smouldering fuel beneath it and raked up flames. Something spluttered and then exploded. There was a shower of bright liquid followed by more popping sounds from within the barricade. The flammable resins trapped in the branches were beginning to explode and ignite. Flames rose high over the top of the statues.

Zanthred could no longer see his comrades on the other side of the barricade. They would have no chance of crossing now. He was on his own.

Zanthred thought about staying and waiting for the flames to die down, but the idea that Feydrin could be killed whilst he was waiting haunted his sense of shame. He hesitantly climbed what remained of the hill, arrow nocked.

He soon regretted the decision. The flames had spread from the barricade and seemed to be taking hold everywhere around him. The smoke obscured his vision and made it hard to breathe. There was no sign of any Sagacious sailors, but there was a huge silent building he took to be the temple right in front of him. He had to get out of the smoke and he deemed its immense black walls the most likely place to offer refuge.

Zanthred stumbled in the temple's mighty doors and found instant relief in the cool clean air. Then he looked up and saw a scene of bloody murder.

A man with a small knife in his hand crouched over the body of a youth. The youth was young indeed, not even a hundred years old. There were many ragged holes in his chest and abdomen through which blood had poured and spread wide across the smooth stone floor.

Zanthred pulled the bow taught.

"Did you do this?" he asked, although there was no

doubt in his mind he was looking at the murderer of a devotee of Solrax.

The Sagacious man looked up slowly and without fear. His eye glistened with the moisture of tears. He wiped at them with a clean part of his sleeve, but they were instantly replaced.

"Yes, I killed him," he said in a remarkably calm voice. "I used to think the story of this war was going to be about emperors and lords. The clash of good and evil armies..." He paused, as if trying to find the right words, "But it isn't. It's a story about me and you and how we're going to live with the things we've done."

Zanthred did not understand a word of what he was saying. "Put the knife down," he commanded, aware his arm was becoming tired holding the bowstring taught.

"My name is Akai. If you kill me, will you weep for me?" the man asked.

Zanthred looked inside himself and balanced the deep sense of morality he had been brought up with against what he found now. He remembered the anger at Kirrie's death. He remembered the fear of the battlefield. He remembered that horrible moment when he had to turn his back on Millie. He had nothing but a kernel of hatred for the man in front of him. A murderer, following a murder with selfish aims. He deserved death.

"No, I won't," said Zanthred.

The Akai's right hand tightened its grip on the knife. "Then I'm sorry, I can't let you kill me."

With speed Zanthred could not follow, Akai's left hand came round and threw a brass incense burner at him. It knocked into the bow just as Zanthred was releasing and sent the arrow skittering into the stonework. Akai charged and all Zanthred could do to fend him off was to hold the bow out like some kind of staff. The two of them wrestled around the stick. Zanthred knew he probably had the greater strength, but he could not pin Akai down. Suddenly, Akai's fist came up with the knife and uppercutted Zanthred's jaw.

Zanthred's head was knocked back and he stumbled to his knees. He expected to find his jaw split in two by the blade, but Akai only seemed to have hit him with the hilt. Before he could get up, Akai punched him in the temple and laid him flat on the ground.

Akai ran for the door and out into the smoke. Zanthred crawled after him, clutching vainly for his wooden club. But by the time he was at his feet and had a weapon in hand, Akai had disappeared into the bushfire.

Zanthred rubbed the side of his head and wondered why he was still alive. It would have been so easy for Akai to finish him off.

"I heard a noise and..."

Zanthred turned around at the sound of a woman's voice. She was dressed like a devotee and even Zanthred with his lead-dull senses could tell her magic potential was immense. Her gaze was fixed on the dead and bloody boy in the middle of the room.

"*Who?*" she asked. But her voice held so much natural authority that it sounded like a command.

"He called himself Akai," said Zanthred. "A Sagacious sailor, I think."

The woman's face contorted into a scowl and for a moment, a fantastic, terrible power welled up inside her and made Zanthred tremble. But within the space of two breaths she relaxed and the rage was forgotten.

"I hope Akai remembered what I told him," she said.

But Zanthred did not understand.

"Are you the priest Feydrin ap Lanlar?" asked Zanthred.

"Yes," she replied.

"I am Zanthred of Icknel. I came here to rescue you."

She raised an eyebrow, noting the injuries to his face, his torn clothing and the conspicuous absence of her 'captor.'

"Thank you for your diligence," she said diplomatically.

Chapter 15

Negotiations

You could tell a lot from a cherno lord by the way they dressed, that was a given. But what Archlord Kamil was trying to say, Duarma had no idea, other than perhaps many of Kamil's courtiers had severe cataracts and needed help finding him. He wore bright red silk robes, brocaded with deep maroon. At his wrist he wore gold armlets studded with red rubies, which stopped the loose sleeves from encumbering his hands. This would have been enough to show he was powerful man with patronage of the Smiths' Guild. But then he had gold earrings wrapped with silver wire, a gold gorget studded with jade, turquoise, amethyst and yellow tigers-eye, and a belt buckle with alloys of yellow, white and red gold. Duarma was glad they were conducting the meeting in the shade of the magnolia trees. Direct sunlight might have blinded him.

"Archlord Kamil ap Hexin, and young Hilsi," said

Duarma. "Words cannot express how glad I am to see you."

Hilsi gave a long low bow, but Kamil only bent momentarily and stiffly. He looked long and uncomfortably at Haddra, then Jandor and finally rested his gaze on Duarma, as if assessing a blade for faults.

"So they made you Emperor after your wife, Duarma?" said Kamil, with a raised eyebrow. "It has a logic." He was informal, almost disrespectful.

Duarma ignored the tone. "Indeed. An unlooked for, but necessary burden. Please, tell us how you came to be here."

Kamil put a bejewelled arm around Hilsi's shoulders, "When my niece here saw what Tisenin did, she knew right away there would be war. And she knew my mind as well as I do. I could not sit in Cathri and let a traitorous wretch like Tisenin make a bid for the throne. So she got straight onto her ship and sailed for Cathri, where I mustered what troops I could from our standing garrison and returned as fast as the wind would let me. It was happy coincidence that we met Tisenin's fleet at sea. I'd say we managed to burn about half of it before they escaped. Although, alas, not the traitor himself."

Hilsi developed a big childish grin at the praise her favourite uncle gave her. It was hard for Duarma to believe that this young girl had exercised more foresight than him and all his advisors.

"My dear Hilsi, I must confess, when you disappeared so suddenly we thought you had fled from fright. We have done you a grave disservice in your absence. I am honoured to have you back in my court."

Kamil frowned and crinkled his nose. "You think I would send such a timid creature to be my ambassador? Hilsi has my full confidence in all matters and it would serve you better to regard that rather than regard her age."

"I can see that now, Kamil," said Duarma.

"One should perhaps introduce exceptional people one's self," said Haddra.

Kamil and Haddra shared scowls. Kamil had a reputation for being just as cholic as Haddra. They were both in their senior years and governed large, distant colonies, which were always under threat of war.

"Personally I find it *quaint*, that you have enough time to leave your realm and make the voyage to Serra so often. I am always detained by pressing duties at home," said Kamil. "Jandor, is it not so with your mother?"

"I will not be drawn into your arguments, my Lords. We are all here now and that is the only thing that should concern us," said Jandor.

Haddra reluctantly sucked down his venom. "You speak with your mother's sense, Jandor. Kamil, I am of course grateful that you have come personally when the need is greatest. And I am fond of any man who has had a go at killing Tisenin. Let us speak of war before politics."

"I have brought nineteen ships, each with a crew of three-hundred-fifty sailors. Among them are a thousand veterans and twenty engineers wise in war craft."

"Unfortunately the extra troops will avail us little at the moment. We have scant food to supply all our forces. Would you object to the majority being sent north to Kelmor to weather the Hurricane Season?"

"Not at all, although I am disappointed not to be allowed a second crack at Tisenin," said Kamil. "Nevertheless, my engineers can use the time to construct machines of war. They can make mangonels that will set a galley alight at a hundred paces and trebuchets that can bring down a wall at two hundred."

"It would be more useful to us if they spent their time helping to repair the road and widen the bridges between here and Kelmor," said Duarma. "That will allow us the gather supplies during the Storm Season."

Kamil frowned, "You want to waste my engineers building roads?"

"Are they not skilled at it?" questioned Haddra.

"Of course they are!" snapped Kamil. "But I'd sooner send them home than see their true talents insulted." He fixed Duarma with a glare, daring him to defy the resolution.

Duarma looked away, unable to sustain the gaze. Jandor and Haddra fidgeted uncomfortably at this sign of feebleness in their Emperor. Duarma felt the sudden, pressing weight of his premiership. He had no idea how to deal with open defiance like this. During night hunts, Duarma had seen skilled mages using bursts of bright light to transfix their prey, and that was how Duarma felt now; transfixed by something he did not understand and could not see past.

How would Kirrie deal with this? He did not know — it had never happened to her.

"Very well, build your war machines," conceded Duarma.

Kamil smiled triumphantly, "As you say, my Emperor."

"But perhaps when the hurricanes are done, you might spare a few to repair the bridges? After all, you can scarcely build a trebuchet with no wood coming into town," suggested Jandor.

"Humph, very well. That seems reasonable," agreed Kamil.

"In the meantime, your ships will be useful in helping us blockade Efrandi during the remaining sailing months. We aim to prepare an army and supplies for an attack on Efrandi at the first opportunity next year," said Haddra.

"A strategy I can agree with," asserted Kamil. "In that regard my cargo might help. I have brought every spare ingot of iron and bronze in Wettan. It should be enough to keep your smiths working into the night for a few months."

That roused Duarma from his melancholic slump. "Kamil, that is good news indeed. You have just given us a strut to raise the canopy of victory."

Kamil slapped his hands together and licked his lips.

"Excellent! I have also brought some bird nests for

a feast tonight. I trust you found the last lot to your liking?"

"Uh-I apologise Archlord Kamil, I did not sample your gift. It was received just after Kirrie died and I was in no mood to appreciate it."

"Ah! Then I have the pleasure of being in your company as you try it for the first time!" said Kamil. "There is but a single place where they may be harvested. A tiny island lying between Quri and Cathri. It is riddled with limestone caves and the only things that live there are birds and bats. My stewards must climb a hundred metres to the roof of the caves to cut down the nests. But the taste is definitely worth it. I hope my fellow lords will be joining us as well?"

"I can delay my return to Delfuri by one more night," said Haddra.

"Unfortunately, I must decline," said Jandor. "I think we have the best chance of turning Tisenin to surrender when defeat is fresh in his mind. I will leave this evening and sail through the night."

"Oh? You expect him to give himself up?" questioned Kamil.

"Perhaps," said Jandor. "Perhaps."

* * * * * * *

When the conference was over Kamil and Hilsi retired to some private quarters and Kamil began to remove the weighty gold jewellery that festooned his person. Off came the gold gorget to reveal an old ingrained sweat stain, and off came the belt, to reveal a burn hole where an ember had singed the beautiful crimson fabric of his robe.

"Ah, it's good to have that lot off!" exclaimed Kamil.

"You looked like a clown today," tutted Hilsi. "You should not have worn your best clothes in the battle with Tisenin. Or at least you could have explained your appearance, the Emperor would have understood. Now they just think you are a vain hoarder."

"I'd rather they think that than insult the man who made my robe with what I have done to it. At the time, I merely thought one should dress with respect for your enemies. I could not face Tisenin in a leather apron and blacksmith's gloves."

"Perhaps you should have some armour made?" suggested Hilsi.

"A few more bits of jewellery and I will have all the armour I need."

Kamil sat on a cushion and begged Hilsi to help him pull off his boots. She knelt beside him and started to undo the buckles.

"So what do you make of Haddra?" asked Hilsi.

"I like him," said Kamil. "He speaks his mind. Honest. Practical. I think he will like me as well, in time. There will be no trouble from him."

Hilsi raised a questioning eyebrow. She had obviously not seen quite the same exchange of words. But she was willing to accept that what passed between old lords was not necessarily restricted to the words spoken aloud.

"And Duarma?" she asked, wrenching one boot away.

Kamil gasped in relief at having cool air wash over his suffocated foot.

"Duarma is different. He is still a slave to the memory of his wife. And weak, leaning on those around him. He knows he has no real authority to rule. That lies in the bloodline of Elsiren. We must goad him as necessary, if the situation warrants it. I do not trust his judgment."

Kamil gasped again as Hilsi removed the second boot. Without being bidden, she filled a basin of water and began to wash her uncle's feet with a soft cloth.

"The real man to watch is Jandor. He seems very wise and able-tongued. I believe he could sway Duarma to any course of action, given time. But whether he could do the same to Tisenin? I am not sure," said Kamil.

"If any man could do it, I am sure it is Jandor," said Hilsi. She smiled to herself as she spoke.

"Oh? Does my favourite niece have a crush?" chuckled Kamil. "The girl who has turned down every feather ever presented to her?"

Hilsi's smile vanished and she stared down into the watery basin, letting her long black hair hide her expression from her uncle's view.

"He spoke well, that is all. And you know I have sworn myself to metallurgy until I have mastered my first art," refuted Hilsi.

"Fine intentions, but wait until you hit your first

oestrus. You're no less a slave to what's between your thighs than anyone else."

Hilsi let go of her uncle's feet and dumped the cloth into the basin with an unceremonious splash. She carried the basin to a shelf on the other side of the room, still refusing to let him see her face.

"I am not the only one. They say Tisenin lives as a celibate," she said, intending to defend her lifestyle choice.

"Ha! Hardly a sound endorsement!" mocked Kamil. But then seeing that Hilsi did not appreciate the same humour, he moderated his tone. "For what it is worth, if you could charm Jandor I would approve of the match. He is handsome and wise, as are you. The age difference does not matter so much. In the scheme of things, you are both still young."

That seemed to brighten Hilsi up. She was still young enough to wear her every emotion on her face. Kamil was in no hurry to see her harden into the woman she must one day become.

"I will go to the kitchen and supervise the cooking of the soup," said Hilsi.

"Thank you, my young niece. With you there I know it will be perfect."

"It is just such a pity that the soup is so vile. It has the texture of phlegm."

"I know, I know," said Kamil shaking his head in sympathy. "I have no love for it either. But we must maintain the pretence. It was important before. Now, with the war...we need a distraction."

* * * * * * *

Jandor's caravel was towed into Efrandi's harbour by a small rowboat that helped it to weave in between the many damaged galleys moored on the quays. Jandor kept careful count of the number of vessels Tisenin still had left. It was early morning, but already the heat was building into the kind of oppressive shell that turned grasslands to desert. The sea birds – usually cacophonous – sat quietly on the forest of masts, stifled by the heat and confused by the lack of fishing expeditions.

A troop of soldiers was waiting for him. Jandor was the sole person allowed off the caravel and none of the soldiers would answer his questions, no matter how innocuous: Tisenin was keeping a tight noose on the flow of information. The guards took him up to Tisenin's mansion on the outskirts of the town. Outside was a crowd of petitioners, most of whom looked to be in mourning for loved ones. Some regarded Jandor angrily, but others were pensive or pleading. He could tell from their eyes that there was an appetite for cessation in the town. Still, they stayed silent as Jandor was conducted through them. Then one hoarse voice shrieked out from the crowd.

"Ask about my father! Ask about Kesith ap Woodrin!"

The owner was a young woman, a mite thinner than was healthy and with clothes that were once rich, but now looked unloved and tatty. A guard made to grab her, but several members of the crowd interposed themselves and made it obvious that if the guards laid a hand on her, the guards would have to lay hands on all of them. At the same time one elderly woman begged the girl to hush. The girl was swayed into silence and the guards backed down.

Kesith ap Woodrin. Jandor had met the man once at Kirrie's court. He was a cousin of Haddra, from the senior branch of the Woodrin dynasty that had stayed in the Hublands. He was a powerful and an ardent supporter of the Ban. The kind of person Tisenin would have been obliged to silence before raising an army. Jandor stored the information in a box labelled 'useful' inside his head.

Jandor was taken through the mansion's courtyard – the usual place for such meetings – and into the relative privacy of the main hall. The hall was made of white marble imported from Serra and hung lavishly with intricate tapestries and purple and black banners bearing Tisenin's coat of arms. There was a grand walnut table in the centre of the room with five people seated at it. The one at the head was Tisenin.

"Welcome Jandor. I am glad it is you they sent to ask for my head," said Tisenin. "Please, have a seat."

Jandor bowed, "Thank you, Archlord Tisenin ap Elsiren."

Jandor took a seat and scanned the other faces. They were all grim-set, but he recognized them all from previous Magnolia Courts. There was Adrin in his trademark lizard coat and Dago, two of the minor nobles of Efrandi. Dago's new look surprised him; she had tears tattooed under her eye and her hands were bound in bandages. Then there was Janjula ap Lunis, the Lord of Hern and Paramount of the Lunis clan. Jandor was not surprised to see her, given she was a known sympathiser of Tisenin's. But it was unfortunate, because her presence symbolised that the Sagacious League was not confined to a single city. She had chosen to celebrate her prematurely greying hair by braiding it into striking dichromatic plaits. At her back she had a woollen travel cloak. It struck Jandor because it was of Lansissari manufacture. The people of Hern – the ever-rainy 'grey city' – loved Lansissari cloaks because of their waterproofing. The fact she was wearing it now meant she had only just arrived before dawn and had not had a chance to change.

The big surprise was the fifth person; Roldern ap Sunnar.

Roldern was the Lord of Icknel. He had been there the day Kirrie died and had gasped with the rest of the Quri lords. But he had kept out of the following politics and had departed for Icknel at the first opportunity. He was a middle-aged man with a reputation for being an absentee lord, spending most of his time hunting and feasting, rather than ruling. However, no complaint about him had ever been laid before Kirrie, suggesting he had good stewards and a certain charisma with his subjects.

"Jandor, let me introduce Adrin ap Foras and Dago ap Keldron, commanders of the Sagacious League.

This is Paramount Janjula ap Lunis, head of the League in Hern and Roldern ap Sunnar, who comes to us from Icknel as a neutral observer."

"A neutral observer?" question Jandor.

"Yes," said Roldern. "I have come here for clarification on matters. I am yet to acknowledge Duarma as the Emperor and wish to hear the arguments from both candidates before committing myself. I hope you will understand this position?"

No, not at all, thought Jandor, *Tisenin's actions are transparent enough*. But he wanted to maintain cordiality for the negotiations and so tempered his response.

"A judicious approach."

A servant in a hooded robe appeared with a tray of food.

"Ah, good. Jandor you must be in need of refreshment after your voyage and I would not have you negotiate at a disadvantage," said Tisenin.

The servant brought over the tray and started to carefully place the food in front of Jandor. Jandor tried to catch the man's eyes to say 'thank you,' but the hood obscured them, almost as if he were deliberately avoiding contact. Then he took the tray and stood obediently behind Tisenin.

Jandor looked over the fare set on the polished flames of the walnut table.

Tisenin explained the provenance of each item. "The last cherries of the season from the Broken

Mountains. The first grapes from the Vintner's Coast. Salted sturgeon liver from the Outer Isles and some apricot sherbet with ice from the Karlsha Mountains."

It was a rare assortment. Grapes and cherries were never ripe at the same time. Sturgeon could only be found in certain northern river mouths. And ice! Ice was so difficult to transport in the hot Hublands that it could rarely be found more than a day's travel from a mountain. Janjula must have brought it with her from Hern. It would have taken a whole galley full just to get a few glasses worth.

Jandor sipped at the cool, sweet sherbet and mused on the meal. It was an assortment of luxuries from all over Jewasri. Tisenin was showing that his power reached across every corner and cove of Jewasri. And also that there was no want of supplies in Efrandi; they were still actively importing extravagances.

Then he is ready to surrender.

Jandor reasoned that Tisenin was making a show of power, subtle, but still a show. If he were really strong, he would do everything he could to make himself look on the brink of collapse. He would hide ships, send Janjula away, heap empty grain sacks at the door and beg for clemency. He was devious enough for that. Then when the troops arrived from Serra, ill-prepared and over-confident, he would ambush and crush them.

No, Tisenin was feigning strength in order to get better terms for surrender.

"Tisenin, my Lords," began Jandor. "Your army is

crushed, your fleet is broken and your philosophy has been rejected by the people of Serra. It is time to surrender yourselves to the clemency of Duarma. He has made a generous offer – all participants in the rebellion will be forgiven if they surrender their arms, accept his authority and deliver Tisenin to him for judgment."

Adrin and Dago scoffed, but Tisenin kept quiet, staring straight at Jandor. He looked like an old philosopher, considering the truth of every statement before replying.

Is the sky really blue? Can I know I exist from the ghost of my own thoughts?

Finally, Tisenin broke his meditation. "This is not 'generous.' This is asking for a return to the day of the Magnolia Court, as if hundreds of thousands of Duarma's subjects had not defied his authority. You say our army is broken, but that was just one small army. For every man that died, there is another willing to stand in his place. Young volunteers flock to the city every day and Paramount Janjula has already brought an additional ten thousand from Hern. You say our navy is broken, but these are just ships, and ships can be rebuilt. You say our philosophy has been rejected, but has it even been put to popular assent? No, a group of scared old aristocrats have used their authority to cajole the masses into following a course of action that they will not live to see the outcome of."

"And what then, would be your terms of surrender?" asked Jandor.

"You can have my life, that much I am resigned to. But it is not for Duarma. He has no legitimacy as Emperor. I'd sooner accept the rule of his horse."

"Do not presume to pour scorn on Duarma. *You* took his wife, Tisenin. Can you imagine how that feels? Kirrie had just promised him a child, he would have been a father before the next gathering."

Whilst everyone else in the room bit their lips, blinked a little longer than usual, or showed some other sign of guilt, Tisenin was as solid as ice. There was no shock or compassion in his eyes.

You knew! Thought Jandor. *Oh no...was that what all this was about? Please let it not be, because that is too horrible even for you!*

"It is not a question of personal grievance. The institution is defunct," clarified Tisenin. "A court selected by lot must elect a new council to rule in the Emperor's stead, with a free hand to manipulate the Ban if that is what the majority decides. Hereditary rights should be abolished."

"And yet you rule the Sagacious League as a tyrant?" accused Jandor.

"No, not a tyrant. We took a poll by lottery and I was elected to lead," said Tisenin. "I do not claim to be Emperor."

But you know people will follow you because of your name anyway, Tisenin ap Elsiren, thought Jandor.

"And did anyone stand against you? Tell me, where is Paramount Kesith ap Woodrin? Was he allowed to compete?" said Jandor.

Tisenin betrayed just a crack of dismay at Kesith's mention.

Adrin slammed a hand on the table, "No one stood! People were free to choose Kesith if they wanted! The truth is the people of this city love Tisenin. There was no one else we would rather have lead us out of thraldom."

"In any case, what you propose is not surrender, it is conquest by another means," said Jandor. "Can Efrandi and Hern really stand against Serra, Kelmor, Sunnel and Gerloth? And now the whole of Cathri? You cannot win against that alliance. You had one chance to seize power and it has failed. Resources and soldiers now flood to us, whereas within a day or two, your ports will be blockaded. And need I remind you that Hern lies on a narrow isthmus? A thousand soldiers could hold it and cut your two cities apart."

Janjula nervously twitched her fingers; she probably had not considered that the people of Hern might have to fight on their own soil.

"Not everyone has picked their sides," said Tisenin. He glanced conspicuously at Roldern.

Roldern shrugged, "Let me be frank then, now everyone is here. My people are inclined to reject the Ban, as am I. But we will not throw our blood in with a losing cause."

"You are right Tisenin, that not everyone has picked their side. I see people in your streets re-evaluating their decisions," said Jandor. "They are stinging with grief and thinking that perhaps they would rather be mana-blind than lose more loved ones."

Tisenin again took on the air of an ancient thinker. This time Jandor would not let Tisenin have the initiative of the discussion.

"Let us speak of compromise then," said Jandor. "We are both in a worse position than before the Magnolia Court and we both need to act upon the other's wishes. I speak now not as Duarma's ambassador, but as an observer at court. Duarma will gladly resign, he has no appetite for command. But not before you are dead Tisenin. So submit yourself to his authority and burn your remaining ships. But keep the Sagacious League as a separate, passive dominion. Once that is done, and you are dead, he will probably be willing to consider your reforms."

"You ask a lot that you cannot give your word for," said Tisenin.

"I can give my word to fight for your plan after you are gone," said Jandor.

"It is not enough. We have tried for hundreds of years to force a popular ballot on the Ban by non-violent means. Why would Duarma agree now?" said Tisenin.

"Because you have made the Empire weak," said Jandor.

That seemed to speak to something in Tisenin.

"*If* I were to agree to your plan, there would have to be certain assurances. First, we will agree not to build any fortifications if Duarma agrees that no armed force can approach closer than Adlan. There will be no blockade of Efrandi," said Tisenin.

"If you come back with me today, that is guaranteed," said Jandor.

"Secondly, the Mages' Guild would have to be bound to the decisions of the ruling council, not allowed to govern itself," said Tisenin.

"Duarma and Haddra would like nothing more, although for different reasons than you, I suspect," agreed Jandor.

"Thirdly, the captives from the battle must be returned to Efrandi without asking us to disarm first," said Tisenin.

Oh no...I did what I could, Jandor mentally lamented.

"There are no captives to return. They were executed on the battlefield," said Jandor.

"*Executed...*" repeated Tisenin incredulously. "How many?"

"Six-thousand," admitted Jandor.

Adrin and Dago kicked their chairs away and began pacing the room. There was violence in their movements, barely restrained. Janjula and Roldern just sat aghast. The hooded servant behind Tisenin leaned forwards and whispered something in his ear. For a millisecond, Jandor thought he saw a tiny smile play around Tisenin's lips.

"You must understand," implored Jandor. "We had no way of keeping them. We were already starving with the refugees and Duarma gave them a chance to speak in their defence before..."

"—Duarma has proven his worth!" cut in Tisenin. "I will not negotiate with that butcher!"

"You are no better Tisenin, you killed the Emperor Kirrie in cold blood! And you were the first to take up arms. One of your men even killed a devotee of Solrax on Adlan."

"Six-thousand lives Jandor! How can you compare!" blurted Dago. She was incandescent with rage. They could all see her mana spinning in wild circles – the mage's equivalent of grinding her knuckles into the table.

"Jandor, we have nothing more to discuss, you should return to your ship," said Tisenin.

Jandor rose to leave, knowing he had failed utterly in his task. But he had to make one last attempt. "Tisenin, your port will be blockaded and a mighty army will come for you. This does not change anything."

But it does, Jandor knew in his heart.

None of them dignified his remark with a response. The hooded servant took Jandor by the arm and led him away.

They were in a vestibule outside the hall when the hooded servant stopped.

"Jandor, I apologise for this ignoble end to your duties as the Fidelis ambassador, but there is another role you may take on, which might yet make a major difference."

"Who are you, who speaks of politics and hides your face?" said Jandor.

"Sometimes a person must speak without worry,"

said the servant. "I know you tried to change Duarma's mind about the executions. I know this simply because you are a good person and that is what a good person would do. I think you have been considering if Duarma is the best person to lead the Empire, but have been reluctant to do anything that might prolong the conflict. Am I right?"

"I will not debate with a man who ambushes me in a doorway," said Jandor.

"Then let me say my piece quickly, because I already know your reply. You will not do anything to hurt Duarma now, not when victory is close. But if the scales should tip against him, you would be in an ideal position to make sure they tip the whole way. When that day comes, you will have significant thanks and influence in the Sagacious League."

"I will not betray my Emperor," said Jandor.

"No. At least not until he betrays *you*." The servant slipped a letter from under his robes and pressed it into Jandor's hands. "You are still your mother's emissary? Ensure she gets this and vouch that all the facts herein are true."

Jandor opened the letter and skimmed the contents. The servant must have penned some of it when Jandor was distracted by Dago's outburst. It was a summary of the rebels' manifesto with a hastily added account of the atrocity Duarma had committed. It ended with an appeal for aid.

"She will not answer this," said Jandor.

"But she will get it?"

Jandor did not respond, but instead continued on his way back to the ship.

Damn you, you know I'll deliver it.

****

Tisenin was smiling for the first time since he had returned to Efrandi. He smiled until he noticed Paramount Janjula staring at him aghast.

"Forgive me my dear Janjula, I do not smile at the death of six-thousand of my followers, but I smile because their martyrdom has given us the only chance we have to attain the bigger goal of freedom from the thrall of the Ban. I knew each of those men personally and I know each one was prepared to die for what was right."

"I hope you are not becoming inured to death Tisenin. My city stands ready to fight, but I am not prepared for it to be led into a slaughter," said Janjula.

"Certainly not. How have the people of your city taken the news that you have joined them to the Sagacious League?" asked Tisenin.

"About half welcomed it. The other half took to the sea and abandoned Hern. In the Outer Isles it is difficult pressing people into things when there are as many boats as buildings and everyone has a relative in five different ports."

"In the long term, it will be good to have a city of a single opinion," said Tisenin. "Speaking of which, Lord Roldern, what say you now?"

Roldern slowly rose from his chair. His face was grave. "My sympathies lie with the Sagacious League.

I have kept aloof from the struggle through a desire to keep my people from harm. But now Jandor has come to us and openly admitted Duarma has committed this act of barbarism. I cannot stand idle. You should consider Icknel to be a member of the Sagacious League."

Tisenin bowed towards the Icknel lord. "Your friendship is welcome, Roldern ap Sunnar. Will your people follow easily?"

"Some will resist. People have already been arming on both sides," said Roldern.

"Then there will be some necessary bloodshed," said Tisenin. "But people will understand now. After the massacre of Sagacious believers, our followers will be prepared to do what is necessary. We must scour Jewasri and Icknel, forcing the Fidelis out. We will tell them to leave or put them to the sword. Have no fear, they will leave. Then we take their property and use it to furnish our armies. We can put grateful commoners in charge of estates and be sure all the produce will come straight to us."

Quinias re-entered the room and threw off his hood, abandoning the aspect of a servant.

"What did Jandor say to your proposal?" asked Tisenin.

"He was reserved but receptive. I believe our message will reach Archlord Serenus well enough," said Quinias.

Janjula shook her head in dismissive anxiety. "To return to your last point Tisenin, what does it matter how much in the way of supplies we accumulate? We cannot beat the veterans and iron of Cathri combined with the mages and manpower of Quri."

Tisenin began to pace and a steely gloss was apparent in his features. He had been thinking a lot about that.

"No, we cannot. But the woodsman fells the sturdy oak with skill far more than strength. I have a plan...First, we will fortify our cities. The one thing we don't lack is stone. Then we rebuild our fleet with custom warships. Faster, stronger, taller. Shipwrights come to me each day with suggestions. Of course, we rearm our soldiers. Those crossbows the Cathri sailors used impressed me. With power like that they could pierce a horse's skull with ease. And Dago has shown us some magic that has such destructive potential, it won't matter that we have fewer mages. I trust I can rely on you to teach that spell to all the mages who stayed with us?"

Dago nodded her head, "Gladly. But Archlord, I'm sure I speak for the rest of this council when I ask what good all these changes will do for us, other than prolonging the war? We need to strike to end it."

Adrin nodded enthusiastically as well.

Tisenin stopped dead and looked from person to person. "I had no plan until my dear Lord Roldern came to our side. The control of Icknel gives us a precious bridgehead in Quri from which our armies can march by land. The rocky coves of the Peril Isles are the ideal place to hide ships and frustrate the junks and carracks of our enemy which rely on the open ocean. We could move a small army with ease, despite their blockade."

As Tisenin continued to explain his plan to his followers, Quinias remained silent at the back of the room. Although Quinias's expression did not change, he was smiling inside. It was a good, audacious plan. He carefully noted each lord's face to see if any of them were wavering from the ultimate goal. Janjula and Roldern were frightened by the sheer boldness, but Tisenin paid close attention to their concerns, spoke high words and gradually wooed them back to the plan.

My protégé, how well you have learnt! You can charm ice and confound fire! thought Quinias.

Finally Tisenin came to the conclusion. "And there you have it. What do you think?"

"Plausible," said Adrin.

"Justified," said Dago.

"I think, I should set sail today," said Quinias.

And they all agreed.

* * * * * * *

Akai sat alone on the deck of Quinias's galley, mending worn ropes and checking tackle. It was not captain's work, but he found the habit was hard to shift. The rituals were easy; they gave him time to think.

He had not dared tell anyone what he had done, but from the blood, he was sure Quinias had guessed. Killing a man had not been as devastating as he thought. It was like sex. The lead up and fantasy of it was more momentous than the act. There was no hate for the boy, perhaps a twinge of guilt, but he had not cried for him since escaping Adlan.

Of course, that was what Feydrin had warned him of.

It hurt more seeing the scorched hulls and vacant moorings around him. He had known many of their crews, worked the cargo routes with them and shared snippets of advice whilst unloading catches. It was bitter hearing how they had been defeated on land, then ambushed at sea. The street cafes and social clubs where the debates of the day were held now carried muted rumblings of discontent and contrition towards the new Emperor, Duarma.

Akai did not know what to think. He was not willing to give up his belief in Tisenin.

"You know they killed the prisoners? All six-thousand."

Akai was shaken from his reflection and turned to see Quinias and another man standing behind him.

"They did what?" asked Akai.

"They killed all the prisoners they took in the battle," repeated Quinias.

Akai dropped the rope he was mending. "How bloody minded can they be?"

Quinias shook his head. "Proof if ever any was needed that the old aristocracy cannot be trusted to make sane decisions. Tisenin is convening an assembly to inform the people of Efrandi. In the light of this atrocity, he has decided we will rearm the League and try again."

Akai got to his feet and nodded sternly. "Good, I shall go immediately."

"No Akai, we have another task," said Quinias. "This is Lord Roldern ap Sunnar. We will be escorting him back to Icknel. The Fidelis forces will be closing in on us soon, so we must leave today."

Akai bowed to the lord, "An honour to have you aboard."

"I hear Tisenin trusts you personally. That is all the recommendation I need," said Roldern. "He looked around the vessel. "Very small, so it is. I trust I will be given the Captain's quarters?"

"I apologise my Lord, but I sleep with the crew. There are no Captain's quarters," said Akai.

"It will be even more cramped when your entourage and the soldiers join us. You may have my map room for your privacy, it will take a hammock nicely." said Quinias.

"Humph, that will be acceptable I suppose. Make sure plenty of mint and ginger is brought aboard, I suffer from seasickness terribly," said Roldern. "And at least one child with a sweet voice, it soothes me best."

Akai and Quinias exchanged glances.

"I shall add it to the manifest," said Quinias. "And now please excuse myself and Akai, we must talk about how to arrange matters."

"Very well, I shall inspect the vessel," said Roldern. "I have quite a few you know. I'm quite the collector, although I scarcely use them."

Quinias tugged Akai aside so they were out of earshot of the hold.

"I'm afraid Lord Roldern must be indulged, his assistance will prove vital to our cause," said Quinias. "Tisenin tells me he is a delight when hosting a soirée, but a little ignorant when it comes to running a war."

"Turning Icknel would be a major coup," said Akai.

"Indeed, but that is not our sole mission. You, and the sailors you gather, must be prepared for a long stay at sea. We will not be able to return to Efrandi once we leave," said Quinias.

"Where are we going?" asked Akai.

"I cannot tell you."

"Regardless, I am glad to go. And I will find sailors also willing."

"Good Akai, I knew I could count on you. Which brings me to this." Quinias took a wrapped bundle of cloth from around his arm and presented it to Akai. "I spoke of your deeds on Adlan to Tisenin and he told me these presents were long overdue."

Akai knelt on the deck and unwrapped the cloth. A bright bolt of purple opened up in his hands, shimmering like layers of onionskin and as soft as down. It was a silk cloak coloured with precious dye from the Peril Isles. Wrapped in the cloak were two further objects. Firstly a bronze short sword coated in a layer of tin so it shone like silver. The last object was the most valuable though: Two small cylinders of brass, made so one slotted inside the other. Akai did not understand until he held it up to his eye. It was a spyglass made with lenses of polished quartz. They were sought after by every sailor in the Empire, yet finding crystals with enough clarity to be useful was next to impossible, to say nothing of the slow grinding needed to polish them.

Tisenin had rewarded him greatly.

"I shall not let this faith shown in me go unwarranted," said Akai. He wrapped the cloak around his shoulders, proud to be wearing Tisenin's colours.

"Akai, up until now I don't think I have placed enough trust in you. You are a man with unique talents that I admire. Within a few minutes of meeting Tisenin and Feydrin you had managed to charm them."

"I think they befriended *me*, not the other way around," corrected Akai.

"That is entirely my point. You have a humble affability which puts people at ease. In times like this, making new friends is as important as galleys and spears. I want to use that talent."

You can get in people's heads and make them do whatever you want, but they will not call you 'friend' afterwards, is that it?

"Then I am at your disposal Quinias. But first let me be a friend to you. You can tell me to mind my own business if you wish. Your left hand, why do you keep the missing fingers hidden?"

Quinias raised an eyebrow, surprised Akai had noticed. He slowly stretched the hand out between them, revealing the two shortened fingers. The little one was badly mangled, with twisted pink lumpy scaring at the tip. The other seemed to have been mended much more skilfully, with a shiny hood of black hairless skin over the stub.

"I lost these in a silly incident when I was a child. Yet I would rather not speak of it or be reminded of it any more often than I have to be. I suppose when people ask me about it, it reminds me of my mortality and how far from perfect I am."

So it is pride that makes you hide your missing fingers? You said it yourself; love and pride are the two things that never fail to hurt us. It was actually reassuring for Akai to know the distant and cunning Quinias had an all-too-common weakness.

"I'm sorry for bringing it up," said Akai.

"It is no matter, I'm actually impressed you noticed," said Quinias. "It makes me more certain that I am right to see you as a potential emissary. But for now, here is a list of the special provisions we will need, *in addition to Lord Roldern's mint and ginger.* I trust you to find a crew and everything we will need."

"Consider it done."

Quinias left Akai to fulfil his duty. But Akai paused for a moment on the dockside.

He wants me to be an emissary? What's this that I feel? A warm and exciting glow of importance. To be picked! Oh to be picked! But then a deep disquieting fear. I never even wanted to be Captain; what might I have to do as an emissary?

Akai picked up the short sword and held it so the

sun flashed along its keen silver blade. It made him feel powerful and special. He wished he had been at the battle of Quri with this blade in his hand, fighting with his Sagacious brothers.

But then he saw his hands trembling.

Akai was three hundred years old; it had been a long time since he had been forced to admit he did not know his own mind.

Chapter 16

Voyage Beyond

Millie and Hanuru sat tight-lipped in the back of the boat. Their hands were tied, they were dehydrated and had been given little to eat except raw fish since Killwa took them captive. Their only way of protesting this condition was to ignore the constant flow of flattery and witticisms that emerged from Killwa's lips.

The gang of eight escapees had proven to be very industrious. They had managed to navigate north past the busy port of Serra without being detected. They had felled several saplings with fires and cut them into a mast with nothing more than the dull blade Millie had given them. They cut the nets to make rigging and wove a sail from their clothes using grass as thread. It had taken a long time. But fortune had been with the escapees. No sooner had they finished the sail than a strong constant breeze had picked up, taking them from the Red Coast towards Efrandi. Hanuru could feel that the breeze was magical, although she did not know what that might mean.

Currently Looshan was in charge of the sail whilst Killwa stood at the back, hunting for sharks. He had carved a bone point using Millie's knife and lashed it to a stick to make a kind of harpoon. He held the harpoon in one hand and with the other dangled a piece of string with fish guts into the water. He had been standing absolutely still with one foot on either side of the boat for hours now. From time to time Hanuru could see a devious desire cross Millie's face; she wanted to nudge the back of his knee and plunge him into the waves. But that would get them nowhere; the others would just row the boat back for him and he would be considerably less well-disposed towards them. Hanuru had to admit, that to Killwa's credit (as much as you could talk about an abductor's credit), so far he had treated them with dignity. Hanuru also knew the only reason Millie had not tried to sabotage them so far was that there was no doubt in Millie's mind that Killwa was capable of treating them much worse.

Killwa shattered the peace in an explosion of movement. His harpoon thrust down into the sea and immediately he recoiled, bringing up a metre long shark. The beast was merely injured and its gapping, toothy maw gnashed wildly at Killwa. But Killwa did not flinch for a moment. He took Millie's knife, grabbed the shark by the gills and began sawing through its head. The shark thrashed in agony for a few moments, but Killwa was quick and strong; he had severed its spine in seconds.

"Phew!" exclaimed Killwa, as he dumped the shark's body onto the boat's floor. "Only a baby but it will feed us today. Nice change of flavour, eh Millie?"

"Raw shark and raw fish are all the same to me," dismissed Millie.

Killwa threw his hands into the air in mock exasperation. "Millie, my dearest, I do these things for your benefit and you reject them! It saddens my soul. What will it take to make you smile?"

Millie held her hands up, "Cut these bonds and I will smile for you."

Killwa sat down and relaxed his stiff muscles against the side of the boat. He took out a little whetstone and began honing the knife blade. The knife had seen so much use and re-honing since constructing the mast that it was now a full centimetre shorter than it had been. "Oh no Millie, I think I have your measure. If your hands were free you would tear our sail just to spite me. But I am a kind man when in a position to give kindness. I will cut for you the choicest pieces."

"It is not much of a kindness when it costs you nothing to extend it," said Millie.

"I would quite like the fat from around its fin," said Looshan, knowing that was the portion Killwa intended to cut for Millie.

"Sorry Looshan, you will have to have the dark meat, same as me," said Killwa.

But suddenly Looshan was not interested in the

conversation about who got what portion. He was on his feet, straining towards the horizon.

"I see sails, lots of sails," said Looshan. He started to count them.

Hanuru glanced up for just a fraction of second, seeing white speckles on a hazy horizon. "One-hundred-fifty-two," she announced.

Looshan and Killwa regarded Hanuru with surprise, and even more so when Looshan finished his count and concurred with her. "It seems the quiet one has her uses as well," said Looshan.

"They move in clusters of twos and threes. Those are no galleys, but Serra-built carracks and caravels," said Killwa.

And it became obvious to Hanuru why the winds had been so favourable to them. The Mages' Guild in Serra was sending fine winds so the Fidelis fleet could blockade Efrandi.

"We should turn away immediately," said Killwa. "We have a low sail. Perhaps they have not seen us yet."

"North or south?" asked Looshan.

"We could either go to White Bay and beg sanctuary with Paramount Janjula of Hern. Or we can go south to Adlan. I hear some troops were garrisoned there before the invasion of Serra. They may yet be in control of the island."

"We have precious little water left. Adlan is less than a day's journey, but it could take a lot longer to get all the way up to Hern," cautioned Looshan.

"Before we left, I heard our general talking about sending troops to Adlan before they invaded Efrandi," volunteered Millie.

Why are you telling them that! Hanuru wanted to scream at Millie. *We could have been heading back to friends!*

Killwa regarded Millie with curiosity as he continued to hone the blade. After a few seconds he seemed to come to some sort of revelation and smiled. "No, no, you lie. You are a wily one Millie, I saw how easily you fooled those guards who were taking us to our execution. You tell us Adlan is taken in hopes that we run into Fidelis ships on the long journey to Hern."

Millie looked shamefaced.

Looshan shrugged his shoulders and made adjustments to the sail, "South to Adlan it is then."

When the crew's attention was fully fixed on manoeuvring the boat and watching the Fidelis fleet, Millie gave Hanuru a private and devilish look of amusement.

Millie you are a wily one!

They turned the ship so the wind came abeam and headed south. They had not been on the new heading long when Looshan made another announcement.

"I think we are being followed," he said.

"Think! Are we or not!?" demanded Killwa.

Looshan scowled and touched a finger to his milk white eye. "If you want to be sure use your own *pair*, brother."

All of them stared out to the sails on the horizon.

There was definitely a couple of specks getting bigger whilst the rest slowly receded into the haze.

"We cannot risk an encounter. We must try to outrun it. Alright comrades, arms and backs to the oars," commanded Killwa.

The eight of them got out the oars and began to pump them rhythmically at a nice, easily maintainable pace. But the few of them with their makeshift sail were nothing compared to the speed of the sleek caravel that followed them. Within a few hours, the ship was clearly visible. It was freshly painted white, had an eagle figurehead and the coat of arms of Kirrie embroidered on the sails. There were soldiers clustered at the prow, bows nocked and ready. It looked like an arrow skimming the water in slow motion.

"Faster men, faster!" demanded Killwa.

But however much they increased the pace, it looked as if the Fidelis ship would overhaul them. With their captors in the midst of furious distraction, Millie whispered to Hanuru.

"Slip off your sandals, we can jump in the water and be saved. We don't know what they might do if they are forced to use us as leverage," said Millie.

"The water! Oh no, I couldn't! I can't swim normally, let alone with my hands tied," said Hanuru.

"You'll be fine. It won't be long treading water until we get picked up. You can hang on to me if you get tired," insisted Millie.

Hanuru shook her head and thought the situation over. *The water or the hostage takers?* After a moment or two, the answer seemed obvious. Silently she slipped her feet out of her sandals. Millie smiled at getting her way and did the same.

"Alright Hanuru, on three," said Millie. "One...two...three!"

The two of them tipped themselves backwards, over the side of the boat. But at the last moment, Hanuru hooked her foot under one of the benches and stopped the fall. Only Millie landed in the water with a plop.

"HANURU!" Millie screamed.

Looshan bolted to the back of the boat to try and grab Millie before it was too late.

"Forget her! We have no time for a rescue," said Killwa. "Get back to your oar!"

Looshan did as he was told and Mille receded fast from the back of the boat.

Yes, the answer seemed obvious. Millie was better off in the water and Hanuru was better off with the captors. But Millie would never have agreed to leave her, so Hanuru needed her own wiles to get her lover to safety.

You'll forgive me eventually Millie. I know that about you too.

Tears streamed down Millie's face as she trod water. It was not right; she would have rather still been in the boat than out here by herself. Millie knew Hanuru had done it deliberately, because she had a look of compassion, not fear, as she watched her lover fall into the water.

The caravel passed right by her without slowing down, and for a moment Millie thought it would leave her in the water. But it was a vessel weighing almost a hundred tons and was simply taking a long time to slow down. It turned and did a great loop around Millie. One of the sailors dived naked from the ship with a rope tied around his waist. As fast as a dolphin, he swam out to Millie and propped her head out of the water. The sailor deftly swam them back to the ship, and the two of them were hauled aboard.

She sat on the deck, exhausted. One of the sailors cut the bonds on her wrists.

"You're safe now, we'll have you on the ship and back in Serra soon enough," he said.

"We can't go to Serra, we have to follow that boat and rescue Hanuru!" Millie insisted, with a note of hysteria.

"Sorry, my young friend. The ship is in irons. The wind is against us now. By the time we free it up, it will be near nightfall and I dare not navigate these coasts in the dark."

Millie's heart sank.

Oh Hanuru, be safe. Come back to me soon.

* * * * * * *

It was a stifling, painful journey south to Icknel. The season was shifting towards the hottest and most humid time of year. Soon the moisture would give rise to the great hurricanes which ravaged the Hublands and no captain would dare take their ship out of harbour. Whilst every sane individual in the Hublands confined their activities to the few hours after dawn and before nightfall, sleeping the day through in the shade, the sailors had to stay active throughout the day. Akai needed the light to navigate safely; although he was perfectly capable of finding his way with the stars alone in the open ocean, they needed to hug the shoreline so they could restore their stocks of water each evening and the Jewasri coast had a wealth of treacherous rocks and shifting sandbanks that no-one wanted to risk at night.

The fate of Tisenin's fleet haunted every decision they made. Every sail was treated as potentially hostile and forced them to veer off course or hide in a fold of the coast. However, only once did they feel genuinely under threat: As they gave Adlan a wide birth, a cluster of caravels and junks snaked across the horizon. One of the caravels split off and followed them at a distance until dusk, when Akai took the galley in a shallow estuary. They slipped away again before the sun rose and did not see any sign of pursuit the following day.

The coolest place on the ship was on deck, in the shade of the main sail, where the sea breeze chilled the hairs of the skin. But the little galley was packed with sailors, soldiers and Lord Roldern's people, so there were too many of them to recline in the shade together. Most of the time they were forced to stay in the stuffy, airless hold and take their turn on deck. Lord Roldern was particularly caught by this circumstance, since by arguing for his own private room, he could scarcely be seen to abandon it. He did suffer from seasickness terribly for the first week, constantly calling for his servant to make him a cup of ginger or mint tea, depending on the specific locus of his nausea at the time. His condition was not helped much by Akai, who had chosen to interpret his directive of including 'a child with a sweet voice' among the crew in the broadest possible terms. Akai had repaid a very old debt and apprenticed his former Captain's son. At the age of seventy the boy was scarcely a child, but not really an adult. And although the boy had a wonderfully smooth voice, Akai made sure he spent most of his time learning his ropes, knots and all matters nautical rather than singing to Lord Roldern.

Lord Roldern was clearly upset by the 'misinterpretation,' but blamed it on Akai's incompetence, rather than a deliberate act of disobedience. Quinias saw right through Akai's actions, but either approved or chose not to say anything.

Luckily Lord Roldern improved incrementally as the second week progressed and by the third was more or less able to act normally, provided he was infused the correct quantities of mint and ginger. In the third week Lord Roldern chose to take his revenge by regaling Quinias and Akai (the only persons on board remotely worthy of his rank) with tales of his brave deeds on the hunt or amusing tales of fellow nobles' humiliations. Whilst given in good faith, these stories always held the same moral; *you should respect me more*. Quinias unfailingly managed to pluck out of the ether a plausible reason to excuse himself, but Akai was caught listening to Roldern's tales unless the apprentice came looking for advice. Then Akai would take his time to explain things thoroughly. Very thoroughly.

* * * * * * *

"So you see, the good lady Kassita could have had her reputation terribly shamed if I had not been there to keep her secret about the amorous steward," said Lord Roldern, chuckling at the memory. "Ah, she lives in Sunnel now. Oddly, she has not come to visit me since."

It was now week four and it was becoming obvious to Akai why the people of Icknel did not mind that their Lord was an absentee. Having him take an active role in control of the city would have been the much greater of two evils.

Akai felt a wisp of cool, determined wind flush against his cheek. It was coming from the northeast, and instantly he knew they were almost at Icknel. It was the summer wind which blew harder the hotter it got. The winds worked very much in Icknel's favour, since the nobility of southern Quri were forced by the sweltering heat to make seasonal moves to either Icknel or private retreats in the mountains. As far as Akai could see, this was the sole reason Roldern found himself surrounded by so much favourable company.

"My Lord!" Akai cut in before Roldern could start another tale. "We are almost returned to your city. I will have the oarsmen take us in fast. I will have to beg my leave to teach my apprentice how to prepare for entering a port."

"Ah....good! That was a most unpleasant voyage," said Roldern.

Roldern disappeared into the hold to arrange his affairs. The second he was gone Quinias found his way to Akai's side.

"Does he even realise what he is saying?" questioned Akai.

"I doubt it. Do you even realise what you are doing?" replied Quinias.

"Me? What?" Akai was perplexed.

"Every time you swap Roldern for your apprentice. Do not tell me it is merely to avoid the blabbering lord. Are you intending to bed him?"

"Ha ha! If I were fifty years younger, he fifty years older and I wasn't his Captain, maybe! There are not many people I'll turn down, but buggering the apprentice boy is one step over the line of honour for me. No I guess just enjoy teaching him. I've never had a family and there is no prospect of one on the horizon. I guess, I like surrogate nurturing."

"Ack! That is far too noble of you Akai! For my entertainment I was hoping for some intrigue. In just these past few weeks I must have heard every story these sailors has to tell twice already. And in the last week, every story Lord Roldern has to tell three times. My mind grows hungry for more gossip."

"You are very tight lipped yourself. I know you cannot tell us about your...work...but what about your family?" suggested Akai.

Quinias waved the question away. "Little enough story there."

"Where did you grow up?" Akai prompted.

Quinias's hand instinctively came to the two nubs of fingers on his left hand. "I grew up in Jewasri, not far from Efrandi. I moved around a lot in my one and two-hundreds, but went back there in time to meet Tisenin when he was just waking up to his responsibility as head of the line of Elsiren."

Akai nodded in understanding, but he saw more than Quinias was willing to tell. Firstly, Quinias had very deftly tried to make a story about himself a story about Tisenin, pulling Akai off-topic. Secondly, he lied about growing up in Jewasri. The first time Akai had noticed that little tell with the stubs of his fingers they had been talking about Cathri. Not that it meant very much to Akai. *But it is always good to know something more about one's friends, is that not so Quinias?*

"Forgive me Quinias, I was not being wholly disingenuous with Lord Roldern. I must attended to the ship and make preparations for coming into harbour."

"Very well."

Akai took out the crystal spyglass and gazed to the southwest. He could see the city; white buildings stacked one atop the other, climbing up terraces on a precipitously steep hillside. The youths of Icknel, it was said, had the shapeliest calves of any town in the Empire. Akai could not say he had noticed it, but the widows certainly had the most crooked backs. At the very top of the hill was a narrow spire; a shrunken facsimile of the Mages' Tower in Serra. Akai had no idea how it had survived the many quakes that plagued the Peril Isles; it looked like it would topple in a light breeze.

He scanned to the south and saw the narrow strait of water that separated Icknel from the Peril Isles. The isles were a volcanic chain crisscrossed by thin channels and so named because of the abundance of keen currents, whirlpools and jutting rocks that threatened novice captains. Icknel overlooked the sole safe passage through them. All shipping between Serra and Cathri had to pass this way.

As they entered the harbour, Akai ordered the sails taken in and they approached with oars only. The Harbour Master was waiting for them at an empty mooring and they threw their lines to some waiting dock hands.

The galley was sitting so low in the water with its cargo that Akai needed to take the Harbour Master's hand to be pulled up onto the wooden quay.

"Welcome my young Captain, I do not recognise yourself or your vessel. Is this your first trip to Icknel?" asked the Harbour Master.

"No I came here as a sailor many years ago," said Akai.

"What is your business? Commission, trade, or flight?"

Akai was surprised to hear 'flight' as an option; it implied that Icknel was already taking in a number of refugees from the fight to the north.

"Commission," said Akai. "I bring a noble passenger who you will know better than myself."

Akai reached down and gave Lord Roldern a hand up on to the quay.

The Harbour Master bowed deeply. "Uh-Forgive my surprise Lord Roldern ap Sunnar. I did not expect you to return in such a small galley."

"That is quite alright, it would not have been my choice. However there are marauders prowling the sea and we needed a vessel to out manoeuvre them."

"Surely not my Lord!" exclaimed the Harbour Master.

"I have many shocking things to tell. For now, close the harbour, no one is allowed in or out. And confiscate the cargos from all Cathri vessels until further notice."

The Harbour Master looked instantly befuddled. These were things he had never had to do before.

Lord Roldern's retinue made their way off the vessel, followed by the soldiers. The soldiers strapped on their armour, gathered their weapons and looked to Lord Roldern for orders.

Roldern looked round to Quinias. "Quinias, you

have delivered me safely to my city, just as Tisenin said you would. I thank you from my soul. As we agreed, you may have any one of my vessels and whatever supplies you need. I have several to choose from, the Harbour Master can show them to you." Roldern shuffled his feet, regarded the assembled warriors and sighed deeply. He clearly did not want to begin the path he had set for himself. "First, we go to my mansion on the outskirts of the town and gather my good people. Then we go to the hardened Fidelis supporters and...hope they surrender their weapons."

"My advice, Lord Roldern, is to trust my soldiers and move swiftly. Nothing will be won with meekness," said Quinias.

"No. Quite," said Lord Roldern, but he did not sound sure.

Once Roldern and his soldiers began marching out, Akai turned towards Quinias.

"We are taking a different ship?" asked Akai.

"Yes, where we are going we will not be able to stop every day to take on more water. We need something with much more storage."

"Just where are we going?" asked Akai.

Quinias took a map out of his robes and held it for only Akai to see. He pointed to a mark on it. "We need to get here. Can you take me?"

Akai nodded, hiding his surprise. "Yes, I can take you."

"Then help me select a ship."

The Harbour Master showed them where Lord

Roldern's private moorings were. The first vessel they came to was a large junk, clearly of Cathri manufacture. Every panel of wood had been carved with decorative reliefs and painted bright colours. It was clearly intended to be some kind of pleasure vessel, but it looked neglected and ill-used.

"A junk is easily big enough for our needs," said Quinias. "And I doubt Lord Roldern would miss it. Clearly it is intended for entertaining at sea."

"No," said Akai. "It has not been out of the harbour for some time. No doubt owing to Roldern's seasickness. It could take a while to ensure every plank is seaworthy. Besides, I have never served on a junk. I could not captain with confidence."

Next they came to a sloop with sleek lines and a prow like a razorblade. When Akai inspected the sails that had been stowed he found them to be the best kind of Serra silk, although badly folded, as if without regard for the artisanship that had gone into them. Sails were not mere pieces of cloth, but three dimensional sculptures that had to be inflated with the wind and protected from mould and insects. It made Akai a little angry at the Lord of Icknel, who clearly gave his ships no love.

"A racing vessel," Akai declared. "Good for speed, but nothing more."

Finally they came to a clutch of bloated caravels and carracks. Their holds bowed out like pregnant mares. These were the cargo haulers of Roldern's fleet.

They were used to bring in the produce from his many estates in the Hublands; grain from the Great River, olive oil from the Emerald Coast, wine from Jewasri and timber from the rainforests of the east.

After a thorough inspection, Akai pointed to one of the caravels. "This one! It has solid timbers, a sound mast. Good rigging. The hull is clean of barnacles. Two sets of sails already on board. Plenty of cargo space for water and wine. But most importantly, it has a broad stable base, which we'll need, because we're probably going to be sailing right through some storms if we set off at this time of year."

"We'd have more space and a broader base if we took a carrack," prompted Quinias.

"Yes, but not the crew to manage it. If just a handful of our sailors became ill, we wouldn't have the strength to handle the sails or anchor," said Akai.

"Very well, you have convinced me it is a sound choice," said Quinias.

Akai got right to ordering the crew to move the cargo across to their new caravel. There was a lot to go and it had to be stacked precisely in the new ship to preserve its balance. Supplies were also brought directly from Icknel by the dock hands. Water, wine, fresh vegetables and some preserved foods. Among the supplies coming aboard Akai noticed some bolts of second-rate cloth, some crudely hammered apprentice copper work and many, many small enamel beads which were normally exchanged between children.

"Is this right?" questioned Akai.

"Yes, perfectly," said Quinias, holding one of the gaudy beads up to the light.

Akai shrugged and found them a place in the hold.

It took almost all day to load the cargo and towards evening they started to hear shouts and screams from the city. In places, smoke could be seen rising over the hill. The dock hands kept people out of the harbour so no news came to Akai of what was going on, but he could guess.

The hardened Fidelis supporters had not surrendered their weapons.

This would be no bloodless take over like Adlan had been. Things had gone too far.

The sun was already below the horizon by the time the ship was full, but they put out to sea anyway. Where they were going it was open ocean, and the stars would guide them truer than anything else. There would be no stopping off until they reached their final port.

As Akai looked back over Icknel, he could see a great plume of smoke, thicker and taller than the town's spire rising into the sky. Its underside reflected a dull, orange glow.

"I hope everything is going alright for them," said Akai.

"It *must,* Akai. We are obliged to have faith in them, and they in us. Because no part in the plan can fail now."

Chapter 17

Approaching Storms

Zanthred sat motionless on the pitch black floor of the Temple. His breathing had slowed to nothing more than would shiver cobwebs. He could feel the delicate hand of Feydrin on his shoulder and her lips pressed just behind his ear.

"Begin to mould your mana, turn it into a stream," she whispered.

Zanthred mentally saw himself as a whirling pool of bright energy and slowly he teased a glowing thread of it from his chest. He was aware of Feydrin's mana beside him, outshining his own as the sun does a candle. The thread began to waver and recede.

"Ignore me Zanthred, reach out. Find the other one who is with us."

Zanthred refocused and stabilised his mana stream.

There was a void out there, nowhere to reach to. There was a dim glow at the very limit of his ether sense which must have been all the people in the village below them, and minute sparks kept flitting above, which he guessed to be the stunted minds of birds catching insects above his head, but there was nothing godlike to be found. Then he turned his mental gaze to the ether closest to him, to weigh its quality, feel how it moved against his mind; he realised it was not black at all, but a seething sea of dark greys. It had shape and form and current. Slowly he came to see a pattern, a gradient. His little thread of mana followed it back to what he guessed must be its source, already knowing it must be infinitely far away. But as his thread of mana travelled the pattern it solidified and began to look like a deliberate fractal design. There were the structures he could see in Feydrin's mind, but not the birds; intelligence, emotion and intention.

He gasped as he grasped the grandeur of Solrax; at once imminent and transcendent. Timeless and temporal. Living and fleshless. As his thread of mana joined with the creature next to him, he felt it tugged an impossibly large distance away, back to the lost home world of Earth.

At once his mind was filled with images of the great white desert and a ring of naked black-skinned warriors using spears tipped with volcanic glass to protect a handful of exhausted mages. The mages were united in the grand chorus. Zanthred thought he could name some of them: Foras; Woodrin; Sunnar;

Keldron; Lanlar; Lunis; Brazini; Suvix; Hexin. Outside the circle terrors raged; creatures of pure hate and fear fixated on slaughtering all life. And then, the great blue sinuous body of Solrax soaring up into the sky and uniting herself with the spell in a flash of light and etheric mayhem.

The horrors died and Zanthred collapsed, his mana reserves drained and unable to sustain the link. His head fell in Feydrin's lap and she gently stroked his face whilst making soothing noises as one does to a child.

Were those visions real? Were they his own thoughts coloured by the many tales of the days on Earth? Or were they the last memories of the creature Solrax before she ascended to the ether?

"I found Solrax," Zanthred murmured.

"I know, you did well," assured Feydrin. "Practise is all you need now. Practise to build your mana and control."

Zanthred lay in Feydrin's lap for a few minutes until he was quite recovered. *Physically* speaking at least; he felt he had just been through quite a spiritual upheaval. When Feydrin was sure he was okay, she led him out to the temple entrance and they sat on the steps, looking out over the water towards Quri.

"Teacher Feydrin, were those things I saw real?" asked Zanthred.

"I cannot say," said Feydrin. "Everyone sees differently, and most not at all."

"When the Ban comes, will we still be able to worship Solrax?"

"Yes, somehow. But it will not be the same. Elsiren is said to have worshipped Solrax on earth when the Ban was strong," she said.

A breeze picked up off the sea, but only bathed them in warm, moisture-laden air.

"The first hurricane can't be far off now. It's early," said Zanthred.

"I detect a note of melancholy," said Feydrin.

"I had hoped to return to Serra before the seas closed up. I have friends there. But Gargrace wants to keep me here and to train me to be a better archer."

"He works you hard. A few more months of his practise and you will have the shoulders of a lion. I could feel the heat of your muscles as we prayed. But tell me, why is it so urgent that you get back to these friends? Surely they will go nowhere during the Hurricane or Storm Seasons? And five months is not long to be separated."

"I left them with bad words. We argued about the war. I worry that if I stay here for five months, the rift will become solidified," confessed Zanthred.

"No rift is irreparable. You are yet young and this war has everyone testing their convictions. They will forgive you if you sincerely beg them," said Feydrin.

"I hope you are right."

"But gifts never hurt," Feydrin added.

Zanthred chuckled. "I shall bear that in mind! Because I need my friend Millie, she is the only one who knows how to defend my reputation. Last week, a sailor who was passing through burst out in hysterics when I introduced myself. He had heard of a certain humiliation of mine I brought on myself in Chepsid earlier this year. I did not know what to do, so I just stood there looking ashen."

"Ah, the Janistor incident?" said Feydrin trying not to smile *too* broadly. "I thought I recognised your name, but I did not like bring it up at your expense."

"So word came all the way to Adlan?" Zanthred shook his head in disbelief.

"It will be forgotten soon. Chepsid wine will make a wise person fall to singing. It will make them chuckle and dance and say many a word best left unspoken. So the foibles of one are quickly outshone by the foibles of another, and all dismissed lightly. When you go back, this Millie and Janistor will be the only people to remember."

Zanthred laughed heartily. Such things seemed so small and petty now.

"But if I go, who will protect you!" he jested.

Feydrin giggled at the memory of a broken Zanthred announcing his intention when they first met. Then she remembered the other circumstances and sobered.

"But I do not think the Sagacious followers would hurt me now, after I promised not to summon the simurgh," she said.

Zanthred also sobered. "The sailors from the blockade say they saw the people of Efrandi erecting a stone wall around their town and building towers at the harbour. And they say Hern has joined Tisenin in rebellion. If things go badly, this war could drag on for years yet. You would not consider summoning the simurgh if things became dire?"

Feydrin mused for a moment. "No, not me," she said. "I have too much fear for the simurgh and too much hope for my own people...but there is one other who talks with them."

"I am glad this will remain something between cherno and cherno. But you say there is one other?" Zanthred asked, perplexed.

"Pallah ap Foras, my old teacher. Last I heard, he was someone of importance in the Mages' Guild. If things get bad, I mean, *really bad*, tell Gargrace to seek his wisdom."

"Pallah ap Foras?" Zanthred remembered the half blind old man slipping away on an overburdened nag and was filled with another wave of private amusement "...I think he has the same opinion on matters as yourself!"

Zanthred was prevented from telling the story by one of the men from the town who came running up the hill. He stopped next to them, panting hard.

"Whatever is it?" asked Feydrin.

"My teacher, Gargrace has requested all the soldiers to meet him at the harbour. Some Sagacious castaways have arrived and they have a hostage."

Zanthred jumped to his feet, collected his bow and quiver and dashed down the steep cliff path. Feydrin insisted on accompanying him; just as the Sparrow Company unofficially belonged to Janistor, the island of Adlan unofficially belonged to Feydrin, which made everything on it her business.

When they arrived at the harbour, they found Gargrace and the rest of the soldiers standing behind a house about three hundred metres from the end of the quay.

"Get back here!" shouted Gargrace. "Every time they see one of us it sets them off."

Zanthred huddled behind the house's wall with the rest of the soldiers.

"What's going on?" asked Feydrin.

"Some boat full of Sagacious fugitives just turned up in the harbour thinking it was still in Tisenin's control. When we tried to take them into custody, they produced a hostage and put a knife to her throat. They demanded that we stay out of bowshot and prepare a small ship for them to escape to Jewasri. It goes without saying that I'm not sending any allies back to Tisenin. Have a look if you like, one at a time."

Gargrace moved from the corner of the house and allowed Feydrin to look round it, down into the harbour. Feydrin shook her head in displeasure.

"So you'll let them have the girl's life then?" asked Feydrin.

"For all I know she is complicit in this. The people nearest when they landed say she has the aura of a mage and there were plenty of female mages with the invaders. But my guess would be that they will surrender within the day. To get here in the tiny boat they did means they must be low on water, so I will bring them low by thirst."

"Why do they simply not take a ship, now that you have abandoned the harbour?" asked Feydrin.

"The ships have been prepared for resting during the Hurricane Season. No sails, provisions or sundries. Everything seaworthy is already heading back to Serra," said Gargrace.

Feydrin moved away and Zanthred took his chance to look round the corner at the scene. Over on the quayside there were eight haggard looking men wearing nothing but rags. One of them had a knife to a woman's throat. The woman seemed familiar to Zanthred – she was young and unusually short – but he could not really tell at this distance.

It couldn't be could it? Why would she be here?

The man with the knife to her throat bellowed towards them. "You think I don't know that you are there? Come out! Make a ship ready for us now! You think I will not carry out my threats?"

With the knife still to the woman's throat, the man stretched out his hostage's arm and grasped one of her fingers. With a brutal twist of his wrist, he snapped the woman's finger. She yowled in exquisite pain.

When Zanthred heard that voice, however distorted by agony, he knew who the girl was.

Hanuru! How did she get here? What has happened to Millie!?

"I know that girl!" said Zanthred.

"Was that enough for you to understand?" said the man with the knife. He grabbed another one of Hanuru's fingers and snapped it in his grip like a twig. But this time he rolled the broken nub around, so Hanuru's screams were desperate and continuous. "See what you are doing to this girl? It'll be one bone broken every ten minutes you delay. Every ten minutes until one of these ships is ready to put out to sea!"

Gargrace pulled Zanthred away from the corner so he could get a good look at this horrific development. His face had become blank and stern, as it was in the moments when they fought the Sagacious spearmen hand to hand.

"You know her?" asked Gargrace.

"Yes, she is Hanuru, the mage from the Sparrow Company that you asked to join us," said Zanthred.

"Aye, I see it now," confirmed Gargrace.

"I have seen all I can of this war. It sickens me. Forgive me, but I must leave," said Feydrin. Her expression was bitter. "I can no longer see this ending without bloodshed."

"Wait!" Zanthred cried. He fell to his knees and flung his arms around her legs. "I beg you Feydrin. I felt your power, that moment when we first met in the temple. You could end this in a moment. Come to my aid."

"I will not take a life. It is only to the benefit of Karlsha. If those men must kill a helpless woman, then that is their guilt. If you want to kill them, then that is yours. I will have no part in it," said Feydrin.

"Please, she is my friend! I cannot stand here and do nothing, I could not live with that. I could not look anyone in the eye again. Have pity on her! On me..." insisted Zanthred.

A single tear welled up in Feydrin's eye and trickled down her cheek. Clearly her heart was with them, if not her head.

"Of course I have pity, but you confuse the power to act with the right to. Release me Zanthred, look to your own hands," said Feydrin.

"Zanthred, let her go!" barked Gargrace. He peeled Zanthred's reluctant hands away.

"Thank you, Gargrace," said Feydrin.

"Feydrin ap Lanlar, teacher," began Gargrace. "I can tell you little of morals, but I can tell you a lot of war. By saving others, you save yourself. If you fight only for yourself, you kill only yourself."

She shook her head, "What will you do if they continue to torture the girl?"

"Rush them. Hope they do not have courage to do what they threaten. We will probably end with all nine dead," said Gargrace.

"Only one has a knife to the girl's throat. If he were incapacitated, you could spare the other's lives," said Feydrin.

"Perhaps," acknowledged Gargrace.

"...What if I could get you closer and give you a couple of seconds in which to act, could any of you string a bow and put an arrow through his hand?" asked Feydrin.

"I could," said Gargrace. "But how could I get close? They have seen my face and my bow, they know I am an archer."

Zanthred jumped to his feet, "Then send me! I have been training with Gargrace, you've seen me Feydrin. I can make that shot."

Feydrin looked at Gargrace, "Can he?"

Gargrace equivocated. "Certainly he is capable, but not with surety. I would not trust my life to him, not yet."

"Some chance is better than none, I guess." Feydrin put both her hands on Zanthred's shoulders. "Zanthred, know this. If you miss...and Hanuru dies...you will have as much regret in your heart as if you did nothing."

"I understand, but like you said, some chance is better than none," said Zanthred.

"Very well, I will try to help if you promise to try and do this without any death," she said.

"I promise. Thank you so much Feydrin!"

"Hold your thanks until I have proven my use. At my signal, I want you to shoot the man's hand. You will know it if and when I give it." Then she turned to the townsfolk that were slowly gathering to watch the scene. "Someone get me an acolyte's robe, a needle and thread, nine beakers of water and a silver tray to carry them on!"

People ran to their homes and gathered the objects she requested. In just a minute, Zanthred had been stripped and dressed in the acolyte's robe. A single arrow had been sewn into his sleeve, just tight enough to hang there, but loose enough to pull free at will. Feydrin took Zanthred's bow and leaned on it like a walking stick. The loose string would be hidden along the back of the stave, away from the fugitives.

"No good," she declared. "Here, Gargrace, cut the horn collars off."

Gargrace and Zanthred shared a look of distress as he drew his sword and sliced the horn caps from each end of the stave; it was sacrilege to damage a bow as fine as this. But when he was done, the thick, straight body looked just like a walking stick.

A big silver platter was brought out and placed in Zanthred's arms. It was etched with a floral design and polished so finely that he could have used it as a mirror. Nine beakers went on top.

"Now walk behind me, keep a pace back at all times," commanded Feydrin.

With trepidation, they came out from behind the house and slowly walked into the harbour.

"Stay back! I'll kill her if you come any closer!" shouted the man with the knife.

"Dear stranger, I am Feydrin ap Lanlar. Perhaps you have heard of me? I come to offer comfort and negotiate."

"I have heard of you. You are the priest of Solrax." The man turned and whispered to some of his fellows. After some kind of heated debate he shouted, "Approach no closer than fifty metres, you can negotiate from there."

Feydrin gravely nodded to Zanthred, as if to say *'this is the best I can do, be ready.'*

They walked out along the harbour. At fifty metres they could clearly make out the band of fugitives. It was a young, handsome man who held the knife to Hanuru's throat. An older, more muscular man with just one eye stood beside him. Hanuru was clearly in severe distress; her face was contorted with pain and her robe soaked with tears.

"That is close enough!" the man with the knife shouted.

"Dear stranger, what do I call you?" asked Feydrin.

"I am Killwa of Efrandi."

"Killwa, I have brought water for you and your men. I hope that since you have heard of me, you will trust my reputation and accept this gift for what it is," said Feydrin.

"My dear Feydrin, after just these few words I trust you most out of all the women in the world. But I would trust you even more if you would drink from each cup first," said Killwa.

Feydrin took each beaker and drank a gulp, holding it above her head so they could see the water drop into her mouth.

"Good, now set the water down, we will pick it up when you are gone," said Killwa.

Feydrin passed the bow stave to Zanthred and took the silver platter. She placed the tray on the floor and took each beaker off. Her mannerisms were delicate and formal, like a court servant. When she was done, she held the platter loosely in front of herself.

"Thank you, dear Feydrin. But I fear we have little to negotiate. My demands are quite simple and intransigent. One ready ship for the girl's life," said Killwa.

"The garrison commander here is quite intransigent too. He will not let you leave this island, and if you kill the girl, you will certainly die too," warned Feydrin. "You would be better surrendering yourself and begging for mercy."

"Like the six-thousand comrades who were executed by Duarma's mercy? No thank you, dear Feydrin," said Killwa.

"I will vouch for you. My word carries weight," said Feydrin.

"Regardless, I would rather die free and for my beliefs than live as a penitent, never sure where Duarma's wrath will fall and always hiding my head in shame."

"Is that what your fellows think?" asked Feydrin.

"They are my sworn men and I speak for them. As I said, we have little to negotiate. Now, as much as I enjoy listening to your sweet voice, dear Feydrin, the time is soon approaching when I must hurt this poor girl once more because of your commander's vindictiveness against my people," said Killwa.

"You speak like the capital holds up the foundations," criticized Feydrin. "Allow me to make another proposal. Release the girl, and take me as your hostage. Your sin will be less if your victim is willing."

This caused some consternation within the fugitives. Killwa and the man with one eye began raising their voices to each other. At one point Zanthred made out the words, "No Looshan! I am in charge here! We have come too far!" At last they quietened down and Killwa seemed to have exerted his dominance.

"Dear Feydrin, light in the hour of my distress, we have considered your proposal. But we must reject it. Although you should not take it as any stain on your honour, we know you have magic beyond our own and we would not be able to ensure your...*complicity*...in the same way we can with our current guest," said Killwa.

"Is there nothing I can do to make you reconsider? No accommodation you can see?" begged Feydrin.

"No," said Killwa flatly.

"That makes me sad for our race as a whole," said Feydrin.

Feydrin lifted the silver platter up over her face – Zanthred momentarily felt a surge of power like molten metal fresh from the forge being poured over him – and suddenly light burst from Feydrin's hands and bathed the whole world. It was purer and stronger than the sun.

The signal.

The fugitives screamed in pain as the magical light seared their eyes and made them recoil as if from a blow. The silver platter was acting like a mirror, protecting Zanthred and Feydrin from the unbearable glare.

Zanthred lost no time, he had one chance. He

grabbed the top loop of the string, stamped down on the end of the bow stave and barged his shoulder into its middle to bend it enough to fit the string on. The loop caught in its groove and he let the bow snap back. Out came the arrow from his sleeve, nocked and drawn back to his cheek in an instant.

He just had to aim.

Killwa was shielding his eyes with his forearm, still not sure what had happened. Hanuru was in front of him, knife to her throat. That hand holding the knife was a very, very small target. As Zanthred looked, Killwa's look of anguish was turning to one of anger, the hand on the knife tightening its grip. Zanthred sighted his mark, no time to account for wind or stem his tremors. He loosed.

The arrow shot forwards faster than a diving hawk. It stuck in its target true and clean.

It stuck in Killwa's throat.

Killwa collapsed dead. Gargrace led a charge out from behind the houses and archers and fleet Shadow Warriors piled into the harbour. One of the fugitives made a dive for the knife. But the one-eyed Looshan interposed himself with Hanuru.

"Please, my fellows, no more! We tried and failed to escape. We let Killwa try his way, now try mine!" he implored.

The fugitive dropped the knife.

Zanthred did not think, he just found his legs running towards Hanuru and he embraced her in a great bear hug. "Oh Hanuru, Hanuru, I'm glad you're alright!"

"Zanthred? Oh, my dear friend, I am glad it is you who came for me," she was weeping and smiling at the same time. The waves of pain and emotional release were simply too much for her.

Soon the soldiers were among them, binding the fugitives. Zanthred felt a huge slap on his back.

"That was some shot Zanthred! You'll be a decent archer yet!" said Gargrace.

For a moment, Zanthred was happy for the praise, but then he looked round and saw Feydrin. She was distinctly sombre.

"You promised to shoot his hand," she said.

"Ack! There is no accounting for the wind," said Gargrace, defending Zanthred's integrity.

"And was it the wind?" asked Feydrin.

"No, my Teacher," admitted Zanthred. "...But his hand was very small, and near her throat. I had no time to judge my shot."

"You disappoint me Zanthred, you are no longer welcome in my temple," said Feydrin.

And somehow, that hurt a lot.

Feydrin moved away to enquire as to the health of the escapees. As soon as she was out of earshot, Gargrace made his thoughts known.

"I for one salute your deed. I shall speak of it to all who will hear. It should be worth at least one song or poem in the Chepsid tavern of yours."

"I will write it for you," said Hanuru. "...Perhaps Janistor will sing it."

Wise men wear other people's respect. Millie's words came back to him. For the first time since that night in the Perched Sparrow, the future looked hopeful to Zanthred.

* * * * * * *

One of the Shadow Warriors came to Hanuru and made her sit on the floor. He looked at the fingers and began cutting some cloth into bandages.

"This will hurt, but you will not suffer permanently. It just needs splinting for a few months," he declared. Hanuru nodded in understanding and braced herself. The Shadow Warrior pulled her fingers straight and set them in place. She gasped and winced until the bandaging and splinting were done. Zanthred knelt by her. He was keen to talk to her, but trying to be respectful of the injury.

"Hanuru, I must ask..." he began

"Don't worry Zanthred, Millie is fine. She escaped before me," said Hanuru, pre-empting the question.

"Oh, thank goodness!" he exclaimed. "How did you even end up with them?"

Hanuru nervously looked about at the soldiers. "I'll tell you about it later," she said. Luckily Zanthred had enough sense not to ask more. Hanuru put her head on Zanthred's shoulder, "Oh, I just want to get back to Serra, Zanthred."

"I'm sorry, Hanuru, but the last ship has already sailed. We are stuck here until the Cool Season."

"Oh no! But Millie will not know I am alright!" she whined.

Zanthred could only shrug.

"Gargrace, what will you do with the prisoners?" asked Feydrin. "Will you carry out Duarma's directive?"

Gargrace looked at the prisoners and mused. Looshan was sad, broken, and once again in bonds. Despite everything, Hanuru felt sorry for him. He had lost his friends, his cause and now his brother.

"Please Gargrace, give these men a chance. I have no malice against any of them except the one who lies dead," entreated Hanuru.

"Tell me, prisoners, it takes more than luck to escape from Haddra and his veterans. Who helped you escape Serra?" asked Gargrace.

Hanuru held her breath.

Looshan looked Gargrace dead in the eye and said with a voice so full of conviction that nobody considered questioning it, "*No-one* helped us escape."

"Well then, Duarma gave no directive to kill prisoners on Adlan, and I will not make that choice for him. Prisoners, can you work for your food?" asked Gargrace.

Looshan looked around to his fellows and gauged their faces. "We will do what you ask of us, except betray our Archlord Tisenin," said Looshan.

"I need builders and farmers to prepare this land for a garrison over the Hurricane and Storm months. If you will do that freely, and swear to cause no trouble,

I will commute your execution and defend your right to live to Duarma's face. You will be more use to me alive," said Gargrace.

"That, I think, we can agree to," said Looshan.

"Oh thank you!" said Hanuru.

"The first sensible thing I have heard this year," said Feydrin.

Millie! We have not done these things in vain!

Zanthred had been wearing a self-satisfied smile since she mentioned Janistor, and now Hanuru was sure she must look the same. Thinking of Millie and Zanthred jogged her memory.

"Oh, Zanthred. There was something Millie wanted to ask you," said Hanuru. "When we were at the coast, we saw a ship with a courting swan on the sail heading northwest past Serra in the night. Millie said it was from Icknel and thought you might know the owner."

Zanthred's smile instantly disappeared and he developed the same brooding look Millie had adopted as she gazed at the ship.

"Aye, I know the owner. I spoke with the artist as he painted it. It is Roldern ap Sunnar's ship, the Lord of Icknel. And you say it was stealing passed Serra in the night, on the way to Efrandi?"

Hanuru had not quite thought about it in those terms. "Yes, I guess so."

The weight in Zanthred's face said it all without him having to use any more words. It was a look that bore worry for everyone he had ever held dear – parents, friends and mentors – and the growing fear that one day soon, he would be asked to deal with them in the same way he dealt with Killwa.

"Then it means my home town has joined the rebellion."

* * * * * * *

When the caravel was a long way out from Icknel and only a tall plume of smoke like the effluence from a volcano was visible on the horizon, Quinias had Akai gather the crew. Quinias stood on the prow and addressed his people.

"The secrecy of our voyage has been necessary. We have been given a task crucial to the Sagacious League's victory. The journey ahead of us will be hard, but I have confidence in all of you." Quinias paused to gauge the reaction of his crew; so far they seemed stoic about the promised difficulty and eager to be of use to their master. But as he spoke the last line he began worried rubbing of the clenched stumps of his fingers, "We are going to the north of Cathri to find some allies. *We are going to visit the humans.*"

* * * * * * *

Hesiad sat at the entrance to his cave. All morning ships had been streaming past on their way back from the Efrandi blockade to find sanctuary in Serra's harbour. The sky had gone black and wild winds were tearing at the tops of waves. White foam was being whipped all along the beach as high as the cave's entrance. The first hurricane was here and the two armies would have to rest their hostility until the season turned once again.

But for the moment, Hesiad's cave sheltered him from the chaos. He lit a candle and let it settle into a steady flame. He knew this war, this Sundering of kin, could only have one resolution. Tisenin could not be forgiven; there were some crimes that could not be forgiven. And there were crimes yet to be committed.

Hesiad, the disgraced bodyguard, twice penitent, had a plan. He lifted the candle to his face and allowed its hot flame to kiss his skin. He gritted his teeth and refused to scream out. Although his hand shook, cheeks blistered and his nostrils filled with the foul smell of burning flesh, he made sure no part of his face was spared the touch of the flame.

Hesiad had a plan. *Sometimes you have to embrace the pain.*

To Be Continued....

About the Author

Ali Jon is an archaeologist from England who specialises in the Bronze Age. He has a love of all things archaic, especially classical Greek literature. When not digging up long forgotten skeletons, he enjoys running games of D&D for his friends and sculpting new monsters from polymer clay. Ali Jon suffers from dyslexia and publication of this work represents a huge personal milestone for him in overcoming the limitations he once thought he had.

Ali Jon would like to thank *you*, for not only purchasing this book, but making it all the way to the end! You deserve a cookie! By the time you read this, Book 2 of the saga (*The Broken Land*) has probably already been published and Book 3 is in production, so you can keep reading the story right now, if you like. Regardless, it would be much appreciated if you left an honest review or recommended the book to a friend. Then you have Ali Jon's permission to have a couple of cookies instead.

Lightning Source UK Ltd.
Milton Keynes UK
UKHW010811221122
412637UK00018B/762